THE

ONCE UPON A KISS

TAILOR AND THE DEMOISELLE

SUMMER HANFORD

CHAPTER 1

Miss Elizabeth Adams, or Betsy, as her parents called her, sat in the upper hall, legs dangling through the railing as she studied the grand entrance of her family home below. Centered over the two-story drop before her, a giant crystal-laden chandelier boasted no fewer than ninety-six lighted candles. Without, fat snowflakes dashed against the leaded panes on each side of the front door. Inside, light blue, silk-clad walls swept upward, their wide-striped texture shimmering in the candlelight. To Betsy's right and left, a set of honey-colored wooden steps, layered over by a pearl white runner, curved downward. The twin staircases perfectly framed the entrance hall below.

Their butler, Mr. Côte, opened the thick front door to admit another masked couple amid a swirl of whistling wind and snow. The quills on their peacock-feathered masks drooped under quickly melting snow. The man nodded to Côte, mumbling unintelligibly as he shucked his greatcoat, which would have tumbled to the floor if Mr. Côte hadn't caught it. The woman giggled madly, as if intoxicated, and Mr. Côte wasn't quick enough to save her bright red cloak from puddling on the marble inlay beneath her feet. He scooped the garment up as they walked down the hallway in the direction of the ballroom and the audible ruckus.

"Are those the last two, do you think?" Betsy pitched her voice loud enough to be heard in the hall below. "The time is nearly midnight. I cannot imagine anyone arrives at a ball to celebrate the new year *after* midnight."

Mr. Côte looked up with a frown. "Miss, you oughtn't be spying on your parents' guests. Where is Miss Chaff?"

As if summoned by his words, Penna, Betsy's nanny-turned-companion, burst from a doorway to Betsey's left, long face red and breath uneven. "There you are."

Betsy smirked. "Penna, you have perfect timing. I do believe the last of Mother and Father's guests have arrived. We have the entrance hall to ourselves. I've devised a fabulous game."

"Game? You're meant to be abed, Miss."

Betsy narrowed her eyes. "I have twenty years, Penna. I may be barred from my parents' festivities—"

"Thank heaven for that," Penna said over Betsy's words.

Betsy raised her voice and kept talking. "—but I am not being put to bed like a child. Tonight is the eve of the new year and I intend to be entertained."

"Entertained?" Penna repeated with asperity. "Was not dosing my tea with laudanum and leaving me locked in your sitting room yesterday entertainment enough?"

Betsy laughed and pulled her legs back through the railing. She stood and shook out her skirts. "That *was* highly entertaining."

"How did you measure the dose?" Penna pressed. "Laudanum is not safe. Who knows what you might have done to me?"

Betsy waved a dismissive hand. "I gave you less than my mother consumes in a serving."

Penna pressed a hand to her heart. "Heaven preserve me if you'd given me what Mrs. Adams takes."

"Ladies, please," Mr. Côte called from below. "Such unseemly talk. Penna, see Miss Adams to her room."

Penna advanced on her, mouth tight and eyes flinty. Outside, the wind howled, even more enraged than Penna appeared.

"I am not going to my room," Betsy said. "You and the other servants are going to play the game I've invented, and if you do not make it so, Penna, I shall tell my father that you struck me."

Penna halted and the color drained from her face. "You would not."

Betsy tossed her light brown curls. Curls to which Penna had diligently applied lemon juice to brighten them until they gleamed with gold by candlelight. Curls Penna painstakingly coiled into perfect ringlets daily, exactly as Betsy liked.

"I am to have a season," Betsy stated. "We are off to London soon. I'm sure I can find a much better companion and lady's maid there. Someone who hasn't known me all my life and does not presume liberties with my tolerance."

Penna compressed her lips again. "So you have said before, Miss."

"But this time, I mean it." Betsy looked over the railing at Mr. Côte. "Not only that, I'll tell my father you steal from him, Mr. Côte, and ensure he finds plenty missing. See what happens to you, then."

Mr. Côte, nearly in his seventh decade, began to cough and sputter.

"I will see half the staff fired without reference." Betsy raised her voice as the wind without shook the leaded panes. "Don't think I won't."

"Now, now," Penna soothed. "There's no need to shout, Miss."

"So, you'll summon more of the staff? To play the game I've invented?"

"Most of the staff are assisting in the kitchen...or the ballroom," Penna replied.

"Well then," Betsy said, smug, "I will march into the ballroom and collect them."

Penna cast Mr. Côte a fearful look. Betsy didn't know the full extent of the mischief that went on at her parents' parties, but she knew her parents relied on the staff, as their sworn solemn duty, to keep her from finding out. In a swish of muslin, she took the nearest staircase down.

"Miss, you can't," Penna cried.

Betsy ignored her, simply hitched up her skirts and continued to follow the staircase's pristine white runner down to the entryway.

At the base of the steps, Mr. Côte stepped into Betsy's path. "Miss, I cannot permit you to enter the ballroom." Worry edged his firm tone. "No decent person should."

Betsy glared. Did he fear for his job, or for her? What exactly happened in the ballroom? She knew they all drank and danced themselves into disheveled states, but not much more. While growing up, Betsy had assumed that, eventually, she'd be allowed to attend and discover what transpired. Over time, however, she'd come to realize she probably didn't wish to witness the absolute foolishness of her parents' parties. Not that Penna and Mr. Côte needed know about her private conclusions on that front.

Soon her parents' proclivities and the servants' lack of suitable respect wouldn't matter. Her grandmother, who owned the entire Rodchamb estate, including the manor house in which Betsy and her parents resided, and all the farmland around the house, and all of grandfather's businesses across India and the Caribbean, had promised Betsy a fortune at the end of the summer, when she reached one and twenty. Betsy would take that money and throw her own parties. She'd hire servants who properly obeyed her.

For now, she planned to be entertained.

She said to Mr. Côte, "Either let me pass or use force to stop me. Either way, you shall be removed from my father's employ." For good measure, she added, "Without a pension."

"Stop," Penna cried. "Oh, Miss, stop. I'll fetch more of the staff. How many do you need?"

Betsy looked up at her in triumph. "As many as possible, and all the pillows from the bedrooms."

Penna frowned. "Pillows?"

"Or not. The pillows are up to you. I am merely trying to be thoughtful, as you constantly badger me that I must." Not that Betsy understood why she must. Thoughtfulness was for poor people.

"What exactly is this game, Miss?"

"Why, racing." Betsy gestured to the curved staircases. "We have here two staircases of equal length. All the staff must take turns sliding down the banisters into piles of pillows. Each winner will go up against another winner, and losers against other losers, until we have a champion and a runner-up."

Penna groaned. Outside, whiteness flashed, followed by thunder, and snow that still pelted the windows in soggy splats. Penna wrung her hands and made no move to do as ordered.

"Banister races are what I want for entertainment to celebrate the new year. I will have what I want, Penna."

"Yes, Miss," Penna said in a defeated voice. She slunk away down the hall.

Betsy faced the aged butler. "You do not have to slide down the railings, Mr. Côte. You shall help me judge. Fetch me a chair."

Stubbornness and indignation warred on the older gentleman's face.

"I said *a chair*, Mr. Côte."

"But Miss," the butler began.

"Mr. Côte," she cut in, "you cannot imagine how important Father's little things are to him. If any were to go missing...."

With a scowl, Mr. Côte marched from the entrance hall, headed in the direction of the dining room. Betsy waited in the hall and wondered if he would return. If not, she would get revenge. She'd drug his tea, too, so he slept through his duties and got dismissed. She would not tolerate insubordination.

Mr. Côte returned with a wooden chair. Betsy considered sending him back for a cushioned chair from the parlor, but the footmen and kitchen boys had arrived with pillows.

Betsy sat in her rigid chair and ordered in a loud voice, "Go upstairs and line up in the hall, all of you. You as well, Penna."

Penna's mouth fell open. "But Miss, I'm in skirts."

"I daresay my father's footmen have seen worse than a glimpse of your legs, Penna."

Penna's face reddened, but she followed the men up, then took a position in the center of the upper hall.

"The winner shall receive a pound. The runner-up will receive five shillings." Betsy leveled a hard look at Penna and pointed to Mr. Côte, who stood beside her chair. "Anyone who Mr. Côte and I deem to be cheating or losing on purpose shall be docked a week's wages." Betsy studied the staff. Most of the men, especially the younger ones, appeared eager to race. A pound was a fine prize, after all. She pointed to one servant at each end of the upper hall, those closest to the twin staircases. "You two first. Get ready to slide."

Exchanging a quick grin, both young men straddled the polished railings. Penna gasped and slapped a hand to her mouth. Betsy ignored her, raised her voice further, and said, "On my mark. Get set. Go!"

The men slid down the banisters at quite a clip. At the center of the curve, the one to the left overbalanced, tipped to the side, and cartwheeled headfirst with a squawk. He crashed to the marble floor. The other young man reached the bottom and slid off into the pile of pillows.

Betsy clapped and laughed. "Our first winner."

The fallen young man groaned and clutched his arm. Mr. Côte hurried to the lad's side. His long form audibly creaked as he dropped to one knee to examine the injured footman. The man groaned again, before another round of thunder drowned out the sound.

"If he has broken something, he's disqualified from racing for runner-up," Betsy declared.

Mr. Côte helped the footman to his feet. Anger radiated from the old butler's face. "I do not believe his arm to be broken. Merely bruised."

"Excellent. He can keep racing." Betsy flapped her hands at the two racers. "Back up you both go, to await your challengers."

"You will go nowhere." Côte's gnarled fingers clasped the young man's shoulder. "Miss Adams, I demand an end to this lunacy."

Betsy folded her arms across her chest. "Or what?"

"Or I shall write your grandmother."

Betsy stilled; even her heartbeat seemed to halt for a stuttering moment. Silence settled on the grand entrance hall. Everyone—each footman, the kitchen boys, Penna— held his or her breath.

Could Mr. Côte truly write Betsy's grandmother? Would Grandma Adams listen to him? He'd been with the family longer than Betsy had been alive. Would Grandmother care about Betsy's silly races? She frowned at the wounded footman, who still coddled his arm.

The front door burst open and a frigid wind gusted across Betsy. She jumped up and shrieked in unison with Penna's cry. Lightning flashed, illuminating a strikingly tall, black-skinned man in the doorway. Betsy stumbled back toward Mr. Côte.

The man stepped aside and a small, wrinkled, darkly tanned woman entered. The gentleman followed. He swung the door closed behind them, blocking out the driving wind and wet snow. The woman threw back the hood of her cloak to reveal neatly coifed white hair. When the tall man doffed his hat, Betsy blinked at his shiny bald pate. The old woman loosened her cloak, and the man removed a layered greatcoat. They were both dressed in the height of fashion.

"Mr. Côte." The many wrinkles on the small woman's face creased upward into a smile. She glanced about the entryway. "Why are so many servants assembled?" Frown lines on her brow dampened her sunny expression. "And the pillows? Is someone sliding down the banisters?" She nodded to the injured footman. "Is that young man hurt? Where is my son?"

Mr. Côte stepped past Betsy and bowed at the waist. "Mrs. Adams. How good to see you. May I take your cloak? And your coat, sir?"

Côte accepted their garments, then stepped back and snapped his fingers. One of the footmen hurried forward to take the damp outerwear from him. On the landing above, the other staff rustled and began to melt away.

"Clear those pillows," Penna ordered before they could all disappear. "And return that chair to the dining room."

Behind Betsy, servants pattered down the stairs to do as Penna ordered. Betsy stared at the white-haired old lady. Her grandmother hadn't returned from abroad since Betsy's fifth year. Since before Grandfather died and left everything to Grandma Adams, rather than to their only child, Betsy's father. Betsy still recalled how angry her father had been.

"Grandmother?" Betsy stammered.

Her grandmother looked her up and down. "My, my, Elizabeth. You have grown, haven't you?" She turned to the tall gentleman and rested a hand lightly on his sleeve as she spoke in a musical language that reminded Betsy of the two months of Italian she'd taken before chasing off her tutor, but which she didn't understand.

"Grandmother, you're here," Betsy said, still stunned.

Grandma Adams lifted her brows. "And you are interrupting me, child. That is not a good display of manners." She returned her attention to her companion and continued in that strange language.

Betsy scowled but stood silently in the middle of the room. Around her, servants quickly set the entrance hall right. Mr. Côte took up his customary position near the front door and stood taller than usual, quite fine in his black suit. Penna appeared at Betsy's side.

The black-skinned man replied to Grandma Adams in the same language she spoke. She laughed and touched the sleeve of his tailcoat. He flashed a grin.

"Elizabeth, this is Mr. Relógio," Grandma said. "We are—"

A riotous roar sounded from deeper within the house. In various rooms, clocks began to chime, ringing in the new year. The roar grew. High-pitched shrieks and cackles clashed against masculine bass rumbles. Grandma Adams grimaced.

She returned her attention to Mr. Relógio. "Perhaps now we shall learn why the letters from my son and his steward have become increasingly erratic and insensible. Come. Let us go find my progeny and his bride." She headed for the ballroom, addressing Penna as she passed. "Miss Chaff, is it not? Keep my granddaughter here. I suspect we will not be long."

Betsy's anger sparked to life. "You cannot order about my companion, Grandmother. Nor have you the right to say where I must remain. I will go where I please, when I please."

Mr. Côte blanched.

Grandma Adams stopped and regarded Betsy with squinted eyes. "How did that young man come to be injured? The one who stood over there when I entered?"

Betsy blinked, startled by the question, then selected her

most haughty tone to reply, "He was sliding on the banister but slipped off halfway down."

"Why was a footman sliding down the banister?"

"I ordered him to. I ordered them all to. I wished to be entertained."

"Do you find the fright and pain of others entertaining, child?"

"How dare you make such an accusation? Of a certainty, I do not. He's the one who fell. I didn't make him tumble." *And I am not a child,* she mentally added, for experience taught her the words said aloud sounded childish. Instead, she infused distain into her voice and asserted, "It is not my fault he's clumsy."

More feminine squeals echoed through the house, followed by more male laughter. Outside, the wind whipped to an even greater frenzy.

Grandma Adams turned back to Mr. Côte. "Where is Mr. Arch?" she asked.

"Attending the festivities in the ballroom," Mr. Côte replied with no inflection.

Mr. Relógio again spoke to Grandma Adams in that indecipherable language.

She nodded. "Have my granddaughter brought to the library. Mass the footmen. We're putting an end to my son's festivities."

"I am not going to the library," Betsy cried. "You cannot come into my home and order me about. What are you even doing here? How do I know you're really my grandmother? You've been gone for fifteen years."

Grandma Adams addressed Mr. Côte, "You have my full permission to summon footmen to assist Elizabeth to the library and keep her there until I send for her. Use whatever force necessary."

Without so much as a glance at Betsy, she started toward

the hallway leading to the ballroom. Mr. Relógio walked at her side, a hand to the small of her back.

"Miss." Penna touched Betsy's sleeve. "Miss, we should go to the library."

Betsy looked past Penna to Mr. Côte. He met and matched her defiant gaze, expression fixed. She didn't doubt he would summon footmen to drag her to the library should she refuse to go. He may even be pleased to do so.

Betsy scoffed at the butler. "I am only going to the library because I wish to hear what she has to say."

Chin in the air, Betsy marched down the hall. Yet, she had a sinking feeling she truly did not wish to hear what her grandmother had to say, at all.

CHAPTER 2

The library, vast and little used, smelled of dust and old paper. Betsy wrinkled her nose. She hated the library, the scene of many arguments with her long-gone tutors. Penna called a footman to start a fire and sent a maid for their shawls. When the maid returned, Penna ordered both the footman and the maid to remain in the room, positioned near the door. With three guards, Betsy made no attempt to leave. That way, she could pretend they wouldn't stop her.

For a time, commotion filled the house. Wind whistled beyond the tall, dark windows, but didn't fully cover the sound of people running, occasionally even screeching or yelling. When the ruckus died, so did the wind. The snowflakes grew smaller and piled gently on the sills into walls of white against the leaded panes. Betsy paced, too agitated to sit with a book as Penna did. Reading never much appealed to her. Why bother with words for entertainment when she could order real live people about?

Finally, when the house had been silent for some time, Betsy glanced at the mantle clock, which reported the hour as half past two. "How long am I expected to remain here?" she demanded.

"What? Who?" Penna started awake, book open in her lap.

"Do you think that evil old witch forgot about me?" Betsy cried.

Penna yawned and said, "We must be patient."

Betsy spun from Penna to the maid, who still stood to one side of the door. "Go tell my grandmother that I will speak with her now."

The maid looked to Penna.

"I give the orders, not Penna," Betsy snapped.

The girl paled but did not move.

"For heaven's sake," Betsy yelled. "Tell her to do as I say, Penna, and remember her, so I can see her fired."

Penna sighed and sat up straighter. "Please do go see if Mrs. Adams has a notion of when she might wish for Miss Adams."

The maid nodded, curtsied to Betsy, and left.

Half an hour later, heavy footfalls sounded in the hall. Mr. Côte appeared in the library doorway. Far from tired, the elderly gentleman appeared invigorated. He said, "Mrs. Adams has interviewed most of the staff. She has the master and his wife with her now. She asks you both to join her in the study." Then he turned and left.

Betsy dashed out after him, but Penna brushed past her and caught up to the old butler. "What is afoot, Mr. Côte?"

He maintained his stride and replied in satisfied tones, "Mr. Arch has been let go. Mrs. Adams plans to banish the family to their London residence, with only a small stipend, and set Rodchamb to rights."

"What?" Betsy hurried to keep up. She didn't mind the first half of Mr. Côte's news, as she loathed her father's steward, Mr. Arch, who reminded her of a salamander, but the second half alarmed her. "Surly, Grandma Adams can't do that."

Mr. Côte cast a disgusted look over his shoulder. "She can do as she pleases. None of you has a penny of your own. Your grandfather left everything to her. Fortunately." He turned into the study.

Betsy retorted, "At least I shall have to endure a small allowance for a short time only, as I will come into my inheritance on my birthday." Though, the eight months now stretched out into endless days.

"I am afraid not," Grandma Adams said as Betsy entered the study behind Penna.

Betsy froze in the doorway. Her grandmother sat in the large, upholstered chair behind the desk. Mr. Côte and Penna crossed the room and stood by the sideboard. Mr. Relógio lounged on a side couch and studied the ledger on his lap.

Betsy recognized her father's head of thinning, light brown hair visible just above the top of the high-back chair in front of the heavy mahogany desk. That greased head hadn't turned at her entrance. Draped over the chair's arms, she also recognized the sleeves of his embroidered silk robe and wondered at his state of undress.

On the couch opposite Mr. Relógio's, Betsy's mother sprawled, asleep. She also wore a robe and didn't appear to have anything on underneath. Face paint smeared her cheeks and the garish red she'd applied to her lips streaked her chin. Drool trickled from one corner of her mouth, as was often the case after she'd imbibed too much strong drink and laudanum.

Penna cleared her throat, and Betsy finally returned her attention to her grandmother. "What do you mean, you are *afraid not?*" Betsy asked.

"I mean, you will not receive your inheritance, Elizabeth."

"That is my money." The volume of her own voice startled her, but Betsy continued. "Grandfather set the money aside for me. You said you would give it to me."

"I did agree to honor his wishes." Grandmother regarded

Betsy with blue eyes paled by age. "Yet now that I see the terrible creature you've become, I have changed my mind."

Betsy swayed. "Changed your mind?"

"You are to go live with your mother and father in London. I will provide the three of you with staff, two new sets of clothing per year, and food. Any staff who wish to leave the London house may, with severance, and will not be replaced. You will each receive fifty pounds a year to spend as you see fit."

"Fifty pounds a year?" Betsy sputtered. "Fifty?"

"Yes," Grandma Adams said with a crisp note of finality.

Nausea roiled in Betsy's stomach. She looked to her father. "Papa, can she do this to me?"

Her father turned to her, blinking, expression dazed.

"She can," Mr. Côte said.

The sick feeling crept up Betsy's throat. "But...but, Grandmother...Grandmama, I haven't done anything wrong. I swear."

Her grandmother nodded. "Indeed, the staff tell me my son's one good decision has been to shelter you from the more dissolute aspects of his and your mother's amusements. We can only—"

"You see," Betsy broke in. "I am not like my parents. I don't deserve their punishment."

"However," Grandma Adams cut in, "I have also observed, and been informed of, your lack of appropriate education and pursuits, *and* of your selfish, spoiled, and ill-mannered behavior. Therefore—"

"Who says that?" Betsy glared at Mr. Côte.

"I fear you are beyond redemption," Grandma Adams continued. "At twenty, you can certainly be held responsible for your actions."

Betsy looked about the room again, but no one spoke. Mr. Relógio turned a page in the ledger. Penna stared at the floor. A soft snore left Betsy's mother's mouth. Betsy swallowed.

A new idea occurred to her. "What of my season? I was to have a season. Now. This year. In London. I could find a husband."

"You are certainly welcome to do so. Your parents may direct as much of their fifty-pound allowances to the venture as they wish. If they're wise, they'll apply every penny in the hope you secure a husband who can support them."

Betsy's father made a strangled sound.

"I can't have a season with only fifty pounds," Betsy protested. Bile scalded the back of her throat as she dared to ask, "What of my dowry?"

"Rescinded."

The room spun.

Penna hurried to Betsy's side and grasped her arm. "Is there nothing to be done?" Penna whispered.

Grandma Adams frowned. "Done?"

Penna squeezed Betsy's arm tight. "She is not bad. Simply… undisciplined." Penna gestured to Betsy's parents. "Certainly, she isn't like them."

Grandma Adams leaned forward in her chair and steepled her gnarled fingers. "No one else has spoken a word of good about you, girl."

Betsy's stomach twisted. Who among the staff would speak well of her? She swallowed again and lifted pleading eyes to her grandmother. "I can change, Grandma. Truly I can. I can learn. I —" She choked back a sob. "I can be better. Please don't send me to London to live in a townhouse with them, with only fifty pounds a year. Let me stay at Rodchamb."

Grandma Adams studied her, tanned face unreadable. Mr. Relógio closed the ledger, looked up, and spoke to Betsy's grandmother again in that language Betsy couldn't quite place.

Grandma Adams shook her head, expression stubborn, but Mr. Relógio continued. Grandma Adams replied, her tone one of disagreement even if Betsy couldn't understand the words. Mr. Relógio answered in his almost musical voice.

Betsy took in the lines about Mr. Relógio's mouth and eyes, unnoticed before against the backdrop of his nearly black skin. Something about those lines, though nowhere near as deep as the ones that etched her grandmother's face, and his gentle, soothing tone spoke of wisdom and maturity. She realized he might be her grandmother's age, not her father's. For the first time, she wondered what Mr. Relógio was doing here. Why had he accompanied her grandmother to Rodchamb? Why had either of them left the Caribbean sun and sailed to England in the middle of winter? She recalled the intimate way he'd put his hand on her grandmother's back. Was her grandmother as debauched as her parents?

"Why are you even here?" Betsy wailed.

Grandma Adams leveled a hard look at her. "You must learn not to interrupt your elders when they're speaking, Elizabeth."

Betsy took a gulp of air. "Yes, Grandmother."

"I came here, among other things, to see you, child. It seemed irresponsible to settle such a large sum on you without assessing your character, especially in view of your father's and Mr. Arch's disturbing lack of clarity or, in fact, intelligence, in their correspondences with me."

Betsy glared at the back of her father's head. This was his fault. She opened her mouth to yell at him, but quickly clamped her lips closed, rather than interrupt her grandmother yet again. Betsy would do anything to get her inheritance back. Even refrain from telling her father what she thought of him.

"I thought I was prepared for the worst," Grandma Adams continued. "I was wrong. Things here are far more neglected than I'd imagined. We spent the day touring some of the tenant farms. Some are vacant. All are dilapidated. The roadways are in ruins, rendering some holdings unreachable."

Farms? Roads? Betsy worked not to frown. Who cared about farmers? Her inheritance was what mattered.

"Then, I come here to find half the staff as depraved and immoral as your parents, the other half harried to the point of mistreatment. Your father and Mr. Arch have neglected and abused Rodchamb and our people to a point near destruction." She sighed and sorrow eased some of the harsh lines of her face.

She lowered her hands to the desktop and looked to the wide windows on the east side of the room. "Your grandfather and I spent little time here. Not as much as we ought, but I do love this place. When we first wed, I lived here for five years while raising your father before I joined your grandfather on his travels. I used to keep a rose garden outside those windows, for your grandfather to enjoy when he was home. I've never managed to grow roses like that on the island."

Betsy said, "I...I'm sure they were lovely."

"Under the previous steward, my rose garden was kept up. When we visited, the roses were always lovely."

Betsy recognized the opportunity intrinsic in the nostalgia that tinged her grandmother's voice. "I could tend them, if you let me remain. Come spring, I can put the rose garden right. I swear I will."

Her father let out a maniacal laugh, his puffy hands clutching the arms of his chair.

Grandma Adams curled her lips into a hard smile as she refocused on Betsy. "Oh, you will, child. You will do that and more. I offer you a final chance. Your parents will depart for London tonight, but you will remain and manage the estate. You'll oversee the manor house, the tenants, the roadways, and the land, and you will do so using only the income Rodchamb generates. Without raising rent for the remaining tenants. You have until your birthday to restore order to the estate. Eight months. Until then, I shall take residence in the dower house, and you will manage here. If you succeed, you get everything. If not, I'll search our relations for a suitable owner for Rodchamb, and you will be left to find a husband to support you."

Betsy stared. A reprieve. Fresh dizziness washed through her. She clutched at Penna. Mr. Côte scowled.

But what a reprieve. "How am I to manage everything?" She'd never so much as set a dinner menu.

Grandma Adams shrugged. "I care not, but I reiterate that you may use only the funds Rodchamb generates. No loans."

Her father giggled like a child, and Betsy belatedly realized he'd imbibed at least as much as her mother, if not more, considering he'd not uttered one coherent word during this entire conversation.

Betsy's legs trembled. "How…how will I even know where to begin?" She choked down tears. "I will never succeed. It's impossible."

Mr. Relógio spoke to her grandmother again, who replied with a nod. From his pocket, he produced a wrapped package, then stood and crossed the room. He halted in front of her and proffered the small box to Betsy.

She craned her neck to look up into his dark eyes. "Th-thank you." She released her hold on Penna to accept the box.

Mr. Relógio dipped his head gravely in acknowledgement and returned to his seat on the couch.

"Open the box," Grandma Adams ordered.

On shaky legs, Betsy walked to the desk, set down the gift, then stripped the cloth wrapping away to reveal a carved wooden box. She glanced up at her grandmother, who nodded, then she lifted the cover from the box.

Inside rested a rose, each petal formed of a polished seashell, shimmering mother-of-pearl lining set upward to capture the flickering light. Betsy lifted the rose to find a gold chain strung through the petals. A gold bead at the top of the rose held the petals down, their chain attached to a thicker one, that one a necklace. Unlike the mother-of-pearl lining of the petals, which faced upward, the underside of the rose was satiny and pink, like the last blush of sunset. The rose pendant was the most exquisite object she'd ever seen.

Grandma Adams held out a hand. Reluctantly, Betsy passed her the necklace.

"I brought this for your birthday." Her grandmother opened the clasp. "Because I loved my rose garden, and the memory of English roses." She unhooked the chain, then slid free the shorter, narrower one that held the rose. "All these years, I remembered you as a stocky girl of five. A rosy-cheeked, smiling, sweet little girl." She worked off the bead. "And when I finally returned, what should greet me but the worst sort of hoyden."

Grandma Adams tugged at the rose and the petals spilled free. Betsy gasped as they clattered onto the inlaid desktop. She reached out in protest.

"Hand me the box," Grandma ordered.

Betsy frowned but slid the little wooden box across the desk. Her grandmother swept the petals up and dropped them in, then closed the lid. She stood and held out the two lengths of chain and the golden bead.

"Take these."

Betsy accepted the bits of gold, pathetic and disarrayed without the rose. Much like Betsy's life.

"You are correct," her grandmother said. "Even the most competent manager could not fix Rodchamb by the end of August. I will not judge you on the completion of the task, but on the steps you take."

"Steps I take?" Betsy repeated.

Grandma Adams stared at her, and Betsy realized she'd interrupted, again. "Yes," Grandma continued. "Mr. Relógio will remain here to watch you. He will not assist you. Simply observe. Every time you do something right, he will give you a petal. If you do something horrendous, he will give you no more until you right your wrong. If you can rebuild the rose before your birthday, that will be proof enough that you have changed. That you deserve Rodchamb."

Betsy stared at the little box resting on the desk. Mr. Côte gave a quick, derisive sniff. Betsy's father tittered.

"Are we agreed?" Grandma Adams asked.

With no other option, Betsy nodded. She frowned at the box. By the end of August, she would rebuild the rose.

CHAPTER 3

Standing before his makeshift easel, Isaac paused in adding the final brush strokes of golden yellow to the sun in his painting. He listened to his mother's melodic voice filter from the house into the garden. She loved to sing. Some of the villagers found her odd, perhaps even off putting, but he understood this expression of her joyous nature. So long as his mother flittered about their home, garden, or shop singing, all was well.

She spun into the garden, an empty laundry basket on her hip. Still singing, she swirled along the clothesline and gathered bedlinens into her basket the way a honeybee collected pollen. Auburn hair, touched by gray, swished about her shoulders as she twirled in time to her song. Her tresses whirled with her, half curled, half not.

Isaac smiled at the sight of her. She must have gotten distracted before finishing her hair. As she worked, her voice rose with lyrics she'd undoubtedly invented. Isaac watched her do her chore, each disappearing linen revealing her before she danced away behind another. Even as she approached her fourth decade, Isaac understood how his mysterious father had been swept past reason by love of her, though Isaac doubted he would ever know for certain why the man had left. Were he jaded, he might assume any man who would take advantage of a girl not yet out of the schoolroom was bound to leave.

Isaac returned his attention to his painting. His daily quest to capture that which he deemed most beautiful in the world. Today, the sunrise. Tomorrow, a yellow-winged butterfly tasting nectar. The next, a songbird in her nest. Spring always proved full of wonder, of so many scenes to capture, the land finally freed from the grays, browns, and muted blues of winter. Focused on the rapidly changing sky, Isaac painted.

"Oh Izzy, how lovely," his mother said at his shoulder.

She set down the basket of clean wash at her feet and stood next to him. Isaac kept his attention on the thick paper before him. He'd nearly completed the scene. Painting transported him that way. He became so immersed, he no longer realized he was painting. The subject before him simply expanded as he worked, there the next time he blinked his eyes.

"But Izzy…" she said, and he closed his eyes, knowing what she would say next. "How can you attempt a sunrise without using red?"

"Thusly." He gestured to the page then began to clean his brush. He glanced back at his work, the perfection of the technique marred by the absence of that all-important color.

"Izzy," his mother pressed.

"Mother. Please."

She sighed. "Yes, well, you'd best pack up and come in. Don't forget that Dougal Guest is coming by this afternoon to try on his new trousers. You haven't worked very diligently on them, which isn't like you. You don't want to disappoint him with half-stitched trousers." She giggled. "A gentleman cannot go about town in half-stitched trousers."

"True."

She swung away, a new song about half-stitched trousers on

her lips, linen basket held out before her as she whirled, her dance partner.

Isaac continued to clean his brushes. He surveyed the state of his paints, but halted on the red. A final gift from his father, for his ninth birthday. Red paint and a note, with an apology for missing his birthday and a promise to visit soon. That visit had never come. Nor any more notes, gifts, or money. His father, a man whose real rank and name Isaac would never know, had simply vanished from their lives forever. After over a dozen years without a word, Isaac could only assume his father was dead, an assumption to which his mother would, on occasion, agree.

Movements rapid with practice, Isaac stowed his accoutrements. His mother was half right about Dougal Guest and his trousers. Mr. Guest did plan to come by that afternoon to try them, and be fitted for a matching tailcoat, but he wouldn't care a lick if Isaac had finished the work. The suit was the fourth Isaac had crafted for the gentleman that year, and it barely spring. The real reason Guest kept buying suits was so that his sister, Filomena Guest, could work her wiles on Isaac. Slower work on Isaac's part meant more opportunity for wiles. As Isaac did not appreciate Miss Guest's attention, he wanted to finish the trousers.

He also didn't appreciate her manipulations. Miss Guest had stopped buying gowns from his mother when she'd realized continued purchases didn't guarantee access to Isaac. He'd thought staying away would be a kind, subtle rebuff. He hadn't realized that by avoiding Miss Guest, he would end her patronage. He'd also been ignorant of Miss Guest's determination. Instead of buying from Isaac's mother, she had begun to accompany her brother to his fittings, where Isaac couldn't avoid her.

Isaac gathered his materials and crossed the tidy garden. He walked past the clothesline, noted that his mother had taken in nearly all of the dry bedsheets, and entered their small kitchen.

She stood within, stirring a pot of porridge while she stared out the window, humming. Her interest could shift in a moment and their breakfast could burn. Isaac hurried up the narrow steps to his room, left his painting supplies, and raced back down.

He completed making the porridge and served them both. After they ate, he brought in the rest of the wash, then folded and stowed the linens. Once he cleaned the kitchen, he headed out front to sweep the walk. The air held the soft warmth of spring, and a cheerful bustle filled the streets of the village. As he swept, Isaac waved to passing carts, the shop girl across the street who gave a quick wave back, and the baker. He greeted tradesmen on their way to work, servants on their way to their masters' homes, and farmers hauling goods for the market.

The exterior of the shop in order, he returned to the workroom, where his mother busily draped peach ribbon along the full skirt of a pink and yellow gown she'd designed for a special client, Lady Ellen. Isaac frowned as he passed. When had they ordered that shade of ribbon? In the kitchen, he stored the broom, collected gloves and a bucket, and walked back out to the little garden to turn some soil. He'd need to begin planting soon. Once he finished tending their vegetable patch, he restocked the wood for the oven and drew fresh water.

Finally, seated in the workroom, where his mother now added lavender bows to her confection-like concoction of a dress, he took up his tailor's work with another frown. He definitely didn't recall ordering the pricy fabric from which his mother crafted the bows. She continued to hum, so contented in her work that he decided not to ask how much she'd spent on the new silk trimmings. From time to time, she burst into song, leapt to her feet, and danced about the gown. Then she'd settle once again into merely humming as she worked. Isaac just smiled and stitched in time to her improvised tune.

He finished the trousers before luncheon, which he

prepared and served. His mother, intent on her work, didn't notice when he set a plate of food near her. He wanted to ask about the strange, sheer, stiffly boned cloak she'd added to the gown, but didn't care to interrupt her work when she seemed so happily productive. Instead, he went to the front of the shop. He was organizing ribbons when the door to the street swung open.

Filomena Guest swept in, her brother Dougal a step behind. Through the front window, Isaac glimpsed the small gaggle of gentlemen who'd taken up position on the sidewalk in front of the shop. Two and twenty, stunning, well dowered, and daughter to His Majesty's Lieutenant for the County of Cumberfordshire, Filomena Guest featured in many a young gentleman's plans and dreams…but not Isaac's.

Miss Guest halted six inches too close to him. "Good afternoon, Mr. Bell."

"Good afternoon, Miss Guest, Mr. Guest," Isaac said.

Miss Guest jabbed an elbow into her brother's ribs.

"Dougal, please," Dougal Guest said. "I ask all my friends to call me Dougal."

"Thank you, Mr. Guest. I have your trousers ready." Isaac gestured to the back of the shop. "I'd be happy to show you to the dressing room to try them on?"

Rather than step out of the way, Miss Guest smiled to show perfect, even white teeth. "Then come right back out with him. I must inspect your work and assist Dougal in selecting material for the tailcoat." She smushed her mouth into a cute little grimace. "I cannot count on Dougal to select anything *en mode* on his own."

Dougal shrugged and laughed.

"You can, however, count on me, Miss Guest." Isaac kept both voice and expression bland. "Your brother is in safe hands if you have other errands." He nodded toward the front window. "I believe you have more than enough admirers to escort you about town and carry your purchases."

Miss Guest tittered and tossed her head. Her curls swung back to show her long neck. A lovely glass cameo, the silhouette of her departed mother, hung from a chain to rest upon her décolletage. The tribute would have been more touching if Isaac didn't know Miss Guest had one in every color, to match all her gowns.

She rested a hand on his forearm. "Oh, Isaac, you sound jealous."

He frowned.

She snatched back her hand and covered her mouth. She regarded him with startled brown eyes. "I beg your pardon. I meant, Mr. Bell." She shot her brother a slanted glance. "Pretend you did not hear that, Dougal."

"Consider it unheard."

Miss Guest squinted at her brother. "Go try on your trousers, Dougal, while I look through fabrics." She gave Isaac another bright smile.

Dougal, always amiable, shrugged again. "Lead the way, Bell."

Isaac escorted Dougal Guest deeper into the shop. After his mother greeted their customer, Isaac gently ushered her out of the back rooms, so the gentleman could change, sending her to the kitchen with her long-forgotten lunch.

The trousers fit to perfection, as Isaac had known they would. To Dougal's credit, Isaac never needed to resort to padding or extra darts, or any such artifice. Simply sew the best, in the best fit, and Dougal Guest would make the work look good. Much as Dougal's sister used to do for Isaac's mother's eccentric gowns.

Dougal studied his new trousers in a tall mirror and nodded in satisfaction. "Excellent work, Bell. Really could have fitted out the tailcoat at the same time. I don't know why Filomena insists on turning it into so many trips."

"Don't you?" Isaac asked dryly.

Dougal grimaced in sympathy. "Look, man, why not give in and court her? She'll bore of winning your attention in a week or two. Your refusal is what drives her. Well," he laughed, "that and the rumor that your father is a duke."

Isaac snorted. "Duke. Nabob. Author. Earl. You know my mother. The story changes with her whims. All I can say for certain is he dressed finely, had excellent penmanship, and spared no expense when he sent gifts."

Dougal shrugged broad shoulders. "Regardless, why not court Filomena for a bit? My father has labeled me a dandy for purchasing so many suits, and I'd rather have a new mount, for what your work is costing me. Not," he said quickly, "that your skill with a needle isn't worth the price. There's simply a limit to the number of new coats a man needs, and what's the harm in showing Filomena some attention?"

"The harm?" Isaac raised his eyebrows. "What if she doesn't tire of me? We'll end up married."

"Would that be so terrible? My sister is a fine-looking, well-connected young woman with ten thousand pounds. You could certainly do worse."

"I don't hold your sister in that sort of affection."

"You mean, you don't love her." Dougal snorted. "Love. A batty way to pick a wife. Give me connections and coin any day."

Isaac couldn't help but chuckle.

"Dougal," Filomena called from the front of the shop. "Whatever is so amusing? Do come out and show me Mr. Bell's fine workmanship."

"Right, off we go then." Dougal Guest took one last satisfied glance in the mirror and strode from the back room.

Isaac lagged a moment to tidy the dressing room, then ducked into the workshop to deposit a cushion of pins.

"There you are." His mother stood in the kitchen doorway.

"Yes. Here I am." He didn't point out that, as he'd come in earlier and asked her to leave the back rooms, she should know exactly where he might be found.

"I finished the gown, you know." She pointed to the confection of lace, ribbon, and layered skirts on which she'd been working for nearly a month. The flamboyant gown stood in the middle of the workroom, between them.

Isaac said, "Of course, well done," and studied the gown more closely. Though the skirts puffed unfashionably large, overall, the dress seemed rather too small for most ladies. Then again, Isaac didn't know Lady Ellen. He decided he must trust his mother's talents.

"I already hired Mr. Belgica to take me to the fitting." His mother clasped her hands before her, eyes alight with excitement. "Philippe and Philippa are very pleased to go on the adventure. I've been to see them just now and braided ribbons in their manes to match the gown."

"That's splendid news, Mother," Isaac said, but wondered if she'd yet touched her lunch.

Once his mother delivered the gown, he hoped she would return to her normal work. She'd focused exclusively on the ridiculous amalgamation of ribbons, boning, and silk. Since it was impossible to persuade her to do anything she didn't want to do, he'd had to work late into the night while she slept in an effort to keep as few clients as possible from waiting on their orders. He also remained anxious to see if the mysterious Lady Ellen—who'd written and sent her measurements but never visited the shop—liked the dress. He'd already braced for his mother's sorrow…and the damage to their account book.

"You know Lady Ellen invited you to come, as well," his mother said.

"You know I cannot. Someone must mind the shop, and I have much work to do." Also, as his mother hadn't seen fit to show him Lady Ellen's missives, he had no idea if he'd truly been invited. Mother heard what she wanted to hear and said what she preferred to be true. More often than not, that manipulation worked for her.

"We'll leave at first light, I should think," Mother said lightly. "You have plenty of time to change your mind."

"But I won't." Isaac lowered his voice to soften his rejection. "You needn't take the trouble of leaving so early. You'll have to stop at an inn regardless."

Mother shook her head. She'd managed to curl several more locks of hair, but some still fell loose and straight over one shoulder. "We can make the drive in one day. We will go through the forest."

Isaac stilled. "No."

She started to turn away, then paused. "No?"

"The roads on the Adams' estate are nearly unpassable in the best of weather, and we've had a damp spring. And there are clouds brewing to the west."

"Maybe they have repaired the roads."

"Why would they? No one has put any funds into that land in a decade." He firmed his voice. "Mother, I forbid you to take the forest roads. I will tell Mr. Belgica as much." The carriage driver would listen to him over his mother. Belgica couldn't wish to attempt the drive across the Adams' neglected lands any more than Isaac wanted the attempt made.

Mother looked down. "We cannot afford to pay for lodging for me, Mr. Belgica, *and* the horses."

"Certainly, we can. I'll count out the money from our reserve."

She raised beseeching eyes that shimmered with unshed tears. "I used the funds to buy the very best materials for Lady Ellen's gown."

Isaac stared, unable to breathe. He should have moved the funds. He should have hidden her key to the little safe. He should have known….

He inhaled deeply. "Regardless, you cannot take the forest road. I will pay for the inn." He gauged his private savings to be about equal to the task.

"Oh, Izzy, I couldn't let you do that."

He tried to smile. "You can, and you will. Your safety is worth the expense. You may repay the funds to me once Lady Ellen pays you for the gown." Which he prayed she would.

Despite his even manner, his mother's lower lip began to quiver. "I'm sorry, Izzy. I don't deserve such a good son." With a wail, she rushed back through the kitchen door.

"Mr. Bell," Filomena called once more from the front room, tones dulcet.

Isaac glanced in the direction his mother had disappeared. Guilt urged him to go after her and beg forgiveness, but frustration—and some anger—made him want to shake her and force her to admit that she knew full well tears incited contrition on his part. He closed his eyes and reminded himself that the occasional lucidity he glimpsed in her eyes didn't mean she truly understood. He opened his eyes and mustered the neutral expression required face his customer.

Miss Guest sauntered through the doorway. "No one else is here? I thought I heard a woman's voice."

"My mother." He indicated the opposite door. "She's returned to the kitchen."

Miss Guest didn't halt her languid steps until she reached him, eyes sparkling. "Do you mean, we are alone?"

"Highly inappropriate, I agree. Mother!"

To his relief, she appeared immediately, tears already gone. "What is it, dearest?"

"I believe Miss Guest is looking for you."

His mother rushed forward with hands outstretched. "Miss

Guest. How wonderful. Have you finally returned for a new gown?"

Isaac didn't miss the quick spiteful look Filomena cast him, but she permitted Mother to clasp her hands.

While Miss Guest worked to extract herself and his mother tried to show her the new gown she'd created, Isaac escaped to the front of the shop. No matter what Dougal advised, Isaac had no intention of being caught by Filomena.

CHAPTER 4

His mother's luggage in hand, Isaac stepped from the shop into the predawn light to find the carriage she'd rented already waiting. To the west, storm clouds roiled, the gray mass streaked an angry red by a sun not yet visible to the east. As Mr. Belgica dozed in the driver's seat, Isaac began to secure his mother's cases to the rear of the conveyance. At the front, the two stocky Clydesdales, Philippe and Philippa, snorted and pricked up their ears.

When he finished loading, Isaac went to scratch the horses' forelocks. Each responded with a friendly nudge. In the dim light of the new day, he took in their carefully braided manes, decorated with expensive ribbon, and shook his head. Before his mother could appear, Isaac walked back to the driver's seat, where Mr. Belgica snored, wrapped in his cloak against the morning's chill.

Isaac climbed up onto the step to better garner the driver's attention. "Mr. Belgica, a pleasant morning to you."

Mr. Belgica's head popped up. He rubbed his eyes. "And to you, Mr. Bell. What can I do for you? Are your mother's cases ready?"

"I already stowed them, thank you, but you should know, Mother has enough funds for you, her, and the horses to stay at an inn tonight. She may try to convince you to take the shorter route through the forest on the Adams' land. Don't let her. You know how treacherous those roads are."

Mr. Belgica tipped his head in acknowledgment. "I'll see we take the long way, Mr. Bell, and oh, my girl wants to know if she can keep them ribbons." Mr. Belgica pointed to team harnessed before him.

Isaac glanced again at the pricy strips of silk. They would forever smell of horseflesh. He nodded. "She may, and thank you for humoring my mother."

Belgica rolled his shoulders and sat straighter. "No harm in letting her."

Except the loss of work time and ribbons. If Lady Ellen didn't like the gown.... Isaac nodded to Belgica again and jumped down. If Lady Ellen didn't like the gown, Isaac had best have current orders ready as soon as possible. He'd more faith in his skill and speed with a needle than in his ability to ensure his mother didn't spend frivolously in the future.

His mother swung open the shop's door, movements made awkward by the wrapped gown she clutched to her side. Isaac hurried to help stow that all-important package inside the carriage. Despite the rising sun, the morning darkened as the western cloudbank roiled nearer.

"I shan't be away long," Mother said as she slid on her gloves. She clasped her hands in glee. "Lady Ellen will simply adore the gown. Absolutely adore it."

"Yes, Mother, but shouldn't you wait until the storm passes?"

"Certainly not. I have an appointment to keep. Rain is only water."

Isaac frowned, but his mother climbed into the carriage. She patted the gown on the seat next to her and smiled fondly.

Isaac closed the door, rapped on the side, and stepped back. The carriage started forward.

He waved and called, "Safe travels," but his mother's face didn't appear in the back window.

Isaac stared after the carriage for a moment and nearly shivered with an inexplicable sense of foreboding. He shook off the feeling and entered the shop. He'd best sweep the walk before the rain.

Due to the weather and his pending workload, Isaac forewent the pleasure of painting for the day. Instead, he went about his chores, ate his breakfast, and set to sewing. He needed to complete Dougal's tailcoat and a mounting pile of his mother's orders. As he sewed, Isaac tried not to worry over their complete lack of funds.

His mother would need two days to reach Lady Ellen, plus a day there, and two back. If no one else came seeking the services of a tailor or modiste, and Isaac worked all available waking hours, he should be able to finish the outstanding work before his mother returned. If he could collect payment on every completed order, they wouldn't have to borrow, even if Lady Ellen didn't like her dress.

If Lady Ellen *did* like the dress.... Seated in the workroom, bent low over a table to pin seams, Isaac permitted a moment of hope. If she liked the dress, and paid in full, they wouldn't have to fret over money for the remainder of the year. They'd be free to order finer fabrics. For Mother to try one or two more of her fanciful designs. If Lady Ellen had friends who saw the gown and wanted one of their own....

An image of the purple, yellow, peach, and pink extravaganza his mother had created flashed to life in his imagination. Outside, thunder sounded in the distance. Isaac shook his head to dispel his daydreams and lit the candles on his worktable. The day, which should be brightening by now, only grew darker.

The front door's bell jangled. Isaac looked up from his work to find his candles had burned low. Without his mother's constant motion and voice to anchor him, he'd sewn, much as he painted, without conscious thought for the work and the day had nearly passed. He scanned the tailcoat, afraid his needle had wandered off with his mind, and found all in order. He glanced at the mantel clock. He'd missed the hour at which he usually ate lunch, as the time showed nearly two. He needed a cup of tea, at least.

"Mr. Bell," Miss Guest called. "Mr. Bell?"

Isaac stood, back stiff. "Coming," he replied, and snuffed out the candles. He blinked yet again in the sudden darkness, then looked to the window. Fat droplets of rain splashed against the glass.

"Mr. Bell?" Filomena Guest opened the workroom door and squinted into the gloom. "How can you see to work? It's nearly dark as night in here."

Isaac hurried across the room to keep her from entering. He'd no mother to save him now.

"Filomena, come back here," Dougal Guest ordered from the front room. "You can't keep wandering off into the back of the shop. Such behavior is not proper."

Isaac reached the doorway and said to Filomena, "The room is dark because I only now snuffed out the candles." He motioned for her to proceed him to the front of the shop.

Dougal stood by the front door, next to a sopping umbrella he'd leaned against the frame.

Isaac said, "I'm surprised you dared to venture out in this rain."

Dougal grunted as he swiped droplets from his sleeves. "Filomena insisted."

"I'm afraid your effort is wasted. I don't have your coat ready," Isaac said.

"I told her you wouldn't. Hardly been a day."

Miss Guest, who didn't appear at all rained on, tittered. "But we are Mr. Bell's particular customers." She puckered her lips into a pout. "I assumed he'd make a special effort for us."

Behind her, Dougal raised his gaze skyward in silent supplication.

Isaac said, "I am sorry, Miss Guest, Mr. Guest. If I'd known the tailcoat to be urgent, naturally I would have devoted my time exclusively to the garment. But even so, I couldn't have had so elaborate a piece ready for a fitting in only a day."

"No trouble, Bell. No urgency at all." Dougal looked at his sister, expression stern.

"Oh no, no trouble," Filomena echoed. "We can check back again tomorrow." She took two steps and halted before Isaac. "Your mother is away, I hear, so you may need someone to look in on you." She lowered her voice and gazed at him through her lashes. "Someone to take care of you."

"I'm surprisingly capable," Isaac said. "Comes of not having a father, I suppose."

"Oh, but you did have a father." Cupidity sparked in her eyes. "A duke, I shouldn't wonder, by the looks of you. So tall. Upright." She lifted her hand to hover near his face. "Such full, dark locks."

Dougal cleared his throat. "No offense, Bell, but what would a duke be doing in our little corner of Cumberfordshire?"

Annoyance flashed across Miss Guest's features. Then she dropped her arm and flashed a quick grin. "Well, an earl at the least. Everyone says so."

Isaac's chest tightened. He had no wish to discuss his father with Filomena Guest, but he said, "No one knows. People only caught glimpses of him when he used to visit my mother. I haven't seen him since I was a lad of eight, and he stopped writing some time ago." After he sent the red paint.

"Well, we'll find out, don't you worry." She patted his arm.

"Connection to any of the peerage is always desirable, even if only a viscount."

"What about a baron?" Dougal leaned against the door-frame, crossed his arms, and regarded the back of his sister's head with wry amusement.

She shrugged. "Being the bastard of a baron would be something, I suppose. Better than of a common man, to be sure."

"To be sure," Dougal repeated dryly.

Isaac had much work and little patience for Miss Guest's attempts to beguile him. Over her head, he cast Dougal a beseeching look. Normally amiable to his sister's whims, or at least preferring to indulge her in lieu of enduring the brunt of her displeasure, today Dougal seemed an ally.

Dougal nodded. "Filomena, the rain is only getting harder. We should let—"

Thunder clattered. On the street, a horse screeched in fear. Something large hurtled against the outside of the shop door. Dougal jumped away from the door with a startled oath. He tried to regain his balance, but still bumped into his sister, who collided with Isaac.

Isaac seized her slim shoulders, then mentally cursed when Miss Guest clung to him and wailed, "Oh Isaac, hold me."

The door flew open. Wind gusted into the room with a swirl of rain. The candles in the shop flickered and half guttered out. With another oath, Dougal fumbled at his side and Isaac realized the other man reached for a pistol he didn't carry, likely a habit from his time on the Continent. Isaac squinted in the lack of light and discerned a sodden Mr. Belgica huddled in the doorway. A flash of lightning illuminated Philippe and Philippa outside.

Isaac's blood went cold. Where was the carriage? Where was his mother? Isaac pushed Miss Guest aside and lunged toward Belgica. The man braced an arm against the doorframe. Isaac took in his pallor and the dark gash on his forehead.

"Gods man, what happened to you?" Dougal asked.

At his side, Filomena gasped.

Isaac supported Belgica around the waist, pulled him into the shop, and shoved the door closed. "Where is my mother?" he demanded.

Belgica shook his head. Water dripped from his drenched clothes. "I don't know, Mr. Bell. I don't know."

"What do you mean, you don't know? Where is she?"

"We were in the forest when—"

"The forest?" Isaac broke in, voice so harsh he hardly knew it as his own. "I told you not to take the forest road."

Belgica blanched. Thunder clapped again, and he winced. "Aye, but your mum paid me extra to take the route, heaven help me."

Hardly able to breathe, Isaac reiterated, "Where is she?"

"I left her in the forest."

Dougal swore.

Isaac swallowed, trying to clear bile from his throat. "Alone?"

Belgica nodded.

Isaac released the man and surged toward the door, but a strong hand on his shoulder held him back.

"Find out what happened first, Bell, so you know where to go charging off to," Dougal urged.

Isaac turned back to Belgica, fists clenched.

"She paid me to take the forest roads," Belgica protested and took a step back.

"That money was for room and board," Isaac grated out.

"Aye."

"Do you mean that you disobeyed a direct request from Mr. Bell?" Miss Guest stepped up beside Isaac. "How dare you? He should have your hide. My father will hear of this."

"How dare I?" Belgica shot back. "My carriage is shattered,

somewhere in that forest. That carriage is my livelihood. I say Bell owes me."

"He most certainly does not," Miss Guest said. "How you could listen to Miss Bell, when Mr. Bell ordered you to do the opposite, is incomprehensible. And to take money from her to do so? You should be ashamed, Mr. Belgica, and don't tell me you didn't know better, because everyone knows the woman is—"

"Filomena," Dougal cut in.

"But what actually happened?" Isaac said before Miss Guest could begin haranguing again. "Where is your carriage?"

Belgica's Adam's apple bobbed. "I left the carriage, and her in it. I...there was so much thunder and lightning, like cannon fire. The road was so pitted and narrow. I don't even know if we were still on the road. A fallen tree appeared out of nowhere and my team jumped the tree. The carriage crashed into the trunk." He shook his head.

"You crashed?" Isaac ignored the arm Miss Guest wrapped about his and half growled to Mr. Belgica, "And you left her there?"

Thunder clashed again, and Mr. Belgica cowered. "I had to. I was thrown free, you see." He lifted a shaky hand to the gash on his head. "And I chased the horses. I finally caught them far down the road, with the shafts still dragged between them. All worn out, poor beasts. I freed the tack from the wreckage, then led them back, thinking we could each ride one, but—" He swallowed and began to shake. "But—" His teeth chattered.

"Perhaps a dram of something?" Dougal suggested.

"He doesn't need a dram," Isaac snapped. "He needs to tell me what happened to my mother."

"I'll go look." Miss Guest sounded unaffected, for once. "There must be something in the kitchen," she said and hurried off.

Dougal took the driver's arm. "Take a deep breath, Mr. Belgica. How about a seat? There's a chair right over here."

Isaac ground his teeth, more inclined to force the tale from Belgica than soothe him to get news, but Dougal kept up his ministrations. Isaac concentrated on trying to breathe and to remember that Dougal, having served on the Continent, likely knew what he was about. Miss Guest returned with a glass of wine. Belgica drained the dark liquid in one long swig.

Belgica held out the glass. "More, please, Miss?"

Dougal nodded. Miss Guest took the glass and disappeared back through the workroom door.

Isaac took a firm stance before the carriage driver. He folded his arms across his chest and repeated the only question that mattered, "Where is my mother?"

"I went back to the carriage, to get her. I swear I did. But…I lost my nerve. I grabbed Philippe's reins tight, vaulted onto Philippa's back, and we ran."

Isaac threw up his hands. "But what frightened you, man?"

"A banshee—from them old stories. White face. Wild hair. Screeching fit to drive a man mad. You could hear her wails over the thunder. And a great, giant black bucca, come in with the storm from the sea. Manlike, but a towering giant with skin like coal and bright burning eyes. The thunder was all around them, and lightning flashing, and neither one cared. The banshee screeched on and the bucca stood, a statue but alive. Then his glowing eyes settled on me, and that's when I ran." He trembled. "I'm paid to drive people, not to die at the hands of the fey. Like as not, your mother's madness summoned them."

Isaac tried to force speech through his anger. "There are no banshees, you fool. Or buccas. You left my mother to die in the forest."

Belgica drew his shoulders back. "I know what I saw."

Isaac had heard enough. "I'm going to get my mother. Philippe will know on the way." He started for the door.

Belgica surged to his feet. "You're not taking my horse back there to be devoured by a bucca. I'll turn you in for a thief. You'll hang."

Isaac wanted to ignore the man, but he couldn't be charged as a horse thief. When he got his mother back, he'd be no use to her dangling from a gallows.

He swung back to Dougal. "Did you ride?"

"We came in our carriage," Miss Guest said as she finally emerged from the kitchen. "I couldn't find any more wine," she added.

"What say you, Dougal, will you go with me?" Isaac asked.

Miss Guest stopped at her brother's side. "But we need to get home. It's nearly two miles." As if to emphasize her point, another loud clap of thunder shook the shop.

Outside, the horses squealed. Belgica rushed past them toward the door. He said over his shoulder, "Roads are all washed out, Guest. Full of holes you can't even see in the rain. Your carriage will never manage." He yanked open the door, then plunged into the dark.

Isaac slammed the door behind him.

"You see? Our carriage would do you no good," Miss Guest said.

"Dougal?" Isaac repeated.

Miss Guess marched over to stand before Isaac. "If we let you use our carriage, what will you promise me?"

Isaac blinked.

"Filomena—" Dougal began.

"No," she cut in. "Isaac is always putting me off. I made a fool of myself, patronizing his mother's gowns. Isaac knows what I want. Would marriage to me be so terrible? I bring money. Connections."

Isaac locked gazes with her. "Miss Guest, I wouldn't marry

you if we were fresh off the Ark and the perpetuation of humanity depended upon our union."

She balled her hands into fists at her sides. "Then you cannot use our horses or carriage."

"Then I'm going on foot." Isaac sidestepped Miss Guest and headed for the back room.

"What do you mean?" She hurried after him.

Isaac reached the kitchen and snatched up his cloak as he passed through. He halted at the garden door. His back to them, he said, "Lock up for me, Mr. Guest, if you will."

Ignoring Miss Guest's screeches of protest, Isaac rushed out into the rain.

CHAPTER 5

Betsy paused in pacing the thick bedchamber carpet and frowned at the unresponsive woman on the bed. Mr. Relógio sat in an armchair near the window, where he read. Betsy knew he kept part of his attention on her, to evaluate her choices.

Winter had faded, a winter she'd barely survived. She didn't know how to manage her stores. She didn't know from where more food came. She had no money to send to London for supplies, even if that were the answer. Most of her staff had left. Either the promise of new management come August's end —after her presumed failure—wasn't enough to keep them, or they'd gone down the lane to work in the dower house. Some she'd let go, as they'd become indolent. Those who remained did nothing for her personally, but still seemed to care about the manor house. She'd little idea what work they accomplished, only that they keep the house and grounds in some vague state of order.

Now spring was upon them, and Betsy had only earned three rose petals. She had no exact idea how many petals there were in total, but the glimpse she'd had on the eve of the new year suggested at least twenty. Demands made of Mr. Relógio were met with replies in his own language. Betsy had found books on languages in the library, ones she'd been assigned but had refused to study, but without a tutor at hand, how could she know which book held the key to Mr. Relógio's words?

She kicked at the carpet as she walked, then sneezed. How did one remove dust from a carpet? She recalled the staff taking them outside and beating them. Something they'd done when she was still small. How often should one beat carpets? She sneezed again. Apparently, more often than had been done of late. She glanced again at Mr. Relógio, but the dust didn't appear to trouble him. Nothing ever did.

The woman in the bed stirred and Betsy stilled. She wanted the woman to wake. Betsy had considered sending for a doctor but didn't know if the servants would listen to her. She would ask Penna to order one of the footmen to go. Penna proved sometimes willing to give advice and assistance. Betsy would have to get help soon if the woman they'd found didn't wake. She knew Mr. Relógio would judge her lack of action.

Mr. Relógio should give her a petal for finding the woman, no matter why Betsy had been out in the storm. What did it matter if, under Mr. Relógio's watchful gaze, she had quarreled with Penna over the last of the potatoes? Penna had some stupid notion of planting them to grow more, but Betsy had wanted to eat them for her supper, then take more from Rodchamb's tenants. Her grandmother had stipulated that she couldn't raise their rent, but not that she couldn't take their potatoes.

Penna's disappointed expression and Mr. Relógio's frown had told her she was in the wrong, yet again. Betsy had given in to a fit of anger and raced out into the raging storm with Mr. Relógio at her heels...and that particular choice had turned out rather well. She'd found the wrecked carriage, the driver and horses gone, and an unconscious woman inside. Then a bizarre gentleman had appeared, screamed at them, and ridden off. Obviously, the odd little man would be no help to the woman, so Betsy had asked Mr. Relógio to carry her back. For once, he'd seemed to understand her and had done her bidding.

But now the woman wouldn't wake up. Betsy had thought she would, come morning. That's when people woke up, after all. She sneezed again and opened her eyes to find her visitor conscious and alert, finally. From under softly graying auburn locks, the woman studied Betsy with keen hazel eyes.

Betsy rushed to the bedside. "You're awake."

Relief filled her, and not simply because the woman had woken. Betsy looked forward to the chance to converse with someone who didn't know the weight of her circumstances, someone who maybe wouldn't judge her and find her constantly wanting.

"Yes, quite awake." The woman looked about the room. Her gaze halted on Mr. Relógio, who'd lowered his book. Sunlight streamed over him where he sat by the window. She smiled at him, then turned back to Betsy. "Where am I? May I ask your name? Whatever is the matter with your hair, child?"

Betsy raised a hand to the rat's nest atop her head. Penna refused to wash or comb her hair, or lighten the darker sections with lemon juice, or even simply tie back the unruly mass. Betsy had decided to ignore her hair as best she could, and now the matted strands formed a giant tangled mass that stood out from her head in various directions.

"I'm Betsy Adams and...." A little hiccup left her. Nearly a sob. "I don't know how to fix my hair." Tears spilled from her eyes. She fell to her knees beside the bed and buried her face in the dusty coverlet.

The woman smoothed her hair with a gentle hand. "There, there, child. We'll fix that."

A voice filled the room. A lovely, clear, lilting voice. Betsy didn't know the tune. The words sounded nonsensical. Something about little bluebirds and bows, but peace washed through her and she stopped crying. She lifted her head to find the woman wore a happy expression as she sang. Betsy smiled back with trembling lips.

"There now," the woman said. "All better."

Betsy nodded. She stood, wiped her cheeks with the heels of her hands, and plopped down on the side of the bed. "Thank you."

The woman started to slide upward but grimaced.

"What's wrong?" Betsy asked.

Alarm skittered through her. If the woman was hurt, had Betsy somehow made her injury worse by sitting on the bed? That possibility seemed likely. Ever since her grandmother dismissed her parents to London, Betsy seemed to make everything worse. She cast Mr. Relógio a worried look, but he'd gone back to his reading.

"It's my leg," the woman said.

"Is it…will you die?" Betsy whispered.

The woman blinked then laughed. "Of a twinge in my leg? I hardly think so. I have two, after all, so how important can one be?"

Betsy glanced at her own legs. She enjoyed having the use of both and thought both rather important. Her mind flashed to the young footman who'd fallen from the banister the night her grandmother arrived. He'd likely enjoyed having the use of both of his arms, and she'd risked all four of his limbs for a silly game.

"Oh dear. You're sad again. How can we rectify that?" The woman regarded Betsy with concerned eyes.

Betsy thought her face the kindest she had ever seen. Every line, faint though they were, spoke of cheerfulness. Crinkles around her eyes. Indentations curving upward from her mouth.

No worry had drawn harsh marks across her forehead or between her brows. Betsy thought back to the flash of intense assessment in the woman's eyes when she woke, an expression incongruitous to the sunny one before her, and decided she'd imagined it.

"Do you think…." Betsy drew in a deep breath, touching her hair again. "Do you think you could help me with my hair?" She didn't dare glance at Mr. Relógio, sure he'd frown.

"Of a certainty, my dear, as soon as I wash and dress." The woman looked about the room again. "But where are my cases?" She covered her mouth with her hands. "Where is the gown? The gown that was with me in the carriage? And Philippe and Philippa? And Mr. Belgica?" Eyes wide, she asked Betsy again, "Where am I?"

"Oh, yes, I forgot you asked," Betsy said in a rush. "You are at Rodchamb Manor. My…my family's manor, only right now I am the only one here. I am Miss Betsy Adams, as I said, and that is Mr. Relógio. We rescued you from a carriage last night, in the storm." She recalled the scene and frowned. "There was a man with two horses. He rode off with them. I didn't see anyone else. Are Philippe and Philippa your friends? Children?"

The woman shook her head. "Philippe and Philippa are Mr. Belgica's horses."

"Oh, then they must be well. He took them with him."

"And the gown?"

Betsy shook her head. "We didn't search for luggage." She gestured to the window, a bright sunny day without. "We can go check now?"

The woman clasped her hands together and rewarded Betsy with a bright smile. "Yes, that will be lovely." She took in her quilt-covered form. "I do think this dress is unfit for gadding about, though. May I borrow a dress? From whom did you borrow that dress?"

Betsy frowned again. "This is my dress." She blushed and folded her hands over a large stain on her skirt.

"Oh dear. That's not right. The fit is no good. That gown is much too large, Miss Adams, and the color does nothing to show off your lovely complexion and, well…that dress is simply no fun at all."

The dress hung limp and dingy from her form, for she'd lost considerable weight once the cook refused to prepare meals for her. More stains spattered the gown than the large one she now covered. Her cheeks heated.

"But no matter," the woman said. "We can set that right too. I am a modiste, you know. We'll have you in something equal to your loveliness in no time at all."

Betsy's hope surged. "Truly?"

"Definitely, but first, may I borrow a gown and," she looked at Mr. Relógio, "would you please excuse me, sir, while I ready for the day?"

He angled his head in acknowledgment and stood. He tucked his book under his arm, crossed the room, and went out into the hall.

The moment the door closed behind him, the woman said, "He's a handsome one, isn't he?"

Betsy looked at the closed door, then at the woman. She'd never thought of Mr. Relógio in that way. He existed as her adjudicator and constant shadow.

"He's so old," Betsy said.

The woman laughed. "We all grow old, Miss Adams, if we're fortunate enough." Then she burst into song again: "Olden golden, folded too. Wrinkled crinkled, me and you."

Betsy stared at her.

The woman gazed back with an open, pleased expression.

Heat crept up Betsy's neck as she realized she'd blundered yet again, and surely Mr. Relógio had observed as much before departing. "I'm sorry…I never asked your name."

"Miss Bell. Marcia Bell, the modiste."

"It is very good to meet you, Miss Bell," Betsy said. "I'll fetch you a gown."

"And soap and water?" Miss Bell asked.

"Oh yes. Certainly."

Miss Bell began humming. Again, Betsy didn't know the tune, but the song lilted with joy and sparked a similar emotion in her. She rushed from the room to find Mr. Relógio seated in a chair at the far end of the hall, now reading by the light of the window there.

"I must fetch Miss Bell a gown and soap and water," Betsy called and hurried away.

The gown would be easy enough, for Betsy had many. Extra pitchers she could find in the kitchen, though she'd happily lend Miss Bell her own. Soap, though…Betsy had used up hers months ago, and then what she'd found in her parents' chambers, and Penna wouldn't tell her where to find more in Rodchamb's endless cupboards and closets. Fortunately, from her occasional attempts to discover what the house held, Betsy knew where clean linens were kept, at least the ones for washing. She'd grown bored with sorting through Rodchamb's storerooms before locating any for the tables and beds.

Some household items had been taken by the staff when they quit or when Betsy sent them away, like the crystals from the chandelier in the entrance hall. Someone had lowered the fixture, but not to change the candles. They'd left the chandelier down and now the armature hung there at eye level, stripped of all beauty, a constant reminder of Betsy's inadequacy. Other items, she suspected, had gone to the dower house for use by her grandmother. She scowled at that thought and tromped off to the kitchen.

She'd trekked down the lane once with snow thick on the ground and hunger gnawing at her insides and peered through the dower house windows at suppertime. Her grandmother and Mr. Relógio had sat inside, bathed in cozy yellow firelight. They'd dined and chatted in that strange language—likely discussing his daily report on Betsy. Mr. Relógio had poured them wine, and Betsy's grandmother smiled and resting a hand on his sleeve as she seemed wont to do. Betsy had longed to pound on the door and demand to eat with them, but pride, and the fear that her grandmother would take the act as capitulation, had forced her to tromp back to Rodchamb's grand, hollow mansion for a dinner of stale bread and sprouting potatoes. How she hated potatoes!

Betsy stomped down the hall, collected a bucket, then headed through the kitchen and out to the well. She drew enough water to fill a large ceramic pitcher and went back inside to gather one, along with a wide, flat washbasin. The basin clutched under one arm and the bucket and pitcher in hand, she went back upstairs. Aware that Mr. Relógio assessed her manners from the end of the hall, Betsy gently set the items before Miss Bell's bedroom door.

She left them for the time being to rummage in the storage closet from which she took clean towels whenever hers seemed too filthy to use anymore. Betsy had tried to ration herself to one towel per month. Very few now remained, but Mr. Relógio would expect Betsy to give at least one to Miss Bell. Clean towel in hand, Betsy went to her room to collect a gown. She selected green, which should look very well with Miss Bell's auburn hair.

When she reached the door to Miss Bell's room, Betsy peeked down the hall at Mr. Relógio, then politely knocked and called, "Miss Bell, it's me, Miss Adams. May I come in?"

"You certainly may, Miss Adams," Miss Bell trilled.

Betsy pushed the door open to find Miss Bell stood beside the bed, one leg cocked so her foot didn't touch the floor and both hands clutching the bedpost for support. "Your leg. Will it mend?"

Miss Bell studied her torn skirt. "Oh, I daresay it will. The trouble is my knee, you know. Doesn't seem to take any weight. I'd so much prefer if the trouble were with my ankle. Ankles are much more romantic than knees, do you not think?"

Betsy crossed to the bed. "I do not know. I never thought much about either."

"Oh, but you should. Why not? Such things are good to know."

"Being a modiste, I suppose you must consider...knees and ankles."

Miss Bell smiled in agreement but nodded her head at the open door.

"Oh yes," Betsy said and turned to retrieve the supplies. She carried the pitcher and basin to the dressing table, then returned for the bucket, towel, and gown. She placed the towel and bucket by the table as well, then held up the gown. "I thought you would like green."

"I like all colors, except black, but then it really isn't, is it?"

"Isn't what?" Betsy asked.

"A color." Miss Bell made to hobble to the dressing table.

Betsy quickly draped the dress over her shoulder and rushed over to offer her support. "I haven't actually thought about colors in that way, either."

"Well, you should, but not at the moment," Miss Bell said as she took Betsy's arm. "Right now, we must concentrate on your ankles. Are they well turned? If they are, we shall raise your hem to show them. A fetching ankle is a good step to getting a husband." They reached the table and Miss Bell braced her free hand against the carved wood. Betsy stood to the side, to give her more room to wash. "Life is so much easier, they say, with a husband."

"You do not have one?" Betsy asked. Of course, she didn't. Hence, the title of "Miss," despite the fine lines and gray hair.

Miss Bell's expression grew wistful. "No. A husband wasn't for me." She brightened. "But I do have a lovely son."

"Oh. That's...good."

Did a son make Miss Bell a woman of loose morals? A modiste *and* a trollop? Could one be both? If she were a trollop, would Betsy have to send her away?

Miss Bell stared into the dressing table mirror, eyes unfocused. "Such a handsome gentleman, my Izzy's father. So kind and good. Always sending beautiful gifts for Izzy." She launched into another strange song.

Betsy stared again. Miss Bell, she realized, was a bit odd. Yet, so very nice. So happy. Not only that, she gave of her happiness freely. Betsy hadn't met anyone so cheerful in...she didn't know how long, if ever. She liked Miss Bell. What did it matter if the woman wasn't quite...normal? Besides, Miss Bell must stay for at least a time. She couldn't walk.

Miss Bell leaned against the table and twisted her hair into a neat knot. "...and once I'm crisp and clean, then we shall see what is yet unseen..." she sang as she reached for the water bucket.

Worried Miss Bell would fall over, Betsy dipped down and grabbed the bucket handle. She lifted the bucket and poured water into the basin and pitcher.

Miss Bell thanked her, then ducked her head to splash water on her face.

Betsy set the bucket aside and asked, "Do you think we can really fix my hair?"

"Oh yes, dear, we'll do that." Miss Bell dabbed her face with the towel.

"And, maybe, one of my gowns?"

"Certainly, my sweet Miss Betsy Adams," Miss Bell sang.

"Miss Bell, do you know how to make bread? Or, maybe, plant potatoes?"

"I do."

"Might you show me?"

"I'd be honored to do so."

Betsy grinned as she hadn't in months. Perhaps years. Now that Miss Bell had arrived, maybe everything would be well.

CHAPTER 6

Under the shadows of encroaching trees, Isaac trudged down the deeply rutted forest road. He'd walked the forest roads for days, working his way from the westernmost to the east. After that first night, unable to find anything along the roadway Mr. Belgica should have taken, Isaac had gone back to speak with the man and discovered that Belgica was uncertain if, in the storm, he'd made a wrong turn. He couldn't even say how far he'd gone, though Isaac guessed not overly far in the heavy rain, over rutted roads, and in the darkness under storm clouds and these ancient trees.

So, Isaac searched. He left before dawn each day and kept careful track of which roads he'd investigated. He sought the broken carriage. Or spilled luggage. Any sign, really, of his mother.

And each passing day, fear squeezed tighter about his heart. Were his mother well, would she not return? She was distractible, unfocused, given to fanciful behavior, but wouldn't she return, if she could?

When at home, he'd searched his mother's possessions for a letter from Lady Ellen. He sought her address so he could write to see if his mother had pressed onward alone, but had found no correspondence from her. He waited in vain hope each day for her ladyship to write them, as she surely must if his mother hadn't arrived. Maybe today, when he returned to the village by the weak lingering rays of daylight, he'd find the message he awaited. He'd need to use his last few coins to pay the postage, but news of his mother was worth any price.

Isaac skirted a hole large enough to bury a cow and shook his head. How could the tenants take goods to market? How could tradesmen come in to offer their services? Why were the Ada mses permitting Rodchamb's roadways to fall into such ill repair, and for so long?

Everyone knew the roads were only the tip of disreputableness to be found at Rodchamb. Rumors filtered out of the forest about the poor treatment of those beholden to the Adamses. Isaac had met the people who'd packed up and left their land to seek work elsewhere. That very winter, quite a few servants had passed through the village on their way south to London to seek employment. They spoke of a family gone mad.

But not of a banshee, nor a bucca, and Isaac had found no evidence of either, or any other fey. Not that he thought he would. Belgica had simply been scared by the storm or, were Isaac being uncharitable, making excuses for abandoning Isaac's mother.

Whatever the truth, Belgica still refused use of his horses, even had Isaac the funds. Worse, he'd spread tales of evil throughout the village. No one wanted to help Isaac hunt for a woman they all felt was not only crazy, but also touched with scandal and shame. No matter that rumor had his father a duke, his mother remained a wanton woman. Between his mother's reputation, Belgica's ghost stories, and Isaac's inability to offer any compensation, he could stir no help for his search.

Nor could he approach the Lord-Lieutenant or any other

member of the Guest family. Not after how he'd left things with Miss Guest. Isaac rubbed at his temples. He would need to fix that problem. Not only did their shop require the good will of the Guests and their peers, but as His Majesty's Lieutenant for the County of Cumberfordshire, Miss Guest's father could also make Isaac's and his mother's lives quite difficult. He could drive them from the county if he wished. Isaac had no delusions that Filomena Guest would be content with rejection.

He continued to scrub at the tension in his forehead but walked on in the muggy air that still lingered, even several days after the passage of the storm. Very faintly, a soothing murmur reached his ears, and he dropped his arm. He breathed deep of musty earth and moldering leaves, then stopped. The murmur wasn't random. A lilting rhythm pattered through the notes.

Isaac lengthened his stride, skirting gouges in the road. The murmur consolidated into singing. A song he knew. One no one else could know, the tune being one of his mother's inventions. He broke into a run. Over his increasingly ragged breath, he could hear her song, her voice not alone.

Far down the rutted road, an open black iron gate emerged from the gloom on the right side of the roadway. He reached the gate, which hung open from tall stone pillars. Up ahead on the road sat Belgica's carriage, half overturned, three of the four wheels broken. His mother's cases were no longer tied to the back.

Isaac stopped, panting. His mother's voice came from somewhere beyond the gate to his right. He decided the carriage could wait and turned to jog up the drive.

He raced between trees planted at even intervals. Forest giants, their trunks stretched wider than Isaac stood tall. Their bulky, gnarled roots heaved the sides of the roadway upward, almost as if the trees cradled the drive. Their broad limbs crisscrossed over the road and combined with half-unfurled leaves to block the sun.

As he burst free of the trees, Isaac discovered a vast stone manor house and knew he'd reached Rodchamb Mansion. He looked across a sweeping lawn in dire need of a trim but saw no one. The singing still sounded far off, so he veered from the drive and headed around the house. His skin prickled as he raced by rows of lead-paned windows, as if each beveled diamond held an observer to his trespass, but a glance showed only his face reflected over and over.

He rounded the corner of the house to the rear and found several more oaks and a waif-thin young woman. Hair the color of dark honey cascaded in a silken rivulet down her back. She wore an ill-fitted dress and swung a broom at a rug draped over a low limb. Dust puffed upward. The young woman broke off her singing with a delighted laugh, then struck the rug again.

To her right, his mother sat on a blanket beside rows of freshly tilled earth, legs stretched out before her. She leaned sideways and appeared to be planting seeds, her voice raised in song with the young woman's.

To see his mother unharmed and happy filled Isaac with joy.

Then confusion.

Then anger.

Did she not realize the pain his worry her disappearance had caused?

Isaac sucked in air to steady his nerves. Anger never proved useful with his mother. He uncoiled his clenched fists and continued to breathe slowly. A breath in. A breath out. He must harness his emotions. Ever since the night his mother had decided his father would never come back, the night she'd nearly burned down their shop in a fit of misery, Isaac had realized that one of them must behave calmly. One of them must speak with care and thought. That one would never be his mother. Across the lawn, she continued to sing and work, while the young woman savagely beat at the rug, her glee almost maniacal.

Under control, Isaac pulled out a handkerchief and blotted sweat from his brow. He tucked the square of cloth back away, then straightened his coat. A swipe returned his hair to order, disarrayed from his dash up the road and around the house. He glanced at the slender woman with the broom, her back still to him, and hoped he appeared presentable.

As he started forward Isaac noticed that, in the shade of another tree, a tall, black-skinned gentleman in an exceedingly fine suit sat on a bench, his expertly tailored wardrobe a stark contrast to the young woman's obviously borrowed dress. The gentleman held a book, but watched Isaac through dark, assessing eyes. Isaac dipped his head in a nod of acknowledgement but kept his steps aimed for his mother.

"Izzy," she cried as his approach finally garnered her attention. She held up her arms but didn't rise. "You found me. Help me up."

"Mother," he managed in an even tone and reached down to pull her to her feet.

Once upright, she held him tight for a moment, then released him and bent to sweep up a cane from the blanket on which she'd sat.

"Are you unwell, Mother?" The last vestiges of his hurt warred with worry as she leaned heavily on the cane.

She grimaced, but somehow still maintained her cheerful demeanor. "My knee doesn't seem to be quite right. It's terrible for dancing."

"Terrible for...." He trailed off. He was calm. Rational. Not full of anger, at all. "Mother, I have been beyond worried for you. I've been searching for you for days. I thought...that is, Belgica said...Mother..." he beseeched.

"Well, I couldn't very well walk home, and I didn't want to write because I didn't want you to have to pay the postage." She tipped her head to one side. "If you've been searching, who's been minding the shop?"

From the corner of his eye, Isaac noted movement to both sides as the young woman and the well-dressed gentleman converged on them, but he kept his focus on his mother.

He willed her to understand. "No one has been tending the shop. I have been searching for you. Mr. Belgica came back with wild tales of the storm and the carriage crash, and I thought you were alone in the forest, possibly dying."

"Oh, my poor boy." She patted him on the cheek. "But how silly of you. If I were dying, I would let you know."

Isaac closed his eyes and prayed for patience.

"This is Izzy?" a breathless voice asked to his left. "From the way you speak of him and his love of painting, I thought him a mere boy. A child of perhaps ten."

Isaac turned to take in a woman of about his own age of two and twenty. Eyes the color of bluebells bathed in sunlight met his gaze, and bowlike lips pressed into a mild frown.

He bowed. "Isaac Bell."

The young woman performed a curtsy in obvious need of practice and said, "Miss Elizabeth Adams."

"But everyone calls her Betsy," his mother added, then gestured to her left. "And this is Mr. Relógio. He doesn't speak, but he's here to see that Miss Adams behaves."

Isaac, halfway through a bow to Mr. Relógio, raised his eyebrows at that declaration. He straightened to find Miss Adam's cheeks gone scarlet. He looked between the two, saw a glimmer of mischief in his mother's eyes, and realized she'd deliberately tormented the girl.

In an effort to forestall whatever game his mother played, Isaac said, "It is very good to meet you both. Perhaps you could tell me what my mother is doing in your care, and whatever is wrong with her knee?"

"We rescued her," Miss Adams said quietly.

"Nothing is wrong with my knee, Izzy. I have lovely knees. Your father always said so."

Isaac would have prayed for more forbearance, but he could feel Mr. Relógio's scrutiny and didn't want to give the impression his mother dismayed him. "Nothing is wrong with your knees, Mother, but you do not appear to be able to use both to full advantage at this time."

"Oh, yes. That's because I twisted one when the carriage tipped over." Before he could comment on that bit of information, she grabbed his sleeve, face radiant. "We saved the dress, Izzy."

"That's good," he said, but Lady Ellen's order seemed the least of his concerns. "Mother, I'd like to take you home."

"No," his mother said but her refusal was drowned out by Miss Adams.

"I forbid it," she practically screeched.

Isaac turned to Miss Adams in shock. "You forbid me to take my mother home?"

Miss Adams, face quite pale now, nodded. "I need her."

"And she needs the care and comfort of her home."

"She is very comfortable here," Miss Bell snapped.

"Children." His mother's soothing tone grated. "There is no need to argue." She placed a hand on Miss Adams' arm. "Betsy, dear, I cannot remain."

"But, Miss Bell," Tears flooded Betsy's eyes. "I need you."

"I know, dear, but I simply cannot stay a moment longer."

Isaac could little imagine why the spoiled daughter of rich, neglectful landowners required his mother, but it pleased him that, for once, she chose to see sense. "I am certain you can find someone else to fulfil whatever services my mother is rendering?" Isaac cast a questioning look at Mr. Relógio, but the gentleman remained silent. Isaac continued, "My mother is injured and must return with me."

"Oh no, dear. I'm not going with you, either," his mother said.

Isaac started and stared at her.

"I am going to Lady Ellen's. With the dress," she stated. "I don't know what possessed you, leaving the shop untended, but we've no more money. Even your personal savings are used up. I must take the gown to Lady Ellen and hope she pays, or we face ruin."

"Mother, you've no means of getting to Lady Ellen," he said.

"Certainly, I do." She faced Miss Adams. "Betsy will loan me her horses and carriage, and a driver."

Miss Adams shook her head. "Why would I? I want you to stay." She jutted her jaw at a stubborn angle. "I need you here."

To Isaac's left, Mr. Relógio let out a nearly imperceptible sigh. Was this the sort of willful behavior the gentleman was meant to curtail?

Mother took Betsy's hand and smiled. "Don't worry, dear. Izzy will stay and help you. He's much better at these things then I am. He manages our home and shop beautifully."

Isaac stared at his mother again. "I will...stay here?"

"You manage a shop as well?" Miss Adams asked.

"He's managed ours since he was nine," Isaac's mother said proudly.

"Really?" Hope suffused Miss Adams' features. She made a vague gesture. "You know about finances? Do you know how to grow food?"

"I know how to grow the food we require," he said, confused. "Why do you need someone to manage finances?" He looked about, just then truly taking in the overgrown lawn. The rug Miss Adams had been beating. The lack of wash on the lines outside what must be the kitchen door. How only a small portion of the soil in the garden had been turned. Most of all, the lack of any staff. Even when he'd come up the drive, he'd seen no one. "Are you and Mr. Relógio here alone?"

Miss Adams glanced at Mr. Relógio, who remained impassive, then cleared her throat. Twisting her hands tight together before her, she said, "We aren't alone. Some of the staff remain, and Mr. Relógio goes to the dower house every evening for dinner, and that's where much of the staff ran off to. They're all loyal to my grandmother, but not to me. They don't want the house to go to ruin, but they won't help me with a thing." As she spoke, Miss Adams' voice rose in octaves, inching closer and closer to tears. "At first, my companion, Penna, tried to help but...but she says I am too mean to her, and now even she won't help me." With a strained sob, Miss Adams covered her face with her hands.

His mother patted Miss Adams on the shoulder. "Izzy, how could you? You've made her cry."

Isaac shook his head. "I made her cry?" He asked Mr. Relógio directly, "Would you please tell me what the devil is going on here?"

"He won't tell you," Isaac's mother said. "He doesn't speak."

"Then you tell me, Mother."

His mother continued to pat Miss Adams on the back. "Betsy must order the house and get the planting in and manage the tenants. If she cannot, her grandmother is going to take all this loveliness away from her." Her sweeping gesture encompassed the house, the yard, and the trees and fields beyond.

Isaac took in the dilapidated state of the property yet again. He thought of the terrible roads he'd walked. The grandmother should take charge of the estate herself, if possible.

"And I don't know how to do anything," Miss Adams wailed. "I am going to fail, and Grandmother will kick me out of my home and make me live with my parents and take my dowry and no man will want me and I shall die. I'll be so miserable, I'll die."

His mother wrapped an arm about Miss Adams and glared at him. "You see what you have done with your obstinance,

Izzy? Now Miss Adams is going to die." His mother burst into tears and sobbed in concert with Miss Adams.

Isaac swallowed a curse and turned again to Mr. Relógio, who betrayed only the faint impression of wry amusement. Isaac narrowed his gaze. Somehow, though Mr. Relógio reportedly didn't speak, Isaac had a strong suspicion he did understand.

Miss Adams grasped Isaac's coat sleeve and regarded him through watery blue eyes. "Please, Miss Bell, if I might speak with your son for a moment, in private."

His mother snuffled and procured a handkerchief from a skirt pocket to wipe her face. As she lowered the square of cloth, sorrow fled her features, her leftover tears the glitter of sunlight after a storm. "A splendid idea. I am certain you can make him see that he must stay and help you."

Miss Adams' lips trembled. "I can only try, Miss Bell." She tugged on Isaac's sleeve and pulled him away, in the direction of the rug-laden tree.

As soon as he proved willing to follow, she released his arm. She led him around the tree, so that the rug hung between them and where his mother stood with Mr. Relógio. With the heels of her hands, she dried her wet cheeks. Isaac would have her offered his handkerchief, had he not earlier employed it to remove his own sweat.

"I see my distress did not move you," she said, words crisp.

"My mother is injured and is needed at our shop. She spoke honestly about the state of our finances."

"Yet she also claims that you manage the shop well."

He shrugged. "The gown Mother fashioned for Lady Ellen took much of our resources."

Miss Adams appraised him. "So, it *is* rather important that your mother take the gown to this Lady Ellen."

"I suppose so."

"Then listen well, Mr. Bell. Your mother also gave you an

accurate description of my troubles. My grandmother, who holds the entirety of the family fortune, already banished my parents to London on a very tight allowance. She's given me until the end of August to show that I am both capable of managing this estate and worthy of doing so, or she'll send me off to join them." Miss Adams scowled. "I am not being carted off to London to live on fifty pounds a year with my depraved parents."

He'd thought her quite pretty, until this look of willful desperation formed on her face. "I fail to see how your predicament is any of my or my mother's concern."

Her blue eyes flashed. "Because I can keep her here. She adores me. All I have to do is cry, and your mother will never leave me. You can forget her taking Lady Ellen the costly dress. You can forget her returning to work in your failing shop."

Isaac knew that threat wouldn't prove true, but suspected Miss Adams could not. His mother cared for her precious gowns more than anything else. Food. Keeping the shop solvent. Isaac. Yes, she also cared about Miss Adams right now, but Marcia Bell often fell subject to her own whims. No one knew his mother's mercurial nature better than he.

He opened his mouth to tell Miss Adams as much but paused. He took in the fresh shimmer of tears in her eyes, noted the almost imperceptible tremble that shook her every limb, and realized her hauteur for a bluff. He also remembered that he didn't have any way to safely get his mother to Lady Ellen, where his mother would surely go, regardless.

"Did you even think to have my mother send word to me?" he asked, instead.

Miss Adams grimaced. "Sending word did not occur to me."

"Even though you thought me just a child? You left a mere child with no knowledge of his mother's fate."

She shrugged but reddened. "I didn't think of it," she repeated. She sighed and let her shoulders slump. "I don't think about things. About people. I...I only think about me." She wrapped her arms about her torso. "I'm not the sort of person anyone would want to help, am I?"

No, she wasn't. She was privileged. Inconsiderate. Selfish. But much prettier again, now that the arrogance had drained from her face. "If I remain for a time to help you, will you provide my mother with a carriage, horses, a driver and a maid to accompany her?"

Miss Adams raised her head. "You'll help me?"

Isaac held out a staying hand. "Will you agree to provide for my mother's journey?"

She nodded. "I can send Penna with her. She's my companion."

He raised an eyebrow. "Or you could ask Penna if she would consider going a treat, and if she says no thank you, you could ask a maid."

Miss Adams blinked rapidly. "Yes. I could ask her." She grimaced again. "She'll say yes, I am sure. She doesn't like to be here with me."

Isaac could only imagine Penna's plight. "Will you also agree to always consider my advice, even if you then chose not to follow it?" he asked.

She replied, voice light with surprise, "You mean, you won't insist I do as you say, when you advise me?"

He shook his head. "What would that teach you? You said you must learn to manage this place and the tenant farms. Blind obedience will not help you learn." Tone dry, he added, "Besides which, no matter what you promise in this moment, I doubt you're capable of doing as anyone says."

She flushed. "I agree to always consider what you recommend, yes."

"Then, in exchange, I will remain for two weeks."

She frowned. "I can't learn enough in two weeks. I know spring is important. Penna keeps telling me about planting vegetables." She pointed toward the half-prepared garden. "Two months."

If he left his mother for that long, even if Lady Ellen paid her in full, the shop would be run into the ground by the time he returned. "Three weeks."

"A month and a half?" Miss Adams asked.

"Four weeks." Even his mother couldn't spend all of their earnings before then…could she? And if Lady Ellen wouldn't pay for the gown, well, Mother would need to finish all the local work she'd put off, and quickly. Isaac would impress that dire need upon her before she departed.

"Five weeks?"

"Four," he repeated. "If you cannot learn enough to convince your grandmother of your suitability in a month, you will need someone else to teach you."

Miss Adams mouth pulled down at the corners. "Four, if you agree to putting our deal in writing, so I know you can't go back on your word."

Pique shot through Isaac at the implication he wasn't a man of his word, but he nodded. "If you insist."

Miss Adams nodded and stuck out her hand like a horse trader. "Four weeks, then."

Isaac clasped her offered hand and inwardly winced. Her hand was smooth and without a single callous. Those delicate fingers would soon learn the value of hard work…. he hoped.

CHAPTER 7

Under an afternoon sun that burned off much of the early spring chill, Isaac saw his mother into one of the Adamses' carriages. He knew he had little choice but to let her go. His mother wished to continue on to Lady Ellen's, and nothing short of locking her up would prevent her departure. Isaac had interviewed both Miss Penna Chaff, who would accompany his mother, and the groom who would drive, and found them competent. The groom assured Isaac he could navigate the ruined roads and promised to do so with the utmost care. More than that, Miss Chaff, who seemed in equal parts eager for the reprieve from Rodchamb and guilty about leaving Miss Adams, appeared quite capable, which reassured him. Someone accustomed to managing a spoiled, willful heiress would be able to rein in his mother's more dramatic tendencies.

He turned back from waving farewell to see Mr. Relógio and Miss Adams standing on the front steps to the manor house. Mr. Relógio handed her some small object, which she received with a broad smile and tucked away.

Isaac strode back up the drive to them and halted in front of the steps. "Now, shall we look first at the books, draw up our contract, or meet the staff?"

Miss Adams pressed her lovely bow-shaped lips into a firm line as she thought. "Meet the staff?" she suggested.

"Very well," he agreed. "You must have a ballroom?" She nodded, and he said, "Shall we ask them to assemble there, so everyone will fit?"

She grimaced. "Those who remain will fit quite easily in the large parlor."

Isaac hid his surprise with a brisk nod. He gestured for Miss Adams and Mr. Relógio to proceed him inside. Isaac knew how to manage a shop and a small household, how to plant their little garden, which he'd yet to do, and harvest and preserve their food, but Rodchamb was an immense estate. A mansion with grounds, attached farmland, and tenant farms. He'd hoped more of the staff had remained to help guide them.

They stepped into the entrance hall where, oddly, the carcass of a chandelier hung at eye height. Isaac had nearly run into the armature while carrying out Lady Ellen's gown for his mother.

"Is that lowered for a reason?" he asked.

Miss Adams shook her head. "Someone took the crystals."

"So, I may raise the chandelier?"

"Please do." She sounded quite relieved by the prospect.

Isaac wondered why Miss Adams hadn't raised the fixture herself as he crossed to a panel in the molding, which already stood open to reveal the chandelier's mechanism.

"Are any of the senior staff still about?" he asked as he hoisted the chandelier. "Ones who will know what others remain and be able to organize them?"

"Yes. Our butler, Mr. Côte, and Mrs. Calic, the housekeeper."

She went on to list the name of the cook, the stablemaster, the head groundsman and several other key positions to Isaac's relief. Now he understood how the grounds and manor house remained in some vague semblance of order, even with most of the staff gone.

When Miss Adams finished her list, Isaac asked, "And your family's steward?"

She scowled. "That was Mr. Arch. Grandmother dismissed him. He was as awful as father."

Isaac tied the chandelier's skeleton into place and tried to digest that new information. Miss Adams would describe her father as *awful*? Rumors he'd heard about the terrible treatment of tenants and staff, and other's he'd always dismissed about wild parties, filtered through Isaac's mind.

He closed the door in the panel, which blended neatly into the molding. "Well, then, it seems we should round up the senior staff first and speak with them." He turned to find her staring upward.

She lowered her gaze to meet his. "That is so much nicer. Thank you. I hated that horrible thing hanging right in the middle of the entry."

"You could have raised the armature at any time."

She flushed, cast Mr. Relógio a glance, and tipped her chin into the air. "I had ordered Mr. Côte to see to it."

Isaac raised an eyebrow. "Where might we find Mr. Côte?"

"Are you going to reprimand him?" she asked.

"I am going to ask him to assemble the senior staff in the large parlor and, if that goes well, to then bring in the remainder of the staff."

"Oh."

Isaac crossed to her. "Have you ever tried being considerate?"

Her cheeks glowed a brighter red.

"When we meet the staff, watch how I speak with them, as equals," he said.

"But we aren't equal. You may be, but I am a member of the gentry, and they are my servants."

Isaac pushed a hand through his hair. "You were born into the gentry, but did you ever do a thing to earn that good fortune? To become what a gentrified woman should be?" He strongly doubted she could say yes.

"I...I once had a tutor to teach me languages and another for painting and drawing." She frowned in thought. "There was a dance master and a riding master, and Penna is forever trying to teach me to sew, as if I require the knowledge. I have money. Why would someone with money need to sew? You simply take the money and pay someone—" She broke off.

"Someone like me or my mother?" he finished. "And yet, oddly, you require my assistance, which necessitates my goodwill. You also require the assistance of each and every member of Rodchamb's staff, and of the tenants, which requires their goodwill."

"The tenants, maybe, but I pay the staff to do my bidding," she snapped.

"And have you?"

"What?"

"Paid them."

Her blue eyes went wide. "I...ah...."

"I see," he said. "Maybe we should go over the books first."

He started to leave, but she caught his sleeve. "Please, can we not speak to the staff first?" she pleaded.

He raised both eyebrows. "Why?"

Her breath quickened. Blue eyes impossibly wide, she said, "Because I'm so hungry and I thought, maybe, if you could make the staff return to work, maybe Chef Dramm would make dinner."

"Your cook hasn't been making dinner?"

"He does for the staff," Miss Adams wailed. "He did for me, too, at first, but he said I am too demanding and that I don't understand how to set a menu and now I have to sneak into the kitchen at night and see if they've left me anything, and Penna wouldn't let me boil all the potatoes," she finished on a sob.

Isaac reevaluated her oversized gown and realized the garment was not, as he'd assumed, borrowed. She'd simply lost enough weight to make the dress seem so. "We'll speak with the staff first," he said lightly, to cheer her. "You do get final say, after all. Rodchamb is yours to manage."

She nodded and removed her hand from his arm. She dashed the tears from her eyes and walked down the long central hallway between the double staircases. Isaac followed with their constant chaperone, Mr. Relógio at his side.

Miss Adams swiped her cheeks and squared her shoulders as she led them through the house. Isaac admired the fine carpets, the well-crafted furnishings and, in particular, the masterfully painted artwork they passed, though the lack of candles and the occasional vase of dead, forgotten flowers somewhat diminished the effect. Finally, Miss Adams slowed as they drew near an open doorway. From the smacking, cracking sounds within, Isaac suspected a billiards room.

They strode in to find a thin, elderly gentleman in his rolled-up shirtsleeves and waistcoat, a cue in one hand and a cigar in his mouth. He stood back, watching as a matronly woman in an apron and ruffle-trimmed cap lined up a shot. Her arm whipped forward.

Two balls dropped and she crowed in delight, "Take that, Mr. Côte."

"Well played, Mrs. Calic. Well played," the older man replied.

Miss Adams cleared her throat. The butler and housekeeper turned to her with matching looks of surprise. Mr. Côte grimaced around his cigar, but Mrs. Calic, her expression one of guarded warmth, dropped a curtsy made a touch clumsy by what Isaac guessed was a stiff leg.

Miss Adams said, "Mr. Côte, Mrs. Calic, I should like to introduce you to Mr. Isaac Bell."

Both senior staff assessed the new visitor.

Isaac bowed. "A pleasure to meet you. Miss Adams and I were wondering if we might have a word?"

Mr. Côte sniffed but Mrs. Calic said, "Certainly, young man. What have you come to say?"

Isaac now realized that before any demands were made, amends must be made first. "It's really what Miss Adams has come to say. She wishes to apologize for any previous antagonistic behavior."

Miss Adams whipped around to glare at him. "I do?"

"Yes, you do," he said. "I deem your apology highly necessary."

She crinkled her nose in a rather adorable pout, then spun back to face the two servants. "Mr. Côte, Mrs. Calic, I am very sorry that I have been...difficult."

"And?" Isaac urged.

She cast him an annoyed look over her shoulder. "And...mean?"

"You've been spoiled and ill mannered, child," Mrs. Calic supplied.

"Demanding, disrespectful, willful, and rude," Mr. Côte said.

Miss Adams rocked back on her heels. "Err, yes, I apologize for all of those things."

Isaac stepped forward and touched her shoulder. Her honey brown locks brushed against the side of his hand, silken smooth. "And Miss Adams wishes to do better in the future," he said, but could see they were not yet convinced. He added, "And once we go over the books this evening, she will be issuing some of your back pay."

That last promise brought a smile to even Mr. Côte's weathered face. He pulled the cigar from his mouth. "Will she now?"

"How much of our back pay?" Mrs. Calic asked.

"We must go over the books first," Isaac said.

"You'll find them in the study, Mr. Bell, but I doubt you'll find them in order," Mr. Côte predicted and puffed once more on his cigar.

"We will put them in order," Isaac said.

"By *we*, you'd best mean *you*, Mr. Bell, because Betsy here scared off every tutor her parents ever hired. I'd be surprised if the girl can even add."

"Mr. Côte," Mrs. Calic exclaimed.

Miss Adams eyed the butler, cheeks ruddy with anger. "I can so add and subtract. I can definitely do the math required for there to be one fewer servant here."

Mr. Côte raised a bushy gray eyebrow. "Is that so?"

Miss Adams sputtered with indignation and took a step forward.

Isaac squeezed her shoulder to hold her back. He leaned down and said in her ear, "Let him have this one."

She whirled on Isaac, blue eyes bright and glittering as sunlight that sparkled off a lake. "He insulted me."

Voice low, Isaac asked, "And how many times have you insulted him, and he had to ignore your disrespect, because he was in the employ of your father?"

Her anger intensified, then faltered and fell away. Confusion and shame slackened her mouth. She blinked rapidly. "Many times."

"He isn't a man you can bully into respecting you," Isaac continued in the same soft tone, projecting an air of privacy over their conversation, though he imagined everyone could hear his words. "You will have to earn his allegiance through your deeds."

"I can't," she said, near tears again. "I am a horrible person. I've always been a horrible person. Even Penna can hardly love me, and she raised me."

Isaac shook his head. For all he'd lost, his father, all the hardships of having the whole village know of his mother's disgrace and the sin of his birth, he'd never wanted for love. Flighty as she was, his mother always showered him with affection...when she wasn't too caught up in her work to think of anyone, even herself.

"Miss Adams..." Isaac began.

"I'm sorry." She ran past Isaac and Mr. Relógio and out of the room.

Isaac looked between her retreating form and the two staff members. "I should—"

"I will go," Mr. Relógio said in mildly accented English.

Isaac, Mr. Côte, and Mrs. Calic gawked at him.

"Talking will do the girl no good right now, and you have much to discuss with the staff, Mr. Bell." Relógio addressed the butler and housekeeper. "Listen to Mr. Bell. He is here to help. I will go sit with Miss Adams." Relógio strode away.

"Well, I'll be." Mr. Côte stared after the tall gentleman.

"I suspected as much," Mrs. Calic said with smug satisfaction.

"Yes, well." Mr. Côte shuddered like a dog shedding water. "You wish to speak with us, Mr. Bell, isn't it?"

"About our back pay," Mrs. Calic added.

"Yes. About your back pay. The rest of the staff. The tenant farms. The roadways. Mr. and Mrs. Adams' whereabouts." Isaac shook his head. "But first, could you please tell me what under heaven happened here?"

CHAPTER 8

Betsy didn't slow until she burst through the kitchen door, free of the hateful confines of the house. She'd begged her grandmother to permit her to stay, but now she wondered if anything could be worse than her present life. Even living in a townhome with her parents would be better than enduring insults from Mr. Côte. Even if, in London, her parents would undoubtedly continue in their disreputable ways. Masked balls. Drinking to excess. Lazing away day after day with laudanum-addled brains. On their worst days, they'd hardly recognize Betsy. Or maybe they had changed in London? How much whiskey and laudanum could fifty pounds buy?

Arms wrapped about her torso, Betsy stomped over to one of the large oaks outside the kitchen. Maybe she should beat the rug more? Dust had come out, as Miss Bell promised, and hitting the rug made her feel better. Made her forget for a moment the gnawing hunger in her gut, the stains on her gown and the sinking, sucking understanding that she was not good enough. At anything. For anyone.

She picked up the broom and slammed the stiff bristles against the guest room rug. The resulting cloud of dust seemed pathetic compared to the ones she'd achieved when she had first dragged the carpet down. Betsy tried again but got an even smaller cloud.

She dropped the broom and wrapped her arms about herself once more, then gazed down the hill at Rodchamb's orchard. The limbs of the fruit trees dripped with buds ready to pop open. Betsy usually found the orchard quite pretty, but now all she could do was wonder if fruit trees bore fruit on their own or if some mystical action, one everyone knew about except her, would be required of the manager of Rodchamb to ensure a harvest.

While she gazed gloomily at the orchard, she caught movement to her left. Betsy didn't need to turn. She knew the movement was Mr. Relógio. She'd grown used to his presence in the months since her grandmother's return. Steps silent, he passed behind her, book in hand, and sat on the bench under the other oak tree.

Betsy followed. She perched beside him. He opened his book, something terribly boring about English husbandry. She'd tried asking him how he could read English if he couldn't speak the language, but he never answered. Usually, when confronted with such a question, he wouldn't even look at her, as if he couldn't hear her.

Betsy fished the rose petal he'd given her earlier out of her skirt pocket. The bit of seashell shimmered in the afternoon light. She turned the petal over, never able to decide which side was prettier, the blushing pink outer shell or the opalescent mother-of-pearl interior. She slid her fingers across the pink side and wondered what manner of creature had once made a home out of the shell from which the piece came.

She put the precious petal away, keenly aware how few she'd earned. Her mind ranged back over the day, right up to the point when Mr. Isaac Bell appeared in the garden. She'd never suffer the embarrassment of him knowing such, but he was the most handsome, most perfectly sculpted gentleman she'd ever met. Why, his eyes alone…so expressive and warm. Deeply brown and lined with dark lashes. Even darker than his hair, which fell in waves across his forehead and down to just above his collar. A sigh escaped her.

When she'd first seen him, all Betsy had been able to do was stare, mouth agape. She'd been lucky no drool had dripped out. Fortunately, she'd found the sense to close her mouth before he saw her. She'd sink into the earth if she ever found out that he'd noticed how breathless she'd been, how stunned by his handsomeness.

She grimaced, the memory spoiled because he'd barely taken note of her. He hadn't even looked her way until she spoke. And her all scrawny, dirty and sweaty from taking out her anger on a rug. Worse, he couldn't have missed how her gown sheathed her skinny body like a potato sack. At least Miss Bell had made good on her promise to wash and fix Betsy's hair. True, Betsy's light brown locks hung long and straight, not artfully curled, but at least her hair no longer stood out about her head in a frizzy, greasy halo.

"Miss?"

Betsy lifted her gaze to find a girl of about sixteen, one of the few maids who remained, standing before her. For the first time, Betsy wondered why the girl hadn't left. She tried to recall when the maid had first come to work there, but the maids came and went with such frequency, they blurred together in Betsy's memory.

Betsy blurted, "Your name? What is it?"

"Mary, Miss."

"You're looking for me, Mary?"

"Mr. Bell asked me to come help you ready for dinner, Miss."

Betsy's stomach rumbled in a gurgling growl, which went on for long enough, and loud enough, that her cheeks heated.

Mary brought her hands up to cover her mouth but didn't quite stifle a giggle or hide the laughter in her eyes.

Betsy's face felt like flame. She pressed her mouth into a hard line. How dare this little nothing of a maid, this Mary person, laugh at her?

Mr. Relógio touched Betsy's arm with gentle fingers, but she did not turn to meet his gaze.

"I am sorry, Miss," Mary said. "Only, I've never heard a stomach so hungry."

If Mary the maid didn't stop making light of her, Betsy would kick her out and then *she'd* know hunger. She continued to glare at the maid.

Mary shuffled her feet. "Miss?"

"I can ready for dinner myself," Betsy snapped.

"Yes, Miss," Mary said in a small voice.

What did the maid have to be upset about, Betsy wondered? She was the one who'd been disrespected.

"Then, ah, that will be all?" Mary asked.

"It will."

The maid turned to go. Even without looking at him, Betsy could feel the weight of Mr. Relógio's disapproval.

Afraid he wouldn't give her any more petals if she didn't, Betsy jumped to her feet and hurried after the maid. "Wait, Mary."

"Yes, Miss?"

"I changed my mind. Help me ready for dinner. Please."

Mary smiled. "Thank you, Miss."

"When is dinner?"

"In a little over an hour, Miss."

Betsy pressed a hand to her stomach and kept walking, Mary beside her. "Mary, do you know how to curl hair?" she asked. Maybe with curled hair, Mr. Bell would notice her more.

"No, Miss. I am sorry. I'm a kitchen maid."

"Oh." He would never notice her.

"But I know how to braid, and we could pin your hair up." Mary looked at Betsy out of the corner of her eye and sighed. "You have such pretty hair, Miss."

Betsy preened. "Thank you."

They went inside and up to Betsy's room. Betsy let the girl help her put on a clean gown, then braid her hair. In all the years Penna had braided Betsy's hair before bed, Betsy had never paid attention, but braiding didn't seem too difficult. She watched Mary work in the mirror and resolved to use three ribbons to practice later. Then, she'd be able to do her own hair. Not with gleaming curls, like Penna used to do, but at least keep it tidy. Perhaps braided, her hair wouldn't become so tangled again so soon.

Once her hair was done, she went down to the dining room to find Mr. Bell and Mr. Relógio just outside the doorway. Both gentlemen bowed and a thrill went through her to receive the curtesy due her, especially from a gentleman as attractive as Mr. Bell.

He offered his arm. "You appear refreshed."

Betsy placed a hand on his sleeve, but her heart sank. Refreshed? Hardly the compliment for which she'd hoped. Still, she mustered a pleasant tone and said, "Thank you."

Mr. Bell escorted her into the dining room. Three places lay set at one end of the long table. The dead hothouse flowers that had graced the surface for months had been cleared away, and an elegant candelabra lit the room. Mr. Bell led Betsy to the head of the table and pulled out the chair. It took her a moment to realize he meant for her to sit in her mother's place. He and Mr. Relógio stood until she was settled, then sat on either side of her.

"We aren't to have a formal dinner," Mr. Bell said. "There was neither time nor provisions for such."

"Oh," Betsy said, disappointed. "But there is food?"

Mr. Bell smiled, which made her breath catch in her throat.

"Certainly," he said. "There is much that can be prepared from little, and in a short time."

Mary and another maid entered with laden serving trays. A basket held rolls with steam wafting off them. Betsy's mouth watered at their fresh yeasty scent. A mackerel prepared with mint and fennel lay poached upon an oblong platter. Mary also set down a bowl of pickled vegetables and a smaller plate of thickly sliced yellow cheese and baked eggs. Betsy could barely wait until the maids left before reaching for food.

She took a large portion of each offering. Her hands shook as she broke open a roll and topped the steaming bread with a slab of cheese. She devoured her makeshift sandwich, ignoring the two gentlemen as they took their own portions of the food. Vaguely, Penna's lessons on table manners flittered through her mind, but Betsy cared not. She took up a fork and shoved mackerel into her mouth. Juice dripped down her chin.

Once she'd cleared her plate, Betsy remembered to employ her napkin. She wiped fingers and face, movements slower now. She suddenly appreciated how savage she must have looked. She set her napkin down, took a sip of water, and turned to Mr. Bell.

He ate carefully, of course, but then he wasn't starving. Mr. Relógio, as well, demonstrated impeccable manners. Betsy wondered if he'd dine a second time in the dower house with her grandmother as he made his daily report. She hiccupped, blushed, and took another sip of water.

Mr. Bell gave no evidence he'd witnessed her savagery, and said, "Meeting the staff went well."

"It must have. You persuaded Chef Dramm to cook...for me."

"The remaining staff have returned to their tasks." Mr. Bell carved off a bit of mackerel. "Their numbers aren't what we could hope, but the key staff members remain. You're very fortunate they are so loyal to Rodchamb."

Not to her, Betsy realized. Penna might be, still, but none of the others were, or ever had been. "So, everything will return to normal?"

He shook his head. "Not yet, no. There is much to do. I'd like to start on the books tonight, and to ride out and visit the tenant farms tomorrow."

Betsy frowned. "The farms? Why?"

"To assess their needs."

"Whatever for?"

Mr. Bell regarded her for a long moment, during which Betsy tried not to squirm as a feeling of inadequacy bloomed in her.

"Have you ever seen an illustration of an Egyptian pyramid?" he asked.

Betsy nodded. "We have a book about them in the library." She vaguely recalled a tutor showing her illustrations of triangular buildings with tiny drawings of humpbacked camels at their bases.

Mr. Bell picked three rolls from their place and set them together on the table, then added a fourth balanced atop them. "Rodchamb is a pyramid. Your family and the manor house are the roll at the top." He tapped a lower roll. "This roll is the tenant farms. They provide income from rent and foodstuffs beyond what the manor house's garden, orchards, and livestock can produce. This one is the roadways, for taking goods to market and bringing in what the estate cannot supply. This roll is the staff here at the house."

He met her eyes, and his gaze seemed to will her to understand. "Notice that all the rolls are the same. The one representing your family and the manor house is at the top, but that roll is no different from the other three."

Betsy nodded, though she felt the top roll should be more special. Full of dried fruit or slathered in butter. Her stomach rumbled, already ready for more food.

"Try to take out any of the bottom three rolls," Mr. Bell said. "See if you can without your family and the manor house tumbling down."

Betsy took the roll he'd labeled the staff. The top roll tumbled free. She tore the roll in her hand in half and started eating it.

Around her mouthful, she said, "But farms and roads and the staff are not equal to me."

Mr. Bell sighed. "They are, and while they must provide things to you, you must likewise provide for them, or Rodchamb will come tumbling down."

Betsy swallowed. "Provide them what?"

"Whatever they require."

"What could they possibly need?"

"That is what we shall ride out to see, but for one thing, the staff must be paid. To pay them, you need the income of tenant rent. In order for your tenants to pay rent, they must earn money, which they do by taking their goods to market. They cannot do that if the roads are impassable. Impassable roads are already making Rodchamb teeter. It's common knowledge that some of the tenants have packed up and left."

That made sense. If no one lived on her family's land, no one would pay them rent. Betsy needed that rent to pay her staff, so she had the right to tell them what to do.

She took another bite of bread and frowned. "Did you say ride out?"

"Yes. Come morning. I expect the farm visits to take several mornings."

"I can't ride. We have to take a carriage."

"You can't ride? At all?"

"I never learned."

"Did your parents not wish you to?"

"They did. I said no." She'd thrown a fit about doing as she pleased, and her parents had relented.

She remembered hoping they would try to make her learn. Sometimes refusing to do their bidding garnered their attention, especially if they'd spent money on a tutor. Riding lessons had come later, though, when she was about ten. They'd long since given up by then. All her obstinance had earned was a shrug from her father and a vacant-eyed stare from her mother. Their lack of enforcement had made Betsy sad, because she liked horses, but she'd been too angry that they didn't care enough to make her learn to tell them she'd changed her mind.

Mr. Bell winced. "We cannot take a carriage. Even riding, the visits will take days and some of the roads are impassable in a wheeled conveyance."

"How do you know?" Did Mr. Bell think he knew everything simply because he was so handsome and likeable?

"I walked many of the roads of Rodchamb recently," he replied dryly.

Betsy didn't know what that remark was supposed to mean, but she glared, sure his words reflected a judgment upon her. "You said I get final say. Well, I say you go to the farms and talk with the farmers. I'll wait here and you can report back to me."

He nodded. "Very well. That will give you more time to complete your tasks."

"My tasks?" Why did she feel as if she'd just been tricked?

"Yes. The tasks I promised you'd complete, in order to convince the staff to return to work."

Betsy didn't like the sound of that kind of promise, nor did she appreciate the amusement that lurked in Mr. Bell's devastatingly dark-lashed eyes.

"I do not do tasks."

"Of that I am aware." He returned to eating.

She waited for him to elaborate, but he concentrated on his food. Finally, Betsy could no longer be ignored. "I won't do any tasks," she repeated.

"That is a shame, as your refusal will put an end to enjoying cooked meals, being served at the table, having a maid to assist you, the restoring of the grounds, the—"

Betsy half-growled, half-shrieked to interrupt him, then said, "Very well. I agree to the tasks."

Mr. Bell's pleased expression captivated Betsy and dispelled most of her annoyance. Mr. Relógio set down his fork and fished a petal from his pocket. He passed the small piece of shell to her. Betsy tucked the coveted petal into her own pocket.

Mr. Bell reached for one of the rolls he'd arranged on the table. "We agreed that each member of the staff who returns to work is permitted to select one of their tasks for you to complete, so you will have a better appreciation for what they do."

Betsy pursed her lips and tried to find fault in that logic. Yet, aside from the part where she must do work, the agreement sounded rather fair.

"Such as?"

"To begin with, Mrs. Calic has asked that you go about the house, collect all the dead flowers, and take them to the midden heap."

Betsy sat up straighter, relieved. "That sounds easy enough and...." She faltered, speaking as the thought came to her. "And taking them away will make the house nicer, won't it? I mean, dead flowers *are* rather sad."

Mr. Bell nodded.

A sort of warmth filled her at the way Mr. Bell and Mr. Relógio regarded her just now. As if they were pleased with her. Betsy wasn't accustomed to anything but looks of dislike or even fear from the staff and, from her parents, indifference.

A sudden worry dampened her pleasure. "What did Mr. Côte select for me to do?"

"He asks that you go to the cloakroom, get out all the outerwear that went unclaimed when...." Mister Bell cast Mr.

Relógio a perplexed look. "When, as I understand it, your grandmother routed your parents and their guests from the house."

"What should I do with it?" Betsy couldn't imagine she'd want any of the various coats, hats, cloaks, and gloves. Maybe she could gift them to the staff so they would like her better?

"Mr. Côte has each piece labeled. You are to wrap them, write a note of apology for the late return, and address them for the post."

"But that will take forever," Betsy cried.

"That is the task he has set you."

She scowled. Trust Côte to think of something awful.

"As if any of those people matter," she said under her breath.

"Everyone matters," Mr. Bell said sharply.

"So says you," Betsy muttered and plucked another roll. She bit into it, about to ask what other tasks had been assigned her, and then thought better. For now, best she didn't know.

CHAPTER 9

Isaac rode toward the manor house, eager to take his luncheon with Miss Adams. Three mornings of visits to the tenant farms and he'd yet to complete the task. The Adamses lorded over a vast estate. Rodchamb's restoration would take years but would be well worth the effort.

His visits engendered a mixture of hope and despair. Too many of the farms stood empty, and the occupied ones had become so rundown, considerable funds would be required to affect their repair. The herds must be restocked with fresh blood. More seeds brought in. More farmhands employed.

But the people were good, hardworking folk who loved their land. Those who remained did so because they wanted to. They strove every day to keep their farms alive. As to those who'd left, he'd received multiple assurances that most would return. That they didn't care for life in towns and cities. They simply longed for an invitation and the promise the estate would be put to rights. Isaac had collected the addresses of all those he could, in order to issues such pledges.

He'd also told the tenants they needn't pay first or second quarter rent. He exchanged the sums for the avowal that the money would be reinvested in their farms and that, once the planting was in, each farm would spare some workers to repair a stretch of road. Rodchamb couldn't afford to pay for road repair yet but could excuse debt in trade for service.

Betsy would not be pleased. She wanted money, he knew, but doubted he'd approve of what she might do with the funds should she get them. Better to invest in the farms.

Isaac directed his borrowed mount around a long ditch and to a game trail he'd discovered the day before. More well maintained by deer than the roadways of Rodchamb were by people, the trail cut the corner through the thick trees and would bring him out near the stable, rather than up the front drive. A decent example of horseflesh, his mount only shied once, then took the path as directed.

The trail meandered around broad trunks and across a brook. They splashed through and entered a glade, Isaac's favorite part, for the smattering of bluebells mirrored the color of Betsy's eyes. As he rode through the flowers, he could imagine her there, lines of aggravation melted away by the beauty of the place. How he'd love to paint her amongst the bluebells.

As he rode away from the sunlight-dappled glade and back into the forest shadows, Isaac shook his head. He'd no right to think about Miss Adams' eyes, or any part of her. Not her long neck, nor her silken tresses that, lamentably, she hadn't worn cascading free down her back since the day of his arrival. Certainly not her delightfully curved mouth. He remained at Rodchamb for a specific purpose, and that purpose was not to court a young woman even more willful and selfish than Filomena Guest.

Why, when Miss Guest pressed her mouth into a disapproving expression, Isaac felt only annoyance, but when Betsy did the same, the urge to kiss her lips into a warmer shape nearly overwhelmed him?

Miss Adams, he reminded himself. She was *Miss Adams* to him. He was only at Rodchamb because he had a job to do, so he could return to his shop and not lose his livelihood. And the difference between Miss Adams and Miss Guest was as simple as having known the latter for longer. Once he knew Miss Adams for a time and saw her hauteur and greed refuse to waver, she'd become equally undesirable.

Isaac realized his inattention had permitted his mount to slow to a lazy, plodding walk. With a light kick to the flanks, he urged more speed from the gelding. He had more tasks each day than time in which to complete them, and thus he shouldn't dawdle. The sooner he brought Rodchamb into order, the sooner he would no longer be required. His mother needed him at the shop at least as much as Miss Adams needed him at Rodchamb.

He hoped to hear from his mother today, to know that she'd reached Lady Ellen's safely and gone home safely as well, payment in hand. He wondered if Betsy's companion Penna would return with the borrowed carriage and bring word, or if she would remain with his mother for a time. He hadn't felt entitled to ask, and Betsy hadn't offered Penna's extended services, but Isaac still hoped Penna would remain with his mother so long as he stayed at Rodchamb.

He reached the stable and dismounted, then unsaddled and brushed down the gelding. He could have asked one of the grooms to see to the task, but only the stable master and two young men remained. As they cared for over a dozen mounts, they were rather busy.

After he stabled the horse, Isaac headed for the house. He elected to walk around front rather than bring the smell of the stable into the kitchen while Chef Dramm worked. Glad he'd returned to the village to collect his clothing the day after he'd agreed to Betsy's terms, Isaac went up to the rooms he'd commandeered and changed for luncheon. Before long, he hurried back down and went to the parlor where they took breakfast and their midday meals, only to find the room empty of Betsy.

Isaac swallowed his disappointment and addressed the young woman who now placed the silverware. "Miss Adams has not yet appeared for luncheon?"

The housemaid shook her head. "She's not finished her morning's task."

"Which was?"

The girl's lips twitched. "Clearing the ashes from the fireplaces, sir."

Isaac raised his eyebrows and thought back to his hurried ablutions, trying to recall if the grate in his quarters had been cleared. "Do you know where I might find her?"

"I believe she's in the ballroom now, sir. There are three fireplaces in there and they've not been cleared out since the end of last year."

"Thank you."

She cast him the sort of wistful, appreciative look he often received from women, then said, "I'll come find you when luncheon is served, if you like?"

"Thank you," he repeated, tone neutral. He'd learned better than to encourage those kinds of looks. Isaac left the maid to her work and set out to find Betsy.

He entered the vast ballroom, which fully occupied the first two stories at the end of the mansion's east wing, to see her slender form knelt before the far fireplace. Her lustrous hair trailed in a single braid down her back as she worked to shovel ashes into a large bucket. Squares of midday sunlight illuminated the marble floor on each side of her, but Betsy crouched in the shadow of the hearth.

As he approached, his footfalls tapped out a steady rhythm on the floor, and she turned. She set shovel and brush aside and pushed to her feet. Rays of sunlight caught her hair and lines of gold glinted among the soft browns. She wiped the back of one hand across her forehead.

Her gesture left a smear of ash, but one more dark smudge made no difference among the others. Ash dusted her smooth brow and her slightly upturned nose. Black blotches decorated her cheeks and covered the right side of her mouth. Even one pink, shell-like ear looked gray at the top, dusted with charcoal.

Isaac struggled not to smile. "You've been hard at work, I see."

She grinned, her teeth, at least, still white. "I am nearly done."

She blew several loose strands of silken hair from her face. They immediately settled back into her vision, and she swiped them away with her hand, adding yet more charcoal to her face.

"This is the last room?" he asked.

"And the final fireplace." Her voice held a note of triumph.

"What was your other choice of tasks?" he asked, for sometimes the staff let her choose between more than one of their assigned tasks, to be kind.

"Replacing every candle in the manor, which sounded like a dreadful lot of work." She pursed her lips and puffed at the errant strands again. "But this has been more work than I thought. Do you know, the maids clear the ashes from every fireplace ever day? So, if I go to the library to fetch a book and ask for that fire to be lit, and then go to the parlor to read the book because the library is all musty, and then decide I'd prefer the west-facing parlor over the east-facing one, they have to clear out all three fireplaces and the one in my room and in the dining parlor and the dining room because those rooms are certain to be used as well."

"Indeed." He nodded.

She rolled her eyes. "Yes, well, you knew. You know everything."

"Hardly."

Betsy narrowed her blue eyes. "But you must have some flaw, Mr. Isaac Bell. Everyone does." She waggled a dusty finger before his face. "I am going to discover what is the matter with you."

Isaac caught her hand before she could shake ash all over his crisp white cravat...then went still. Warm, fine-boned fingers curled into his. His heart thumped against the inside of his chest, and he tried to will his mind to work, for certainly he should not be standing there alone with her, holding her hand.

She peered at him over their clasped fingers. "Mr. Bell?"

He forced his mouth to form words. "You've ash on your face."

She pulled her hand free and rubbed at one smooth cheek. "There?"

"Actually, you have ash on your hands too."

She held out her hands, fingers splayed. "Oh dear. So I do. Quite a bit of ash." Her gaze went to the apron she wore, also smudged, then lower to her still-clean skirt.

Isaac read her intention to use the fine muslin to wipe her dirty hands and said, "Do you not have a handkerchief?" He recalled her crying when first they met, no handkerchief in sight.

She blushed. "I burned them."

"I beg your pardon?"

Betsy grimaced. "In January. I burned them."

"To stay warm?"

She balled her hands on her hips and got ash on her gown after all. "How foolish do you think me? For what sort of warmth could one hope from a small stack of handkerchiefs?"

Distressed by the havoc she wreaked on such fine fabric, Isaac said, "You'll ruin your gown. Turn around so I can untie your apron. You can use the clean side to wipe your hands."

She took a startled step back. Her blush deepened even more, an ability which fascinated him. "I can undo the ties."

"Your hands are too dirty. You'll do more harm than good. Turn around."

Startlement sped across her face. She whirled, thick braid flying out to nearly hit him, and presented her back.

Isaac stepped closer. "You've knotted the ties," he said.

She trembled, her ears so bright red they appeared as if they might set her hair aflame. Isaac stilled again, his hands clasped on the ties of her apron. A purpose. He had a purpose here. Ordering Rodchamb. Not studying the long, elegant sweep of Miss Adams' neck. He closed his eyes and drew in a deep breath, which only brought the scent of ash and lemon to his nose. Why did she have such an effect on him? She was simply another version of Filomena Guest. A wealthy, spoiled girl.

"Mr. Bell?"

"What?" he snapped.

Betsy looked over her shoulder at him. "Is the knot that bad?"

"The knot…." His opened his eyes to find his hands now tucked under her apron ties, his fingers pressed against the small of her back. A few quick tugs untangled the ties. "The knot isn't bad, no." He dropped the ties and stepped back.

"Thank you." She slipped off the apron as she turned, then folded the fabric and wiped her hands on the clean side.

Isaac pulled out his handkerchief. "For your face."

"Thank you," she repeated. She dropped the apron to the floor and took the handkerchief.

He gathered himself as he watched her scrub the square of cloth over her face. "Why did you burn them, then?"

"It was January," she repeated, words somewhat muffled as she rubbed at her face. "Penna was still trying to help me, then. She said I must learn to care for my clothing, since the staff wouldn't listen to me or help me." Betsy lowered the handkerchief and met his gaze. "How is my face?"

Somehow, she'd managed to scrub away everything except

the smudge across the side of her mouth. Could she possibly have done so on purpose to force Isaac to look at her lips?

"You have a bit, just there." He touched his own mouth to indicate the spot.

She stared at his mouth and blinked, then rubbed the now-dirty handkerchief on her face, which smeared more ash over her lips. "Now?"

He shook his head and held out a hand. "Allow me."

She passed the handkerchief back to him.

As Isaac folded the cloth to a clean spot, he asked, "How did you go from caring for your clothing...to burning your handkerchiefs?"

"Penna said I must learn to press clothing, but that I must practice on handkerchiefs. She took me to the kitchen and showed me how to heat the iron, then she brought the handkerchiefs in. She told me that once I'd pressed each one, I'd be ready to try something more difficult, like a skirt."

Isaac hesitated, handkerchief in hand. He could take advantage of the moment and kiss the smudge from her full lips if she'd permit him.

"You burned one after another?"

"No. I thought I would teach Penna that I knew better. I put them all in a pile and tried to press them all at once. I reasoned I must need to heat the iron more and then leave it on longer because the pile was thick. I put the iron right in the center of the stack and went to rummage through the cupboards, searching for something to eat. I didn't realize my mistake until I smelled them burning."

She sounded amused but, his attention riveted on her mouth, Isaac couldn't join in her merriment. Instead, he worked to keep all emotions in check.

"I see. So, no more handkerchiefs. Was Penna upset?"

"Not at first." Betsy sighed, her moment of cheer gone. "Not until I declared the entire incident her fault and yelled at her and said I would take all of her handkerchiefs." She sighed again and shook her head. "She should have left me sooner."

Unable to bear the dejection on her face, Isaac cupped her chin. "Here," he said, voice low, and smoothed the clean corner of cloth along her lips.

Her eyes grew impossibly wide. Again, she trembled. Or he did. Isaac couldn't be sure. He slid his hand along her jawline, seeking the silken feel of her hair. He leaned closer.

"Miss Adams. Mr. Bell," a female voice called somewhere in the hallway.

Betsy spun away and this time her braid did hit him, slapping his chest with the momentum of her turn. She took two steps across the distance that separated her from the fireplace and knelt to pick up the shovel and broom. Motions quick and busy, she used the broom to shove a last bit of ash into the squared-off little shovel. She dumped the ash into the bucket in a cloud of dust as the housemaid who'd been setting the parlor table entered the room.

"Miss Adams. Mr. Bell. Lunch is served."

"Oh. Wonderful." Betsy popped to her feet, nearly spilling the bucket as she juggled it, the shovel and the broom. "I'll take these away." Face red again, she rushed past Isaac, past the maid, and from the ballroom.

The maid sauntered across the room, then scooped up the apron and handkerchief. She held them up, dangling from her fingers. "Fancy both of these being on the floor, and all smudged, too." She met Isaac's gaze.

He cleared his throat. "Thank you for letting us know about lunch."

"Don't worry, Mr. Bell, I'll see these are cleaned," the maid called after him as he strode from the ballroom.

CHAPTER 10

Betsy headed out the kitchen door to stretch her aching back and dust flour from her hands. She'd earned more petals in the last ten days than she had in the first ten weeks of her quest to right Rodchamb. Maybe helping to make enough rolls that every member of the staff could have two at dinner that night and another two for luncheon sandwiches tomorrow would earn her another. She certainly hoped so. She'd spent hours kneading dough.

If she'd known Mr. Bell's assistance would mean so very much work…. She grinned. She would still have agreed to their bargain, and not only because she didn't wish to be cast out of Rodchamb and lose her inheritance.

She enjoyed being on good terms with the staff. No one cringed when she entered a room and quickly found work elsewhere anymore. Why, she, Mary, and the other kitchen girl had actually sung a song while they kneaded dough and shaped the rolls. A cheerful, slightly ribald song that Betsy hadn't heard before, but which proved quite easy to learn and far more fun than the dreary arias her music instructor had always supplied.

And they'd laughed with her. Not behind their hands or behind her back. Alongside her.

Still, there'd been a moment, when she'd turned out a bowl of risen dough too near the edge of the table and landed the whole ball on the floor. One of the girls had laughed, and Betsy had gone red, and she'd very nearly lost her temper.

But Isaac's voice came to her. *"When you are very angry, stop and force yourself to smile. Smile, and count to ten, and see if whatever is wrong is truly something worth being angry over."*

Last week, when he first told her that, she could only make it to the count of two. She'd reached ten today. When she had, she'd laughed, leaned down to pick up the dough, and said, "We'll give this batch to Mr. Côte," and the kitchen girls had laughed with her.

Betsy strode a bit deeper into the garden, dusting her hands together, then on her apron. A glance back showed that Mr. Relógio hadn't followed. She didn't know why he'd taken to shadowing her less often of late, but his inattention somehow seemed like progress. He'd also taken to leaving petals from the rose on her desk on days when she knew she'd done well.

Her only sorrow, a slight one, was that Penna hadn't yet returned. Along with the carriage, she'd sent a note that said Lady Ellen had loved the gown and paid in full. After she left her ladyship's hospitality, Penna had returned to the village with Miss Bell and remained there, to assist her, until Isaac came home. Of all people, even including her grandmother, Betsy wanted Penna to see her improvement. And Penna would, once she returned, but her arrival would mean Isaac's departure.

Betsy untied her apron and shook it free of flour. She surveyed the yard. Two giant oaks stood behind the house, the now well-tended kitchen garden beyond them. Farther away, down a sloping hill, neat rows of fruit trees comprised Rodchamb's orchard. Blossoms clustered along their branches, and the air about them vibrated with honeybees. Come autumn, they would have a good harvest.

She settled her gaze on a row of hedges, the dividing line between the functional garden behind the house and the decorative one along the southern side. The hedge was perfectly trimmed aside from one lopsided, rounded bush. Her work. She'd picked hedge-trimming over the other options her groundsman had given her but had found the giant shears much more difficult to employ than she'd anticipated. Still, she would pick a month of wielding the heavy hedge shears over the morning they'd made her empty chamber pots.

She wondered where Isaac might be now. Had he gone out to the tenant farms again, as he had so often? He said the families who farmed Rodchamb's land worked hard and wanted to remain on the rich land of their forefathers. But...they needed help. To her consternation, he'd forgiven everyone the first two quarters' rent. He'd told them to reinvest the funds in their farms but stipulated that each family must help repair a stretch of roadway.

Betsy sighed and retied her apron. Isaac always thought of ways to make people's lives better. Incentives that made them want to work, so Rodchamb could improve for everyone. After his pyramid analogy, he'd next told her to think of the manor as a ship. That no matter how good or bad the captain performed, everyone had to do their part to keep the ship afloat. A good captain made sailing easier and a bad one made sailing more difficult, until they all sank.

But where, with all his worldly wisdom, was Isaac just now? She hadn't seen him since breakfast.

And she liked to see him. What woman wouldn't?

She pulled her long braid over her shoulder and toyed with the end, dismayed by her foolish notions. No need to think about Mr. Isaac Bell's handsomeness. In a little over two weeks, he'd be gone. Still, like a honeybee in the orchard determined to delve into a flower, she felt drawn to him. Steps resolute, she set out around the house. If she didn't locate him by the time she reached the front entrance, she'd go back inside and resume her day's work.

Halfway around the imposing stone structure, she found him tending her grandmother's rose garden. Her heart stuttered as she took in his state of undress, lawn shirt open at the throat, coat and cravat gone, waistcoat unbuttoned. She stared as he cut dead branches from a bush and piled them into a wheelbarrow. Finally, apparently satisfied, he grasped the handles of the wheelbarrow and lifted. Under the thin shirt, his muscles rippled across his shoulders. Not until he executed a wide arc did she realize he meant to head her way. She willed the heat from her cheeks as he sighted her and set the wheelbarrow back down.

"Miss Adams," he greeted.

Betsy's face warmed despite her wishes. "The rose garden isn't on your essentials list," she blurted.

Heaven above, where had that idea come from? Her heart fell into her feet. Why had she issued a criticism? Would he think she didn't agree with the list? They'd made the list together, after he'd gone over the books and visited the tenants.

He pulled off a glove and pushed long fingers through his hair. "I know."

She wished she dared touch his hair. "Then why...." She faltered. She didn't want to seem to criticize him again.

He looked over his shoulder at the garden. At the rose bushes badly in need of trimming and tying back but covered in ready-to-burst blossoms. At the pebble-strewn paths, laid out in pleasant symmetry about four cardinal benches and a central fountain, now hardly discernible through choking debris.

He returned his attention to Betsy and said, "An indulgence. I can picture how the garden once looked, how it could and should look with a little care, and I wish to bring back that beauty." His eyes took on a dreamy, abstract expression Betsy had never seen in them before, but recognized as typical of his mother. "I'd love to paint it."

"Paint the garden?" she asked.

How had she forgotten? His mother had said Isaac loved to paint.

"But even if I don't, the roses will bloom soon," he said. "We will be able to bring them in and make arrangements. They'll be a lovely addition to your afternoon teas."

Betsy narrowed her gaze as that last bit of information penetrated the haze in which his good looks had enveloped her. "Afternoon teas?"

He nodded. "As you do not yet ride and the roads are still in disrepair, you are going to invite the wives and daughters of Rodchamb's tenants to tea. These informal meetings will give them a chance to tell you what they need from you as their landlord."

Betsy's mind reeled. She'd never had anyone over to tea. She hadn't wished to and, peripherally, she'd been aware that proper women did not wish to come to the manor house. She did not know how to serve tea. One of her many tutors had once endeavored to teach her but Betsy, as usual, had rebelled. She distinctly recalled throwing a cup and saucer at the woman. She'd screeched that an Adams had no need for lessons in catering to others.

She must have appeared so ridiculous.

Isaac regarded her. "You've never served tea."

Betsy grimaced, unable to issue a denial.

"No matter. We will practice. I'm sure Mrs. Calic will help, and tea will be a nice way to keep her off her feet more."

"Mrs. Calic needs to be kept off her feet?" Betsy asked.

"Haven't you noticed?"

The touch of disappointment in his tone cut deep. "Noticed what?"

"How she limps by the end of each day. Her swollen ankles. Being on her feet all day, managing the household, pains her. She needs more maids and footmen to do her running and work for her while she manages from her office."

"Oh." Shame washed over her. Would she never be a good person? The sort of person who noticed pained limps and swollen ankles?

"How do we acquire more staff?"

"We cannot, yet. Maybe in the autumn, once the harvest is in and the extra sold and we can expect third quarter rent."

"Oh," she said again, then felt like a fool. Was that the only syllable she knew?

Isaac smiled gently. "How goes the baking?"

She knew he meant to be kind, but his softened demeanor cut her all the more. He looked at her as one would at a child of six, not a woman of twenty, an age he couldn't far surpass. His expression reminded her of the indulgent, barely-shy-of-pitying way he regarded his mother. Definitely not the expression of a man who found her as distressingly appealing as she found him. Mortified by the disparity between that look and how she wished he would see her, she wanted to flee.

She widened her eyes and let out a small gasp to mime surprise. Voice high with distress, she said, "Oh, the rolls. Someone has to brush them with butter when they're nearly done. Thank you for reminding me." She pivoted and raced away.

She rounded the house, out of his sight and transformed her hurried footfalls into angry stomps. Thought of her as a child, did he? As pitiable? Incompetent? Of course, everyone was incompetent when compared to the amazing Mr. Isaac Bell, who'd been running a shop since his ninth year.

She eased her stomps. Why had he taken over managing the shop at age nine? What of his mother? Despite her silliness, surely she could manage a shop better than a nine-year-old? If she truly proved that incompetent, how much did Isaac risk to remain with her for four weeks? What would happen to his tailoring business? For that matter, what of his father, this mysterious man about which Betsy knew only that he'd never married Isaac's mother and had not been a part of their lives?

She wandered back to the kitchen door with slow steps, fiddling again with the end of her braid. She didn't really know much about Isaac, despite his near-constant company for almost two weeks. He knew everything about her. Too much, really. In order to help her learn to manage the estate, he'd asked question after question, and only relented when she insisted he need know nothing about her parents' behaviors that had landed Rodchamb in its current troubles.

She did know he enjoyed painting. His mother, though not the most reliable source, had said as much, and he'd just affirmed the claim. Betsy now hurried into the kitchen. She returned her apron to its peg and, after a wave to the girls and the cook, all but ran through the house to her old schoolroom. There, many an unfortunate instructor had attempted to instill reasonableness in her, until her parents had ceased to squander money on her education sometime in her eleventh year.

She flung the door open, then sneezed. Dust coated the chairs, stools, shelves, and tables. She coughed and grimaced. Watercolors did not give out, did they? They were dry and you added water and could again and again. She recalled at least that much from her early lessons. She sneezed again and wished she'd kept the apron. She began to rummage through drawers and shelves. For once, she would do something kind, without anyone to prompt her.

She found a box of paints, untouched. Elated, she dug out brushes and the heavy paper she recalled her instructor had insisted upon. All unused. She'd never progressed past the bespectacled man's instructions in charcoal drawing, nor had been awarded the dubious honor of a paint brush.

She left the supplies where they were, for she feared Isaac would spot her with them and thus ruin the surprise. She fetched cleaning cloths and water, then washed away the dust and found a wooden box to hold everything except the paper. Betsy took her finds to the parlor to hide them for after dinner. After a little thought, she dusted an easel and added the wooden frame to her stash behind a couch.

For the remainder of the day, Betsy took on the task of scrubbing stains from the hall carpets with unusual vigor. So much excitement filled her at the thought of presenting the painting supplies to Isaac, she even hummed as she worked.

By evening, as they sat for their meal, Betsy could hardly contain her glee. She tried to appear calm as Isaac escorted her to the head of the table but worried he could feel her excited tremble. She'd never given anyone a gift before, but she knew Isaac would love the presents she'd found for him.

Isaac saw her to her seat and took his place beside her, Mr. Relógio across from him. Mary and the other kitchen maid brought in their small supper. They passed the few bowls and plates about, serving themselves.

Isaac picked up a roll and held it up. "They came out well."

"Thank you." Betsy pushed beans, which she'd watched Chef Dramm rehydrate and season, around on her plate, too excited to eat.

"Are you well?" Isaac asked. "You do not seem your usual self this evening."

Mr. Relógio looked up from his own plate and seemed to scrutinize her.

Betsy ignored him and grinned as excitement bubbled within her. "I am perfectly well. Not very hungry, is all."

"Then it is kind of you to keep me company while I dine, as I am starved."

She studied Isaac as he ate. He'd worked the entire day outdoors. She wondered if the break from tailoring pleased him. In another man, she'd take his level of dedication to righting her estate as sign of enjoyment, but she suspected Isaac would work conscientiously at any task.

"Fine weather we're having," Isaac said.

"Do you think so? I find the air rather cool still," she replied.

"As we do not have all the planting in, I'm happy for the temperature. The cool gives us time and we've not yet missed all the rain and moved into the hottest part of the year when planting should no longer be done."

"Oh." She hadn't thought that far ahead.

"But the weather is neither here nor there. I simply endeavored for conversation."

Dismay filled Betsy. "That is my job, isn't it? I am meant to broach topics."

"Not always. Conversations should be a give and take. You begin one, then I do, then you, again. If we had a whole dinner party, you would speak first with the person seated to your right, then switch to the person on your left halfway through the meal."

"I know that part. I did, occasionally, listen to my tutors," she said dryly.

"I did not say you didn't," he replied in a mild voice.

Betsy resisted pointing out that he'd implied she hadn't. "Besides which, you are on both my left and right."

"Not so. Mr. Relógio is to your left."

Betsy studied the tall, comely gentleman, then turned back to Isaac with a shrug. "Mr. Relógio does not speak to me."

"Have you spoken to him?"

"I am uncertain if he speaks English," she shot back, although she felt he must, except not to her. He certainly read English and he always seemed perfectly well aware of what transpired about him.

Mr. Relógio raised an eyebrow and continued to eat.

"Of course, at such an intimate meal, I daresay everyone around the table might speak as they choose," Isaac added.

Silence descended in the wake of that observation, as if to mock it. Betsy sought a new topic of conversation but faltered. She fidgeted with her utensils.

"I spoke to Chef Dramm and organized for tea tomorrow, in lieu of luncheon," Isaac said, at last.

"I should have thought to do so." She pushed her beans around on her plate.

"Not necessarily."

"Did you invite Mrs. Calic?" Betsy asked, hoping he had not, so she might.

"I thought you would like to yourself."

"Yes. I shall invite her."

Silence fell again. Betsy cast about in her mind for something meaningful to say. Something to show she listened. That she cared. Something that indicated that she saw Isaac as a person, and not simply a handsome face and a form that could only be called the perfect advertisement for his vocation. Or, more offensively, as merely a means to securing Rodchamb as her own.

"Why were you running a shop when you were but nine?" she blurted.

He skewered several of the large white beans and put them in his mouth.

Betsy waited.

Finally, Isaac swallowed and said, "Someone had to."

"But surely your mother had been managing the shop until then?"

Isaac nodded. "She had."

"Well, then, why would she—"

He set down his fork. "Do you know, I find I am not as hungry as I first thought."

Betsy blinked. Then the meaning of his words clarified in her mind. "So, we are finished with dinner?"

He nodded. "Indeed."

She hopped up. "We can go to the parlor?"

He wrinkled his brow. "I suppose we might, if Mr. Relógio will excuse us, but why are you so eager?"

"It's a surprise."

Wariness settled over his features. "What sort of surprise?"

"A good one. Come with me. Please?"

Isaac asked Mr. Relógio, "Would you indulge us by excusing our ill-mannered departure?"

Betsy held her breath. Isaac surely wouldn't depart if Mr. Relógio didn't agree.

Mr. Relógio smiled and nodded assent.

"Thank you." Betsy dipped a curtsy for good measure.

Isaac stood. Betsy took his offered arm and walked with him in the direction of the dining room door. She glanced back to see Mr. Relógio watched them with amusement. He lifted his wine glass and tipped it to her in salute. Unsure what to make of that gesture, and too excited to give Isaac his presents to truly care, Betsy urged him toward the parlor.

CHAPTER 11

Isaac let Betsy lead him down the hall, her arm now wrapped about his. He knew he shouldn't permit such familiarity, but he'd never seen her so happy, and to pull away would be construed as rejection. Each time she looked at him, a wide grin plumped cheeks that were still too thin. She'd filled out a little now that the staff provided regular meals again, but he'd like to see her rounder. Her gowns still hung from her frame.

She led him to the small parlor where they usually sat after dinner to review their day and make plans for the next. Candles glowed within and a fire blazed in the grate, bathing the stuffy furnishings in a warm light. As with everything in the house, from carpets to couches, chairs to candelabras, the décor favored expense over comfort or, really, good taste. He wondered if they could sell the lot of it to fund new, less ostentatious, more comfortable furnishings.

Betsy left him in the middle of the room and disappeared behind one of the couches as she dipped low. She came up with a large wooden box. Her grin split her face.

"I have a gift for you, Mr. Bell."

"A gift…for me?"

She nodded and came back around the couch with the box. "Yes. That is, it's nothing, truly. Some things from my school-room. Do not think I went to any trouble or expense. I know that would be frivolous," she babbled, clearly abashed. "That is, I mean them to be nice gifts. I do not mean they're not. They are not cast offs. They're…." She faltered and shoved the box against his midsection, then whipped her hands away as if the wood burned hotter than her cheeks.

Isaac caught the box before it could drop to the floor. "Thank you."

"You have not yet opened the box yet."

"No matter what is inside, the very fact that you thought of me is gift enough, and I thank you." He hoped the box didn't contain items he would be forced to give back. Something expensive from the house. Everything there belonged, in truth, to Betsy's grandmother.

"Are you going to open the box?" Betsy asked, breathless.

Isaac nodded and turned to the couch behind him to sit. He drew in composure with a deep breath, aware that Betsy felt she'd chosen wonderful gifts. No matter what he must ultimately do with whatever he discovered in the box, he must first appear appreciative. Hands squeezed before her, she perched, but angled toward him, on the other end of the couch.

Isaac pulled the lid from the box. Inside rested a rolled cloth bundle and a second wooden box, both stacked atop a lovely porcelain palette. Isaac's hand shook as he lifted out the cloth bundle. He untied the silk ribbon and unfurled the fabric to find a set of beautiful sable brushes, each with its own pocket stitched into the thick cloth. He rerolled the set and retied the ribbon, then laid the bundle beside him on the couch.

He slid the palette out from under the wooden box. The porcelain thin enough to see through, rows of miniature, sunken bowls formed indentations between raised rose vines.

He flipped the palette over to find a delicately painted rose and the maker's mark. He traced the intricate work with his gaze. After he'd admired the palette for a long moment, he set it beside the brushes.

His hands continued to shake enough that he didn't doubt Betsy observed the tremble. Isaac moved the larger box to the floor. He lifted out the smaller box and placed the finely crafted piece on his lap. A single inlaid rose decorated the lid.

"Open it," Betsy urged.

Isaac swallowed. He flipped up the lid to find rows of paints. Whole series of colors, each cake embossed with the maker's mark that declared the expense of the set, even if one could doubt the exquisite construction of the box. He slid a trembling finger over not one cake, but an entire row of different shades of red.

"Do you like it?" Betsy scooched closer until her knee touched his. "There's a drawer, too." She pointed to where a compartment on the front of the box could be slid open. "The drawer contains two bowls for water, a flask if you need to take water with you, and room for the brushes." She looked up at him. "You do like it, don't you?"

Isaac stared into her wide blue eyes and realized he'd never truly seen Miss Adams before. He'd worked to manage her emotions, to focus her body, mind, and spirit on worthwhile tasks, as he always did with his mother. He had years of practice at managing mercurial emotions in others, or appeasing customers. Had he ever spoken to Betsy? Truly addressed her, rather than placate or instruct her? For that matter, did he ever truly speak to anyone?

"Isaac?" she pressed.

"This paint box is the most wonderful gift anyone has ever given me," he whispered.

A dazzling smile erased all worry from her features. A smile that, to his surprise, stood untouched by any hint of smugness.

All she wanted just now, her single goal in this moment, seemed to be his unhindered happiness. He tried to remember a time anyone had regarded him that way.

Betsy jumped up. "I have more." She rushed across the room to drop down behind the opposite couch again. "I couldn't find a bigger box," she added. She produced a thick stack of what appeared to be ready-sized woven paper in a dimension more than suitable for framed art. She set the stack on the sofa and disappeared again to retrieve an easel and, if possible, an even broader grin. Isaac clenched the open paint box and gaped.

She set the easel on the couch and stood before him. She frowned. "You do like it all?"

He nodded, throat too tight to speak.

"You said no one has ever given you so wonderful a gift." She stepped nearer. "That sounded like a good thing, but you look...I don't know." She trailed a soft finger down his cheek. "Not scared, exactly."

Isaac swallowed and forced his hands to unclench so he could close the box. "Stunned. I'm stunned."

She squinted. "That I am being kind?"

"That *anyone* would be so kind."

She flushed. "It's not that kind. I am not using them."

His looked down at the fine paint set, the sable brushes, and exquisitely wrought palette. "Even my father...." He trailed off. He hadn't meant to mention his father.

Careful of the palette and brushes, Betsy settled onto the couch. Again, she twisted so that she faced him. Again, one knee touched his.

"Even your father what?"

"When I was quite young, he asked what I wanted for my birthday, and I said watercolors." Isaac swallowed again against the painful lump in his throat. "He didn't care for the idea. He said painting wasn't a good occupation for a boy and offered me a set of miniature soldiers instead. But I wanted paint." He shrugged. "He knew I would need to work for a living, and that the odds of me making money as an artist were slim. But if I chose to be a soldier, he could have purchased me a commission when I came of age. That would have absolved him of any guilt over my illegitimacy."

Betsy pursed her lips. "But?"

"But I wanted paint." Isaac felt oddly compelled to defend the man he'd hardly known, but who'd been loving on the few occasions Isaac could remember seeing him. He added, "The Society of Painters in Water Colours wasn't even established yet. The pastime had no validity as a profession."

"But he did send you watercolors?"

"He did. He gave me a brush, a few colors, and some paper, and promised an additional brush and color each year on my birthday. I think he predicted that with scant supplies, I'd grow bored and give up."

She blinked. "*One* new color a year? Beginning when?"

"When I was five." His studied the rose carved into the box lid. "He wrote on occasion, but he always arrived in person on my birthday with a new brush and cake of paint. But for my eighth birthday, he sent a cake of red with a note saying he couldn't be with me that year. He also promised to visit soon, so we could paint together."

"And he never visited again? And no paint came on your nineth birthday?"

Isaac ran a hand over the smooth wood of the box but didn't answer.

"And that's when…when you realized he wasn't sending any more gifts."

Isaac hesitated, then cleared his throat and spoke. "For a year, I held out hope he would visit. I kept the red cake wrapped in readiness to use with him, but my mother worried.

She grew increasingly erratic. When not even a note arrived on my ninth birthday, she took the lack as a sign…."

Betsy touched his coat sleeve. Her eyes shimmered with sympathy. "And that's when you began to manage the shop."

Isaac forced a smile and tried to laugh. "Mother had always been fanciful. Subject to high emotions and fits of imagination, but once she decided my father would never come back, the fissure between Mother and the real world widened. That gap remains."

"That is not right," Betsy snapped.

Isaac met her gaze. "It is, I assure you. I know you find her charming and delightful, and she is those things, but she is not…." He paused, not quite willing to admit that he was never quite certain if she understood the ramifications of her actions or if she were truly mad. "She's not capable," he finally continued, "of focusing on anything for very long, except her gowns." And then only her fanciful ones. Not normal, fashionable gowns that were needed to keep the shop afloat.

"That is not what I meant. It wasn't right to foist all that responsibility onto a child. To make you manage everything. You were nine. You mother and father were supposed to take care of you."

"Nine is not that young." Not for a boy who wasn't a member of the gentry. He raised a staying hand when she began to protest. "I had no choice."

Betsy glared at the opposite wall, features hard. Angry. Not at him, he realized, but on his behalf. No one was ever *anything* on his behalf. Not worried. Not solicitous. Certainly not resentful.

Her offered her his hand.

Betsy stared at him. "What are you doing?"

"Thanking you. Give me your hand."

She did, and he brought those delicate fingers to his lips and kissed them. Her hand trembled against his touch. Isaac peered over her fingers and found her cheeks flushed, her breath rapid.

He lowered her hand and gave it a gentle squeeze. "Thank you."

"You are most welcome," she whispered.

"The roses will begin to bloom soon. Let me paint you there, in the rose garden."

She nodded.

With a final squeeze, he released her hand. "Until morning, then?"

Another silent nod.

"And you won't forget to invite Mrs. Calic to tea tomorrow afternoon?"

Betsy shook her head.

Bemused by her silence, Isaac gathered his precious gifts and retreated to his bedroom. He was tired, beyond tired, what with the intense emotion of the evening, but respite wasn't what he sought. At least, not respite from weariness. He needed to leave Betsy before he did something more reprehensible than kiss her pretty fingers. No other woman had inspired such temptation. Mis Guest's face flashed in his mind, and he cringed.

BECAUSE BETSY HAD AGREED TO A PORTRAIT, ISAAC settled into a new rhythm of work over the next several days. He began each morning in the rose garden, which was no great imposition. From the moment he'd discovered the carefully planned plots on the east side of the manor house, he'd longed to put the rose garden to rights. The rose garden had been greatly loved, once.

As he labored in this manner for the fourth morning in a row since he'd accepted Betsy's gift, Isaac couldn't help but reflect that the garden did not constitute, as she had astutely argued, part of his plan to restore the tenant farms, the roads, the house, or even the grounds for that matter. The roses, walks, and fountain feature, even if restored to their former glory, wouldn't improve Rodchamb's finances or Betsy's overall management of the estate, but the rose garden itself could speak to the renewed potential of the place. To show how loved Rodchamb had once been and could be again.

He dug around a thorny bush to loosen the earth so he could remove stubborn weeds. Now that he had paint, Isaac's desire to tend to the garden properly only grew. He would capture the roses in that exact moment of bloom. Those first, bursting flowers. The bright green of new leaves. The garden's fresh colors would play against the white gravel walk, the blue spring sky, and perfectly showcase Betsy in one of her pale muslin gowns, her long hair free of its braid. Perhaps she would even see the painting framed and hung in the parlor. A new painting for a new era at Rodchamb.

He paused, spade in hand, and pushed dark locks off his forehead with the back of his forearm. An era of which he would not be a part, his time at Rodchamb transient. In a little under two weeks, he would be gone. He wouldn't see the orchard bear fruit. Wouldn't help bring in the harvest. Wouldn't have the daily pleasure of witnessing Betsy grow into the wonderful woman she was meant to be.

Isaac sighed and closed his eyes against the sunlight. He breathed in and relished the fine scent of freshly tilled earth, then returned to digging. He would never get the garden ready before the first roses bloomed if he woolgathered. He had far too much to do that morning to squander a moment. Betsy's teas had grown into a daily occurrence, which included the ladies from the tenant farms now, and Isaac didn't like to miss these lively gatherings. As Betsy hosted, he enjoyed watching surety and genuine pleasure replace arrogance and license in her.

Despite his delight in her progress, halfway through his third week at Rodchamb, Isaac asked Betsy to spend the afternoon in the rose garden with him, rather than hosting the tea that day. She agreed so readily, he wondered if her newfound enjoyment of the tenants could have been feigned. Or perhaps she simply wished an honest respite from what had now been six days of tea guests in a row. Regardless, Isaac asked Chef Dramm for a small picnic. He brought the meal, along with a small table and Betsy's gifts to him, to the refreshed rose garden.

He'd just set the items beside the entrance to the garden when he sensed her approach. She walked across the lush grass, now trimmed and tidy, clad in cream muslin, her long braid over her shoulder. What a painting that image would make. The grass so deeply green beneath her swirling hem. The backdrop of the gracious stone manor house on her left, the neat hedgerow behind her, the whole picture capped by cloud-less blue sky.

As she drew near, every step set a new scene. He wished he could paint her in each moment. Against the background of weathered stone. Under the oak trees. In the orchard next spring when blossoms covered every branch again. His gaze flicked to the folded blanket that rested atop the picnic basket. A vision of Betsy reclined atop the red wool, her hair fanned about her head, filled his mind. He would paint her there too. Anywhere. Everywhere.

"Isaac," she said.

His name on her lips brought him back to reality.

"Is it time? You're truly going to paint me?" she asked.

He nodded, perhaps more sharply than intended. "I am."

She tilted her head. "Where do you want me?"

Could those words possibly sound innocent to her ears?

They certainly didn't to his. He cleared his throat. "In the center of the garden, beside the fountain."

She nodded. "May I carry something for you?"

The Betsy of three weeks ago would never have asked to help. Not because she'd been intrinsically bad at heart, but because she'd never been taught to spare a thought for another living being.

"Maybe the paints?"

"I believe I can carry the paints *and* the picnic basket. Is that our lunch?" She tucked the box of paints under her arm and lifted the basket by the handle.

"Yes, but only once I have the composition set. Then, I can work on the background while you set out lunch."

They moved to the isolated center of the garden. Isaac became acutely aware of how alone they were here. He set up the table and easel, a vast improvement over the propped-up board he used at home, then laid out his brushes and paint. As he prepared, Betsy wandered the heart of the garden. Her light steps made little sound on the crushed stone.

"Try standing by the fountain," Isaac said as he studied the symmetry before him.

She took a spot directly between him and the central tiers from which water cascaded.

"Not quite," he said. "Move so you aren't centered."

Betsy took a large step to her right. "Better?"

He nodded. "Much." He looked her up and down, then stepped closer. "Angle your body slightly. No, the other way." He nodded again, pleased. "Now, about your hair."

She touched her thick braid. "What about my hair?"

"You always wear your hair braided," he said. A lovely pink stained her cheekbones. He would have to remember the color.

She raised her chin in defiance. "I like my hair braided this way. It stays tidy."

"Yes, but for the painting you needn't wear your hair thusly."

The pink in her cheeks darkened into a rouge. "I know no other way to wear it. Penna always curled my hair…before."

Isaac studied her. He no longer saw a woman, but a composition. He crossed back to his easel, examined the full scene for a moment, then turned to a rosebush behind him. He took out his pocketknife and cut a large pink rose, then stripped the thorns from the woody stem as he walked back to Betsy.

He passed the rose to her. "If you hold the rose like so"—he cupped her hands about the bloom— "and we unbraid your hair…."

He tugged loose the ribbon at the base of her braid, then raked his fingers through the silken locks and freed them into tumbling waves. He pushed some of its bulk back over her shoulder but arranged the rest to cascade down one side of her creamy décolletage. He pursed his lips and studied his work for a moment, then smoothed his hand along her scalp, above where her hair tucked behind her ear. He slid his fingers through her tresses and let them fall to gently frame her face. He reached to do the same on the other side…and realized she'd flushed again. She stared, eyes large and rounded, lips parted.

Isaac stilled, one hand buried in her honey brown hair. He molded his hand to the shape of her head. "Your ears are pretty," he said, voice low. "But this way, your locks will frame your face."

He slid his hand along the side of her head, then drew his fingers away. Her hair glided smoothly through his fingers to fall in gorgeous waves about her face.

"Th-thank you," she stammered.

Isaac stepped back and Betsy stuck her face into the rose and inhaled deeply. When she looked up again, she appeared more composed. Isaac wasn't. He hurried back to his easel in hopes of hiding his...*infatuation* behind the thick watercolor paper. He willed his hands not to shake as he took the two crystal water bowls from the bottom drawer of the paint box and used the flask to fill them. He selected a brush, then squeezed closed his eyes. He took several slow breaths and rolled his shoulders.

Finally, he looked past the easel at his set composition. At Betsy's perfection. The freed locks of her hair stirred in the gentle breeze. Behind her, water cascaded from the fountain against a backdrop of brilliant blooms and a clear blue sky. Isaac breathed deeply again the scent of roses heavy about him. He dunked his brush in water.

In moments, thought faded. Worry over Betsy's allure left him. Concern for her comfort departed. Everything else dimmed as he plied paint and brush.

CHAPTER 12

Betsy felt as though she'd stood for hours, silent and watching the sun inch across the sky. Her arms ached from holding the rose just so. Her legs had gone numb from standing. Finally, her stomach growled so loudly, she couldn't believe Isaac didn't notice.

She also felt strange to be the center of his attention, to observe the intensity of his scrutiny, yet know he didn't really see her. Didn't look at her. Not as Betsy. Probably as a jumble of lines and shapes and colors, if she recalled any of her lessons properly. He had that same expression she'd seen on his mother's face. So far away. So completely absorbed that nothing existed but his work. That expression made her feel lost.

Yet, earlier, when he'd handed her the rose and run his long fingers through her hair, he'd seen her then. Betsy was certain. For a moment, before he'd retreated to his work, he'd stared at her with a different kind of intensity. The way she dreamed he would. She'd very nearly melted into a puddle on the ground. She'd expected him to reprimand her for trembling so hard that he couldn't paint her.

Her stomach growled again, louder, and dispelled the delicious memory of his intense gaze. "Isaac, when may we have our lunch?"

His brush stilled. He blinked several times. Focused on her. "You may eat." He returned to painting.

"Um, thank you?"

Isaac did not respond.

Betsy huffed and set the rose on the rim of the fountain, then went to the picnic basket. She elected to spread the blanket on one of the benches instead of the crushed stone of the rose garden. She chose the bench behind Isaac so as not to obstruct his ongoing work. Too hungry even to go peek the painting yet, she sat and rummaged through the basket. She pulled out a wrapped sandwich and ate.

After the sandwich and a glass of lemonade, she left the bench and strolled the paths. Would Isaac want her to watch him work? Would he want her to see the unfinished painting? Worried, she crept closer in increments, ready to back away if he protested. He showed no sign that he heard her approach or that she now stood at his shoulder. All at once, she saw her own blue eyes looking back at her from the canvas. Betsy gasped, despite her efforts to be quiet.

He'd made her so beautiful. He'd caught her likeness, and exactly so. Yet, somehow, he'd infused the image with more loveliness than Betsy ever saw in the mirror. Did Isaac see her this way? She wanted to be that woman.

He'd roughly rendered her gown, the fountain, and the walk as well. Now he sketched in the surrounding walls of rose bushes, but he'd yet to fill in the blush of a single rose, even the one she held. Regardless, the painting already mesmerized. She'd assumed him to be good, as Isaac excelled at everything, but she'd no idea he held such brilliance.

A murmured voice caught her attention. She glanced about

the garden. "...alone out here with a young man...." said the female voice she recognized as Penna's.

Betsy turned and walked toward Penna's voice.

"Such behavior is not proper, even if he has wrought an amazing transformation in this garden," Penna said.

"Penna," Betsy exclaimed as her companion came into sight on the path with Mr. Relógio. "I missed you."

Surprise crossed Penna's features, then transformed into genuine warmth. She lifted her hem and hurried down the path. Betsy threw her arms wide but nearly dropped them when Penna neared her and slowed. Then Penna rushed forward into the hug.

Penna drew back and held Betsy by the shoulders. "Look at you." Penna turned her from side to side. "You combed your hair, and it appears as if you've reconciled with Chef Dramm."

Betsy nodded. "I did and now that we get on, I've been learning about planning meals. How one must consider what can be used for other meals if what's prepared isn't eaten, what supplies are currently on hand, and what else can be readied in advance. I'm not very good at putting together a menu yet, but Chef Dramm is wonderful. Mostly, I simply need to stay out of his way and learn."

Penna stared at her, then pulled her into another hug. "I am so pleased you're learning."

Betsy heard the catch in Penna's voice and squeezed her back. For the first time, she considered the pain Penna had endured as her governess. Penna had raised her with love, yet Betsy treated her like a servant. Penna had been there when Betsy drove off everyone hired to help her and watched Betsy go from a cheerful child to a beastly, spoiled, willful young woman. Then, when fate provided Betsy with one final chance, Betsy had lashed out at her. Had Penna had agreed to travel with Isaac's mother to escape the hurt of watching Betsy ruin her final opportunity for a happy life? Betsy had been hurt too. She'd thought Penna just wanted to get away from her, but now she understood Penna's feelings.

After a long moment, Betsy released her and said, "But why are you back? Weren't you planning to stay with Miss Bell until Mr. Bell leaves?"

Could the eccentric modiste be trusted on her own?

Worry pulled at Penna's mouth. She cast a glance at Mr. Bell's back, where he still painted, then lowered her voice. "I came speak with Mr. Bell. Since we returned to the village from Lady Ellen's, Mr. Bell's mother has been…erratic."

"Erratic?" Dread replaced Betsy's joy at seeing Penna.

"Very much so. She took all the money Lady Ellen paid her for that one strange gown, which Lady Ellen did not try on but simply exclaimed over and ordered expensive fabrics with the money. Lady Ellen is such a kind woman, although we caught her unawares as she'd expected Miss Bell much sooner and thought she'd never arrive at all. In any case, Miss Bell wouldn't help with the planting of her garden, and I was able to plant only half. She would not eat, but worked on more strange, puffy gowns and weird, pointy, stiff little cloaks you can see right through. She locked up the shop and turned away all their regular customers, even those who'd already waited some time for their alterations and had already given partial payment." Penna wrung her hands. "I had to come fetch Mr. Bell. I didn't know what to do."

Betsy drew in a sharp breath. She looked over her shoulder to find Isaac staring back at her as his brush dripped red paint on the walk. He blinked rapidly, then plunked the brush into a crystal bowl of clear water. Red seeped from the brush as if the sable bled. Behind him, she saw that he'd only now begun to paint the rose she'd clasped.

He crossed to them. "My mother has done what?"

Penna repeated what she'd told Betsy.

Deep lines creased Isaac's brow. "I must set things right before she ruins us."

"But you cannot," Betsy blurted. "We made a deal. We shook on it and wrote a contract."

Muscles rippled along his jawline. "We did, but I ask you to release me from our bargain. My livelihood is at stake."

In a panic, Betsy tried to think. What could she give him? What would make him stay? If only he hadn't already forgiven the tenants their rent. She could have simply paid him to stay. She needed him.

"Miss Adams, please," Isaac said softly. "If I remain here to help you keep your home, I shall lose mine."

"I'll help." Penna touched Betsy's arm. "I'm here for you now, and I can tell you've learned so much. Moving forward will be easy."

"Easy?" Betsy repeated.

Nothing about life would be easy if Isaac left. The mere thought twisted her gut. She stared at Isaac. His eyes flared with anger, but his frown pleaded with her. If she refused to release him from their agreement, would he stay? Yes, he would stay. That knowledge hurt all the more. He was so good. Better than she could ever be.

A fresh wave of agony rolled through her, so fierce she feared she might crumble. Instead, she squared her shoulders and lifted her chin. She couldn't quite smile, but in her head, she counted to ten.

"My apologies. Of course, you should go to your mother," she said, voice soft but flat. "In fact, I insist you take one of our horses to speed you on your way." She waved a hand toward the stables. "I will...I will burn the contract. You needn't worry."

Isaac squinted at her, as though he suspected a trick. His suspicious look almost broke her composure, but she stood taller.

At last he bowed. "Thank you, Miss Adams. I very much appreciate the loan of a mount. If you send a footman to accompany me, he can bring the horses back."

"A good idea." Numbness spread through her. "And, Mr. Bell, you are welcome to return, once you restore order to your shop." She forced a smile that felt as brittle as dead autumn leaves.

Don't go, don't go, don't go, her mind chanted, but she clamped her lips closed.

He sighed. "I will return as soon as I may. Not because you need me. You have the skills you require. If not in each area, in listening, asking questions, and learning. In kindness." He paused and scrutinized her face. "But I will return, before the roses die, so I may finish your painting."

She looked at his work, surprised to see the painting still there, only her face fully rendered. The rest of the scene faint outlines. Illusion.

"Yes, to finish the painting. What of your paints and…and brushes…." Her vice faltered.

"Please clean and store them for me. I must return to my mother before more harm can be done."

"But I gave them to you."

He'd told her they were the most wonderful gift ever.

"I cannot carry them on a horse. I know you'll keep them safe for me." He bowed again. "Miss Adams." He straightened then bowed to Penna. "Adieu."

He turned and strode away toward the stables. Betsy watched until the rose blushes swallowed his form. Then she covered her face with her hands and tried to hide her tears.

"Oh dear." Penna enveloped Betsy in another motherly embrace.

"An interesting display," a new female voice said, weathered and tattered about the edges.

Betsy pulled back from Penna and wiped her eyes with the heels of her hands. "Grandmother."

Grandma Adams walked into the center of the rose garden, eyes bright and curious. "Your Mr. Bell enacted this miracle? He restored my garden?"

Betsy hiccupped, swiped at her cheeks again, and nodded.

"How very kind of him. He did so beautifully." Grandma Adams crossed to the painting and regarded it for a long moment. "What do you think of this, Henry?" she asked finally.

Mr. Relógio crossed to her and studied the work. *"Ele ama ela,"* he murmured.

Grandma Adams nodded. "I agree, and I daresay the feeling is reciprocated." She began to speak to Mr. Relógio in that bright, melodic language they used.

As they conversed back and forth, Betsy swiped at her remaining tears. Penna, an arm about her shoulders and handed her a handkerchief. Betsy took the little square and blew her nose, then tucked the handkerchief away.

"I'll launder it for you later," she said.

Penna blinked, then squeezed Betsy's shoulders once more. "Come, let us get you inside and bathe your face. You will puff up."

"Yes, but first...I need to clean up Isaac's supplies. His paints...." Her voice caught. She cleared her throat and tried again. "His paints are very important to him."

She worked around her grandmother and Mr. Relógio, who seemed almost to argue. After a moment, Penna joined her and helped clean the paints and pack them up. Once they finished, Betsy began to collect the picnic they hadn't truly had. More tears trickled down her cheeks.

"He will return," Penna smiled encouragingly.

Betsy nodded. "He may."

To finish his painting, he might. She'd seen the obsession in his eyes. Or he might not. Why would he return to a spoiled girl he'd been forced to assist? Betsy offered him nothing. He saw her as a child to be taught and molded. Handsome as he was, he surely had a woman he loved back in his village. Why return to Rodchamb for a mere girl?

"And until he does, we shall carry on, won't we?" Penna said.

Betsy didn't answer, but simply hefted the picnic basket and followed Penna to the house.

She did carry on, though. Through the remainder of the afternoon. On to dinner. Oddly, her grandmother joined them. Fortunately, Betsy had Penna at table as well, as her lady's companion, which gave her some much-needed moral support. Betsy employed all her will and all of Isaac's advice to maintain the semblance of a proper dinner conversation. She touched on the weather and the wellbeing of Rodchamb. She even thought to ask about the Caribbean, but Grandma Adams proved unforthcoming with specific details. Per usual, Mr. Relógio didn't respond to Betsy's questions. Penna filled the more obvious gaps with chatter about Lady Ellen's mansion and her time in the village with Isaac's mother.

Finally, when Betsy could retire for the evening, she declined Penna's assistance and trudged to her room. Betsy had looked forward to having Penna there again to help her with her gowns, to brush out her hair and, most of all, to chat with. But not tonight.

She closed the door to her room, then stirred the dim coals back to life. As she turned to her wardrobe, she caught sight of something on her desk. A small box she recognized as the one in which her grandmother had given her the rose. It rested where she normally left her growing collection of seashell petals.

Fear shot through her when she found her hard won petals gone. Missing, too, were the gold chains and bead. She plucked up the box and opened the lid with unsteady hands.

The complete rose rested inside, restrung. The reunited petals shimmered with opalescence in the firelight. Isaac had helped her for this reason alone, to remake the exquisite rose and reclaim her heritage.

Now, he truly need not return to her.

Betsy snapped the box closed and burst into tears.

CHAPTER 13

Isaac rushed through his early morning chores, intent on opening the shop on time. He'd returned the previous evening and spent hours cleaning shop, workroom, and kitchen. The garden and the account books would require more than a dust cloth or broom to fix, but he'd done what he could.

After a glance at their open orders, and before he'd reordered the premises, he'd all but dragged his mother from another colorful, puffy gown and assigned her the alterations the banker's wife had commissioned over a month ago. She'd worked diligently, though grumpily, all evening, and finished the dress before bed. Isaac intended to deliver the gown in the afternoon, which meant he had the rest of the morning to go over order slips and prioritize the work.

He settled on getting Dougal Guest's coat ready for a fitting. The gentleman likely cared not at all when he received the garment, but his father was Lord-Lieutenant and his sister was vocal in the community. She was also sure to stop by now that Isaac had returned, and he'd rather have some significant progress to show her to keep the encounter focused on business. While he hoped to avoid her that afternoon by being absent with the delivery of the banker's wife's dress, experience told him he couldn't evade Filomena Guest for long.

Isaac took his customary place in the workroom but felt odd to be back in the shop. The room seemed so small and dark, lit only by candles they could now hardly afford and a single window, beside which his mother sewed. Rather than sing as usual, she worked in silence. She cast him repeated petulant looks, which Isaac ignored. His mother may dislike altering old gowns instead of crafting new ones, but the work would prove quick to complete.

In truth, they both worked in stony silence as the morning wiled away and continued through lunch. Isaac knew they should eat but worry robbed him of hunger and his mother never noticed such mundane needs as food. By afternoon, he'd cut the pieces he required for Dougal's coat, then begun to arrange them for pinning.

Isaac stilled his hands and closed his eyes for a moment. How had his mother managed to spend everything Lady Ellen had paid her? He opened his eyes and took in bolts of extravagant, expensive fabrics that practically no one in the village could afford. Try as he might, he couldn't help but look at the gaudy, puffy-skirted gowns that hung on the other side of the workshop.

They fairly dripped pricy ribbons and lace, much of which had been folded and stitched to resemble intricate birds or flowers. The skirts looked like giant, highly decorated pastries —very expensive, shop-ruining pastries. He could only pray Lady Ellen would want to be fitted for at least one of them though, as with the first gown his mother had made, they seemed rather small to Isaac. He could only assume that, in view of the lady's payment, she must be diminutive in stature, which might explain her desire for oversized skirts and attention-garnering gowns.

"I can tell you adore them. You cannot keep your eyes off them," his mother said.

Isaac glared at her. "I cannot keep from looking at them because they represent all our funds for the remainder of the year. Money meant to keep the shop open, a roof over our heads, and food on our table."

She gaped, stilled needle held aloft in one hand. Isaac willed her not to cry. He'd never spoken to his mother that way. He never spoke to anyone that way. Her mouth began to tremble. Liquid welled in her wide eyes.

Isaac jumped to his feet and raced across the room to save the gown on which she worked. He gathered it from her just before she dropped her face to the table with a sob. Her hands scrambled to find fabric, and he snatched another gown out of reach. She grabbed an unused cloth, buried her face, then blew her nose with a gooselike honk.

Isaac set the salvaged gowns aside, then walked around the table and put his arm about her shoulders. She swiveled in the chair away from him.

"You're turning into your father," she wailed.

Isaac jerked back. She never spoke of his father. He'd given up trying to learn more about him from her.

"What do you mean?" he asked.

She shook her head, and he clenched his teeth, sure she wouldn't answer, but then she whispered, "He was kind, and fun, and loved my laughter and my games, until we had you. Then he became so serious. He only wanted to talk about plans for the future." She said *plans* and *future* in exaggerated tones of disgust, as if expletives.

"What plans?" Isaac ventured.

Fabric still pressed to her face, she waved a hand over her head. "Plans," she spat between sobs. "As if you needed your life planned. You were my happy, carefree boy. You liked our playful life together." Her voice choked off into more tears.

Isaac dropped into a crouch beside her. "Mother, I still love your singing and your games and your laughter."

"No, you don't," she cried.

He closed his eyes and counted to ten, as he'd often advised Betsy to do. "Yes, I do. That is why I keep the books. Why I order the shop. So you do not need to worry about mundane tasks that will diminish your happiness. I am sorry I spoke harshly."

If possible, she cried even harder.

Isaac exhaled a long sigh and stood.

"Now you will leave me, just as he did," she moaned.

"Yes, I am," Isaac said, tone even. "I am going to leave you right now and take Mrs. Westcock her gown. I shan't be long. Work on whatever you like while I am out, but please be ready to do more alterations when I return."

Isaac left his mother to finish her cry, for she wouldn't be dissuaded once she began. He gathered the wrapped gown and donned coat and hat. Unsure if his mother would come out of the back rooms should anyone enter, he closed the shop and locked the front door behind him. He set off down the street, the gown tucked under one arm.

He reached the Westcocks' on the early side for afternoon callers, but within the realm of politeness. Mrs. Westcock would expect him to leave the gown with the staff, but that option didn't fit his plans. He wished word spread that he'd returned and put the shop in order and the high-society women who frequented Mrs. Westcock's parlor loved to gossip.

At the front door, he yanked the bell pull, then addressed the butler when he answered. "Is Mrs. Westcock in? I have her gown for her."

The butler frowned but disappeared within. While he waited, Isaac formulated what he might say if told to leave the gown and go. Perhaps he might admit to the slow return and request to check if the measurements remained accurate? Of course, if the lady had increased in weight, such a suggestion could be construed as an insult. Isaac tried to recall the last time he'd seen her.

The butler swung the door open again. "Mrs. Westcock is at home and asks you to join her and her guests in the parlor."

Isaac nodded and entered, then let the butler take his hat and coat. Although he'd sought admittance and an audience before Mrs. Westcock's guests, he felt a sudden unease. He'd fully expected to argue his way in.

"This way, please." The butler led Isaac through the house.

The murmur of voices filtered down the hall. Isaac recognized Miss Guest's voice and grimaced at the butler's back. So much for avoiding her by being out of the shop. Still, her presence solved the riddle of why he'd been so readily summoned to the parlor.

The wrapped dress held before him like a shield, Isaac squared his shoulders, waited while the butler announced him, then entered.

He faced his hostess first and bowed. "Mrs. Westcock, I have your dress ready. Please accept my apologies for how long we held it."

"Oh, Mr. Bell." Miss Guest came to her feet. "We know the delay was no fault of yours."

Mrs. Westcock and the other three women, a gaggle of gentlewomen who always traveled as a group, all nodded.

Mrs. Westcock gestured to her butler. "Take that package from Mr. Bell, won't you? Have it sent to my dressing room. That will be all."

Isaac handed over the bundle with reluctance, jealous that the butler could escape. Under the piercing gazes of the gathered women, Isaac felt a bit like a wounded ram being circled by vultures.

"Yes, well—"

"Mr. Bell," Miss Guest interrupted. She waved a hand to the

empty chair beside the one from which she'd stood. "Won't you sit for a moment? That is, if I may be so rude as to invite him, Mrs. Westcock?"

"Yes, do sit, Mr. Bell," Mrs. Westcock seconded. "We have so many questions."

The three gentlewomen nodded agreement. Isaac tamped down the urge to flee and rounded the low table on which a tea service rested. Once he stood by Miss Guest's side, she smiled and retook her seat. Isaac sat beside her while his hostess rang a small bell.

A maid appeared in the doorway.

"Please fetch a setting for Mr. Bell," Mrs. Westcock said. She turned back to Isaac as the girl curtsied and added, "You really must try the plum cakes, Mr. Bell."

Isaac shook his head. "You are very kind, but, truly, I do not wish to impose."

"Nonsense. With the company you have been forced to keep, it's a wonder you aren't skin and bones, you poor boy."

"Company?" Isaac repeated. Alarm rang through him.

Miss Guest leaned toward him and touched his coat sleeve, face suffused with seeming sympathy. "Oh, you have embarrassed him."

"There is no need to be ashamed, Mr. Bell. It's hardly your fault," Mrs. Westcock said.

He shook his head again. "What is hardly my fault?"

"That you had to spend nearly three weeks in *that place*. Why, Mr. Belgica told the whole village what he saw. The banshee and the bucca. I shudder to think of a trusting young man like you there. Don't you, ladies?"

As one, the three gentlewomen nodded and shuddered.

Isaac plastered on a neutral expression. He recalled Belgica's terror the afternoon he returned during the storm. Isaac hoped the driver hadn't spread too much of that ridiculous tale about the village.

He lifted a brow. "Surely you do not believe in banshees and buccas, Mrs. Westcock?"

"Certainly not, my dear boy," she replied. "But we have all heard the stories. The hedonism. The shameful parties. Why, only this winter, staff fled Rodchamb in droves. Half the tenants have been driven out. Rodchamb is obviously a depraved, horrible place. Not fit for anyone, let alone a young man of your lineage."

Isaac didn't know his lineage and doubted Mrs. Westcock did either. His mother might, but she'd steadfastly denied any knowledge.

The maid returned with a cup, saucer, dessert plate, and spoon. Isaac waited until she set them out and left, then said, "Truly, Rodchamb is a perfectly normal place. In the past, circumstances were somewhat as you describe. I heard the same rumors myself and noted the exodus of staff this past winter. Miss Adams has since been put in charge."

A vision of Betsy formed in his mind, coupled with the memory of her silken locks sliding between his fingers. He couldn't help a small smile. "She's a commendable young woman and has taken the estate in hand. The staff who remain are happy. The forest roads are being repaired." He infused surety into his tone as he addressed Mrs. Westcock who, as the banker's wife, carried considerably clout. "Miss Adams is an intelligent, diligent young woman and I am sure that, should you make her acquaintance, you would find her delightful."

"Delightful?" Miss Guest narrowed her eyes. "Now we have proof. The girl is a wild banshee, and she has Mr. Bell under her spell. There is no other explanation."

Isaac laughed. "I am in no way bewitched."

"Then you have no reason to return."

He hesitated, torn between the truth and what he deemed the wiser reply.

"Oh dear, he is indeed bewitched," Mrs. Westcock said.

"She has enamored our Mr. Bell, the handsomest bachelor for fifty miles. To accomplish in three short weeks what Miss Guest has worked for years to do, she truly must be a banshee."

Isaac blinked in surprise.

The gentlewomen twittered.

"Is that true, Mr. Bell?" Miss Guest demanded. "Are you...enamored?"

"Certainly not," he replied.

"Then swear that you do not plan to return to Rodchamb. Show us that Miss Adams holds you under no spell, or I will label her a banshee and a witch."

The woman had crossed the line of propriety. "She is neither banshee, nor witch," he replied. "As for my being under a spell"—he pinned her with a stare— "you may rest assured, I am not."

"That's exactly what a bewitched gentleman would say," Mrs. Westcock observed.

Isaac recognized the hard edge of jealousy in their eyes, especially Miss Guest's. Even at her most selfish and thoughtless, Betsy had never been malicious.

"He's thinking about the banshee witch," Miss Guest exclaimed. "I can tell by the look in his eyes."

"Miss Adams is perfectly ordinary young lady," he said in a genial tone. "I encourage you to ask my mother, if you refuse to take a man's word."

"The word of his mother?" Miss Guest scoffed. "Like as not, the woman is possessed. We all saw how she acted without Mr. Bell to oversee her. Dancing about her shop at all hours, trailing ribbons from her fingers and singing nonsense. She refused to finish our garments or return our payments. The woman is clearly mad."

Isaac surged to his feet. "You go too far, Miss Guest."

She rose as well and glared. "I do not go far enough," she declared. She hesitated, then added in a gentler tone. "I am only watching out for you, Isaac, as someone must. You've been under the influence of your mad mother all these years, and now you've fallen under the spell of another madwoman. What is to become of you if no one will save you?"

"Save me? If I require saving, Miss Guest, I will save myself."

She leaned close and placed a hand on his arm. "How can you say that? Listen to you, yelling at the sister of your best patron. Embarrassing yourself before your wealthiest clients. It is obvious you need a woman to take you in hand. A sane, respectable woman who will discover who your father is and see that you have the status you deserve."

Through gritted teeth he asked, "You are that woman, I suppose?"

"Certainly, I am. I've been trying to tell you as much for years." She cupped his face. "Oh, Isaac, have you any notion how patient I have been? All for you."

Isaac jerked free of her. "I have been patient as well in politely refusing your advances."

Her eyes flashed. "Why? I am the most eligible miss in Cumberfordshire. Every gentleman wants me. They daily seek my favor, but I am two and twenty and unwed, because I await you."

Pity softened his anger. "But I do not wait for you, Miss Guest. I am sorry."

She yanked her chin high. "Then you are either as mad as your mother or under that witch's spell."

"I am neither." He bowed to the room. "Mrs. Westcock, thank you for your kind patronage, and for the invitation to tea. Please excuse me."

Isaac quit the parlor as Miss Guest sputtered in rage behind him.

CHAPTER 14

Isaac attempted to quell his anger but still pounded down the cobbled streets until he reached the shop. He reached for the front door handle then recalled he'd locked it before he left. He went around back and tried not to notice the garden's disarray on his walk to the kitchen door.

He entered to the sound of his mother singing. The familiar notes soothed him and much of his anger fell away. Miss Guest could think what she liked. No one could be as happy as Isaac's mother could be and, most of the time, he found little harm in her good cheer.

Sadly, most of the time wasn't all of the time. He hung his outerwear on a hook by the door and pushed a hand through his unruly locks. What would he find in the workshop? For his mother to sound that happy, she must be at work on more ridiculous, expensive, useless gowns.

He strode through the workroom door to find her not working, but instead dancing around the room with one of her strange gowns. She sang and twirled...and Isaac began to count to ten. Before he got to five, his mother sighted him.

"Isaac, you'll be so pleased."

"Will I?" he asked with cautious hope.

She hugged the giant-skirted gown close. "We have been invited to Rodchamb for a weekend. But not this weekend. The next. There will be lawn games and a ball, and Lady Ellen will be there. I am to bring five more gorgeous gowns, so it's fortuitous I have so many nearly done, and—"

"How do you know all this?" Isaac interrupted.

A strange pain swelled in his chest at the thought of Rodchamb. How long would it take him to set the shop right so he could return to finish Betsy's portrait? For how long would the roses bloom?

"An invitation arrived, along with a letter from Lady Ellen." She once again held the gown at arm's length as her dance partner and twirled about the workshop.

"May I see them?" He wondered how closely the letter and invitation mirrored his mother's interpretation of them.

She halted mid-twirl, face flushed and bright. "The gowns?"

Isaac needed to count again. "No, the letter and the invitation."

"Oh." She whirled away, back to her dance. "They're in the garden."

"In the garden?" Whyever the garden?

"Yes. I burned them, to set them free, like wishes." She stopped and sighed, expression soft and dreamy. "They floated away to the heavens, and I scattered the bits that didn't want to fly in with the flowers for fairies to find."

Isaac closed his eyes. He shouldn't have left her alone in her sorrow. She'd obviously spent his absence inventing a new reality to restore her happiness, as she'd done so many times before. If a customer didn't care for a dress, by the next morning they adored the garment. Yet she convinced them it could be made even better, so the gown must be redone. Such delusions enabled her whimsical ways.

"I must say, the flower beds are a mess. Penna was very sweet, but not very good at ordering them," she said.

He opened his eyes to find his mother stood still before him, a sweet smile on her face.

"But now that you're here, I am sure the garden will soon be made glorious again." She returned to her dance.

"Yes, I'm certain it will be," Isaac said dully.

He scrubbed a hand over his face, then folded the fabric that would become Dougal's tailcoat, assuming he returned for the fitting. For once, Isaac didn't expect Miss Guest to drag her brother to their shop. The tailcoat stowed, Isaac went to a stack of orders he'd organized by how quickly they could be completed and took the one on the top. He'd get no more work out of his mother that day. That was his own fault. If he hadn't made her cry, she wouldn't have buried her sorrow so deeply in fantasy.

He'd expected her daydream of the weekend trip to last the evening, but she held onto her delusion through the following day and the next. No matter how he cajoled, how he argued, he couldn't shift her from the notion that she must have five more silly gowns ready by the end of the following week. However, as he remained unwilling to bring her to tears again, Isaac could only relent and keep diligent on their *real* orders.

He rose before the sun each day and worked late into the night. He tried to strike a balance between the expense of candles and how quickly he could sew. Once his stitches began to falter, usually a bit past midnight, he blew out the candles and stumbled to bed. He only broke from tailoring to restore the garden and eat but twice a day. Luncheon became a luxury. A distant memory.

Worse, as if en masse, the kind friendly people of the village suddenly had no warmth for Isaac and his mother. Even the girl who worked across the street no longer waved to him in the early mornings. Instead, she ducked her head and hurried inside when he came out to sweep.

Despite his unrelenting industry, money proved difficult to find. Many of their customers refused to pay for alterations on gowns that had been ignored in the weeks he'd been gone, and some said Isaac had been absent longer than they could excuse. The same unsatisfied customers canceled their orders for new garments. In truth, they'd never been as late with orders before, but Isaac suspected the real cause of their apparent shunning was Filomena Guest.

Why had he lost his temper before the biggest gossips in the village, perhaps in all of Cumberfordshire? In one childish tantrum, he'd done more harm to their business than his mother's willful silliness ever had.

The general defection grated beyond measure. He understood the mercurial whims of the upper echelons and he'd expected Miss Guest to hold sway over them. But the remainder of the village folk? No one even wanted to sell him bread. Was Miss Guest so vindictive, so shamed, that she would cow a whole village into turning against the only tailor for miles?

Evidently, she was, and she would, for by week's end no one would meet his eyes when he walked down the street. He continued to deliver altered garments only to be told they were no longer required and, as such, wouldn't be paid for, even at a discounted rate. In those cases, he merely left the clothing, free of charge. He knew the people of the town could ill afford to lose their garments. They didn't deserve to be punished for his error.

After nearly two weeks, Isaac grew desperate. The small payments he'd been able to finagle would see them with food and candles for a time, perhaps into autumn, but not through the winter. And more commissions didn't appear to be forthcoming. He realized he had two choices. Ask Miss Guest to be his wife or take out a loan. Isaac donned his best suit and left his mother to work on her frilly gowns while he headed to the bank.

Situated in the center of the village, the three-story brick bank dominated one side of the central square opposite the Guests' sprawling garden-encircled townhouse. Isaac climbed the wide stone steps of the bank, pulled one side of the copper-clad double door open, and entered the cool marbled interior.

Everyone stilled and stared at him. Men seated behind their desks gaped as if he'd grown a second head. Patrons watched wide-eyed, deposits and withdrawals interrupted. The two burly men, who always stood on each side of the door that led to the bank's vault, glanced at each other in question, as if they might escort him out.

Near the back of the lobby, a clerk rose from a desk situated outside the door to Mr. Westcock's private office. The clerk cleared his throat, rapped on Mr. Westcock's door, and stuck his head inside. Everyone else continued to stare at Isaac. He remained a step inside the double door, uncertain what to do.

Mr. Westcock hurried from his office. The clerk trailed him as he strode across the bank then halted before Isaac. "Mr. Bell."

Isaac angled his head in acknowledgement. "Mr. Westcock."

Mr. Westcock shoved a thick finger between his collar and his neck and tugged, as if he unexpectedly found his cravat too tight. "I don't believe you have any current business in my bank, Mr. Bell."

Isaac blinked. "But I do, sir. I would like a loan with the shop up as collateral."

Interest flashed in Mr. Westcock's eyes, then dimmed. "I am afraid.... No."

"No?" Even the banker, the most powerful man in their village, feared Miss Guest? "I will accept a very generous rate," Isaac said.

"I have no money to loan you, Mr. Bell. At any rate of interest." He nearly choked on the words.

"Not at any rate? Fifty percent?" Isaac would not truly make that kind of deal, even in his dire circumstances. Yet, he still wanted to see if such an outrageous an offer could change Mr. Westcock's mind.

Westcock pulled out a handkerchief and wiped sweat from his brow. "Not at any rate."

"I see." Isaac studied him. Not only wouldn't the man do what was right, he wouldn't even do what served him best. "Well, then." Isaac turned and walked out.

He stopped on the steps and let his shoulders droop. Obviously, he would need to spend some of their meager funds to travel to another town and take out a loan there. Somewhere outside of Cumberfordshire. Somewhere well beyond the influence of Miss Guest or her father.

On the opposite side of the street, grooms led away a carriage from the Guest's home. The hour was somewhat unfashionable for callers. He hoped they burnt their wagging tongues on their tea.

He started to angle toward home, then pivoted back. Isaac knew one person he could ask for money. Someone who wouldn't fear Miss Guest's moods, or her father's influence. At least, not in the way the rest of the district did. Isaac continued to the Guests' townhouse.

The door swung open at his knock to reveal a startled butler. "Miss Guest is not available," the man said. "But if you wish to wait for her in the parlor, I am instructed to bring you in."

Isaac raised his eyebrows. "Instructed to?"

The butler nodded. "Miss Guest left a standing order that you are to be permitted in, Mr. Bell, the, ah, moment you come to your senses and seek her hand." He lowered his voice to add, "But, a bit of advice, sir, if I may? As she is currently engaged, you have time to purchase flowers. I recommend you do so."

Isaac unclenched his jaw to say, "I am here to see Dougal Guest. Is he likewise detained?"

The butler raised a brow. "Not Miss Guest, nor her father?"

"No. Dougal."

"I will see if he is at home, sir."

The butler closed the door in his face. Isaac waited and endeavored for calm, glad the square remained empty so early in the day. Everyone who saw him at this door would come to the same conclusion as the butler that he had capitulated. For the price of his freedom and some flowers, he could make all his troubles go away.

The butler returned. "My apologies. Mr. Dougal Guest is not at home."

Isaac nodded. "I see. Thank you."

"You are certain you aren't here to see Miss Guest or the Lord-Lieutenant?"

"You didn't tell them I am here?" Isaac asked. Bad enough Dougal would know he had sunk so far as to come to their home. He couldn't stand for Filomena to think she might win.

"No, sir. They are previously engaged."

"Then there's no real need to mention I stopped by, is there?" Despite his lack of funds, Isaac pulled a few coins from his pocket and extended them toward the man.

The butler looked up and down the street. The grooms had long since disappeared around back with the carriage and horses. "No need at all, sir." He scooped up the coins and closed the door.

Isaac sighed and started for home. The Guests' enormous house loomed over him as he strode the walk alongside its ornate facade draped in shadow. Isaac reached the end of the house where their low-walled garden began and the morning sunlight streamed down on him

"Psst. Bell."

He halted as Dougal Guest stepped from around a large bush on the other side of the garden wall. Dougal cast a glance up and down the street, then waved Isaac closer.

Isaac frowned, but stepped to the edge of the wall. "What?"

Dougal signaled again. "Come on. Someone will see you."

"If this is some trick to get me alone with your sister, I—"

"Shove my sister. Come on." Dougal grabbed Isaac's arm and yanked.

Of a height with Isaac and much broader, Dougal outweighed him by at least a stone. Isaac had to jump, so he wouldn't tumble over the low wall. He landed on the other side, stumbled two paces and caught himself.

He shook off Dougal's arm. "What the devil?"

"Come with me. Something you need to hear." Dougal rushed into the garden.

Isaac frowned but followed. If Dougal was lying and intended to trap him into compromising Miss Guest, he would plant his fist in the middle of the man's face. He lengthened his stride and came abreast of Dougal.

"I was torn as to whether to warn you, but when they told me you were here, I made up my mind," Dougal said in a low voice as they walked.

"You refused to see me," Isaac hissed, then added, "Warn me?"

"I couldn't very well let you in the front door to eavesdrop on my family. This way, even if my sister finds out you came by, she'll learn you were turned away." Dougal stopped short in front of a tall, well-trimmed hedge wall, and Isaac almost tripped over him. "We squeeze through here. Be as quiet as you can." He melted into the hedge.

Isaac hesitated, but curiosity got the better of him and he and plunged in after Dougal.

CHAPTER 15

Isaac caught up to Dougal in a squared-off section of the garden with tall hedge walls, decorative gravel below foot, and a gurgling fountain in the center of the space. Dougal tiptoed across the gravel. Isaac bit back a laugh and followed. He only hoped he didn't look as ridiculous as the big man.

As they neared the next towering wall of hedges, Filomena Guest's voice reached Isaac. "...I cannot believe what you have been forced to endure," Miss Guest said as Isaac and Dougal halted near the hedge. "Father, can you imagine?"

"Let me see if I have the right of this," said His Majesty's Lord-Lieutenant for the County of Cumberfordshire. "When your father died, Mr. Adams, he left everything to your widowed mother?"

Isaac started. *Mr. Adams?* Betsy's father was in the Guests' garden?

"Yes, Lord-Lieutenant," a man Isaac assumed was Mr. Adams replied in a whiny tone. "The entirety of his business ventures, his properties, and all of his monetary assets. Everything."

A shrewish woman inserted, "And the first thing that

madwoman did was devalue the plantations by freeing the workers and hiring them back. For pay."

"Yet, Mrs. Adams, all reports claim the dowager to be quite wealthy still," the Lord-Lieutenant said. "Though one wouldn't know so by the roadways of Rodchamb or the rumors that come out of the place."

"Rumors," Mr. Adams said with disdain. "Rumors are only so much hot air leaking from the mouths of the ignorant. As to the roadways, the old bat won't give over any funds to maintain them."

"She's had us all but imprisoned in London with only fifty pounds to our name," Mrs. Adams added.

"Oh, that is criminal of her, Mrs. Adams," Miss Guest said. "Do you not agree, Father?"

"But surely the rent from the tenant farms would pay for upkeep of the roads?" the Lord-Lieutenant said.

"When my father died, many of the tenants left," Mr. Adams said in that whiny voice. "They obviously knew better than I what a terrible manager my mother would be, so they fled, leaving us in a lurch without money to maintain the roadways."

"Does it truly matter who is at fault for the roads, Father?" Miss Guest asked. "I am sure that once you declare Mr. Adam's mother mad and have everything turned over to him, he will make certain the roadways remain in good repair from this day forward."

Isaac shot Dougal a thin-lipped look. The other gentleman grimaced in disgust.

"Oh yes," Mr. Adams said. "Yes. I swear it."

"Just as I'm sure you swear to take your daughter in hand once you're restored to your rightful place," Miss Guest continued. "Really, were it me, I would send her away. A little hardship would do the girl a world of good. Do you have any relations in Australia?"

Fury shot through Isaac. Send Betsy away, and just a few short months before she reached her majority?

"Oh yes," Mrs. Adams said. "We promise to send her far, far away."

"For her own good," Mr. Adams added.

"Certainly." Miss Guest agreed. "It is the only responsible thing to do."

Isaac clenched his fists. Dougal closed a hand on his shoulder, and Isaac realized he'd taken a step forward. Isaac eased back.

"But first, we must wrest what is rightfully mine from Mother," Mr. Adams said. "You do agree that she's gone mad, Lord-Lieutenant? No sane person would evict us and put control of Rodchamb in the hands of a mere girl."

"The decision does seem poorly thought out," the Lord-Lieutenant murmured.

"You have that friend, Father. Doctor Fox in Bristol. He seeks patients, does he not? He built Brislington House, a first-rate asylum. She'll be well cared for there. They won't let her mix with common rabble or anything untoward like that."

"All we want is for her to be well cared for and safe," Mrs. Adams drawled.

"You will be generous with Doctor Fox, I'm sure," Miss Guest added.

"Yes, we will be very grateful," Mr. Adams replied.

"Yes, well, I shall take this matter under consideration," the Lord-Lieutenant said.

The shuffle of clothing told Isaac they rose.

"Thank you for your time, sir," Mr. Adams said.

"It has been an honor to speak with you, Lord-Lieutenant," Mrs. Adams said.

More cloth rustled and footfalls faded. Isaac looked at Dougal, jaw clenched. Dougal gestured that they should remain silent.

"You'll write Doctor Fox, Father?" Miss Guest asked.

"You truly believe this woman mad?" he asked.

"Not only mad, but a danger to the region. A disruptive influence. Why, her crazed granddaughter and that Black man she brought here with her nearly murdered Mr. Belgica."

"Murdered Belgica?"

"They menaced him so terribly, his heart nearly gave out. You must write Doctor Fox."

"I will think on it," he said again.

"If Doctor Fox comes here to collect the dowager—"

"To evaluate her," the Lord-Lieutenant broke in.

"Then he should also collect Miss Bell."

Isaac went stone-still. Collect his mother?

"Miss Bell?" her father said. "Is she endangering the community as well?"

"She's quite mad. Everyone knows as much. And yes, she is. She endangers the moral fiber of our youth. She was a man's mistress, Father. Unwed, she shamelessly bedded down with a man and bore his son. Yet we permit her to live among us as if she's not a bastion of immorality and sin. Why, I would never feel safe bringing children into this world, living here, knowing such a depraved woman is permitted to socialize so freely among us. And it's a discredit to you, Father, that she flaunts morality in the heart of Cumberfordshire."

Hot rage shot through Isaac.

"And," Miss Guest added with a note of triumph, "the other gentlewomen of the village agree with me."

"Your requests have nothing to do with a certain young gentleman and his public rejection of you?" the Lord Lieutenant asked softly.

"Certainly, they do," Miss Guest replied without hesitation. "Mr. Bell's behavior showed me how insidious is his mother's immorality. That a reasonable, well-mannered young man with noble blood would champion that mad trull Betsy Adams rather than choose to wed me, points to sinister corruption. We cannot afford for any more youths of Cumberfordshire to be brought under the spell of such women."

Isaac choked.

Dougal shot him a quelling look.

"I will take all you've said, and the Adamses' promise of funds for Fox and Rodchamb's repaired roads into consideration, Filomena."

"Thank you, Father."

"But you would do well to consider what you will do if Mr. Bell still refuses you," he went on. "Or if you wish to wed a man who, someday, could discover what you've done and might hate you for the actions you have taken."

Miss Guest sniffed. "He'll never find out and he will marry me."

"If that is your wish, then that is what I hope for you, Daughter."

Heavy footfalls receded. Moments later, softer ones followed, along with swooshing skirts.

Vibrating with rage, Isaac turned to Dougal.

Dougal took a step back, both hands held out before him as if to ward off Isaac's anger. "I do not agree with her."

"How can she speak that way about my mother?" Isaac demanded. He knew Miss Guest's accusations against his mother held enough truth to be truly deadly. "Or Miss Adams? Betsy is not a crazed witch. She is sensible. Hard working."

"Betsy?" Dougal repeated with raised eyebrows. "So Filomena is right about that part, at least. You are in love with her."

Isaac took a half step back. An image of Betsy rose in memory, nose wrinkled and eyes squeezed nearly shut as she carried a chamber pot at arms' length. Betsy sweaty and tired, hedge shears dangled in hand as she laughed in a mixture of amusement and chagrin at the disaster she'd wrought. Betsy with her hands coated in flour as she helped make rolls in the kitchen. Most of all, the grin that split her face when she'd popped up from behind the couch with the box that held her gifts to him.

Dougal eyed him. "You didn't know?"

Isaac stood mute.

"Well, Filomena noticed." Dougal grimaced. "She is not accustomed to being denied."

Isaac's gut twisted. He'd yet to meet Grandma Adams and had no idea if she could stave off her son and his wife, and protect Betsy, though he suspected Mr. Relógio would help in that regard. Isaac's mother, though…she would crumble under the accusations Miss Guest meant to level on her.

"Your father will give in, won't he?" Isaac asked.

"Eventually." Dougal shrugged. "Filomena will increase the bribes and her badgering until he does."

Isaac clenched and unclenched his fists. A feeling of impotence washed over him. What could he do to stop His Majesty's Lord-Lieutenant for the County? Isaac was no one. A tailor who enjoyed painting.

"Look, reason will prevail, in time," Dougal said. "Filomena will get over her embarrassment. Perhaps take your mother away for a while? Visit London? The city is virtually empty in summer, but—"

"Visit London?" Isaac interrupted with a shaky laugh. "I came here this morning to ask you for a loan against future work. I can't afford London. Even in the summer."

Dougal stuffed a hand into his coat pocket and pulled out several bills.

Isaac shook his head, pride pricked by the sight. "No, I cannot. Not when I don't know when we'll be able to return so I can make good on my end of the bargain."

Dougal thrust the wad of pound notes at Isaac. "My family is at fault. Let me do this."

Isaac shook his head again. "If I need your money, I'll return. Please, see if you can get your sister to relent. I can't imagine why she'd want to be married to a man who...." He caught himself. He'd do no good to admit that his lack of interest had grown into something quite near hatred. "Who will not cherish her or be pleased to be her spouse. She has too many options to settle for a less than perfect union."

Dougal stuffed the money back in his pocket. "She craves your connection to nobility."

"Nobility?" he spat. "Who knows if I have one? That's on the word of my mother. Try pointing that out to your sister."

"I will," Dougal assured him. "But...what will you do?"

"I am going to send my mother away." Maybe he could get her to visit Lady Ellen for an extended time. The woman seemed to like her...according to his mother. "Then I'll warn them at Rodchamb."

"I'll do my best here," Dougal said. "You know the way?"

"I do." Isaac extended a hand, and they shook. "Thank you."

"It's what's right." Dougal released his hand, then walked in the direction of his oversized home.

Isaac hurried from the garden, then forced himself to walk at a sedate pace through the streets. Excessive haste would garner attention and bolster claims of his family's madness and instability.

When he reached home, he entered through the garden and caught sight of a scorched spot on one of the larger stones that lined the walk, marking where his mother claimed to have burned the invitation to Rodchamb and Lady Ellen's letter. Isaac willed himself to forget Miss Guest's all-too-accurate accusations about his mother. He burst through the kitchen door and jogged across the small space, then flung open the door to the workshop.

To an empty room.

He looked about, as if he may have missed his mother at

first glance. Fear shot through him before he realized this Doctor Fox hadn't even been written yet, let alone arrived to cart her off.

He darted across the room to search the front shop and found it, too, empty. He ran back through workroom and kitchen and pounded up the steep staircase that led to their private rooms. His mother's room stood empty, her bed neatly made, covered as always with a quilt stitched in the form of giant yellow daises. The plaster walls, too, glowed yellow, but of a lighter shade that matched her pillows.

He tried to blink away a sudden sorrow. His mother was always cheerful. Always full of life and joy. How could anyone deem her a blight on their community? As far as Isaac knew, she'd only ever made one mistake, loving his father.

He checked the remainder of the upstairs rooms. Even the small storage closet. His mother was nowhere to be found. Isaac returned to the kitchen and went so far as to open the largest cupboards in case she'd hid in one of them. He then returned to the workshop, thinking to search under the tables, when he realized what else had gone missing.

The frivolous gowns.

The five gowns on which she'd toiled so hard, the strange stiff, sheer cloaks, the heaps of ribbon fashioned into flowers and butterflies, the extra lace, even with her sewing box ...all missing.

She couldn't have carried all that on her own. Moving the gowns, awkward cloaks, ribbons, lace, and sewing box would take at least three people, or multiple trips. A carriage would be required to transport the lot.

As he stared at the emptiness, he caught sight of a scrap of paper on her workbench, the corner tucked under a pincushion shaped like a rose. Two strides brought him to the table. He plucked up the note.

•   •   •

LADY ELLEN'S CARRIAGE ARRIVED FOR ME AND THE GOWNS.

HE FLIPPED THE NOTE OVER BUT FOUND NO OTHER words. Isaac recalled his mother's happy words before he'd cast doubt on her. A weekend at Rodchamb with Lady Ellen.

If his mother had gone to Rodchamb, she wasn't out of the Lord-Lieutenant's reach. Besides which, Isaac needed to warn them, as well. He locked up the shop, took his coat and hat, and set out for Rodchamb.

CHAPTER 16

B etsy flattened the bread dough with the rolling pin, then sprinkled on more flour. After Isaac's insistence she carry out the chores given her by the staff, she could now appreciate the hard work that went into all aspects of life at Rodchamb. She'd also learned the joy of creating something with her own hands. But of all the tasks assigned her, from laundering to candle making to summing rows of numbers in the account book and entering expenses in ledgers, she most enjoyed cooking.

All else she'd learned, she would gladly relinquish into more experienced and capable hands, but cooking proved fun. Not simply measuring, kneading, mixing, chopping, braising, and decorating, but the allure of gathering, organizing, and distributing ingredients. The more Chef Dramm taught her, the more she realized that the art of cooking required planning. A creature of impulse for the first twenty years of her life, she now found her time spent in the kitchen both rewarding and soothing.

Dried apples could be rehydrated, sugared, and served as a

sauce with dinner. The leftovers could then be minced and baked into sweet rolls for breakfast. A roast could be served, then the scraps, drippings, and bones saved for stew. The rendered fat could be jellied and saved for various purposes, like aspics. The cold meat could be set out for breakfast, then used in sandwiches. Cuts unsuitable for either went back in the stew pot. Leftovers from those endeavors could feed the staff, and leftovers from staff meals could feed the pigs, though Betsy had decided she preferred the staff to eat better than mere leftovers. After all, Rodchamb could afford to feed everyone well.

Even everyday clippings and trimmings had a useful purpose. Chopped-off stems. Removed peels. Anything. The pigs, chickens, and hounds enjoyed all manner of scraps, of course, but even truly inedible vegetation went into its own pile to sit and wallow until the remnants became dark and unrecognizable, and then could be worked back into the soil for next year's garden.

She simply loved the economy of allocating every bit. The logical challenge of planning meals around the seasons so as not to squander anything. She looked forward to autumn when Chef Dramm and Mrs. Calic promised to teach her about canning.

No new skill could surpass her love of baking, though. When she baked, not only did she organize and cook the ingredients, but she had something indulgent to eat when she finished. Something to be proud of, and to share.

Betsy blinked back sudden tears and stilled her rolling pin. Autumn made her think of the orchard, and spring flowers... and Isaac. She went out early every morning, a bonnet atop her head at her grandmother's insistence, and tended the rose garden. She trimmed away dead buds and pulled weeds, so the garden would be perfect for when Isaac returned to finish his painting of her. But the rose bushes held fewer and fewer buds, and she could not help but wonder when they would flower no more with Isaac yet to return.

"He promised he would," she murmured, and resumed her work.

Penna opened the door to the garden and smiled at Betsy in the kitchen. "Miss, come see, they're rehearsing the play."

Betsy looked down at her dough, not so much to check the thinness as to hide the tears on her cheeks, and found the dough actually needed checking. Her mind on Isaac, she'd rolled the dough much too thin. She peeled it up off the floured tabletop.

"Miss?" Penna asked.

Betsy kept her face angled toward the table, and said, "I must roll the dough back up and put it in the cold room. I'll be out in a moment."

Penna came around the table and put an arm about Betsy's shoulders. "He will return. His mother is here, and she says he'll follow."

Betsy dropped the ball of dough in a puff of loose flour, then used her apron to dab her cheeks. "You know it's impossible to believe anything Miss Bell says. She's a dear woman, but her mind is rarely fixed in reality."

Penna squeezed her shoulders. "Well, then, take Mr. Bell's word for it. He promised to return. Surely, he wouldn't miss the ball? Your grandmother sent out invitations nearly two weeks ago.

Betsy nodded, but she wondered how much work Isaac must have yet to do, without his mother's help. Nor was she insensible to the fact that Miss Bell had obviously spent all of her time working on the many costumes Lady Ellen had ordered. That type of specialty work must pay well, but if Lady Ellen had given Miss Bell the payment directly, which seemed likely, Isaac and his shop might never see any of the money. For all Betsy knew, his mother would fold the banknotes into ships and float them down a stream.

"If he doesn't return, why, come the end of August you are a woman grown. You can go to town and see him." Penna pursed her lips. "With me along. We do not want to ruin your reputation."

Betsy raised her head at that suggestion. "If he is not back by the end of August, I will most certainly *not* go to him." She pulled away from Penna and gathered the dough into a ball, then dropped the sticky mass into a bowl. "I have some pride, you know."

"Oh yes, I am aware…though some would call your pride stubbornness."

Betsy draped a tea towel over the bowl. "I can hardly go chasing after him and beg him to remember his promise to me."

"Why not? Do you not want him back?"

"I do." Betsy bit her bottom lip. "But surely, if he doesn't return by my birthday, it's because he has somewhere else better to be." *Or* someone *else better to be with*, she mentally added.

She went to the cold room and deposited the bowl, then leaned her forehead against the edge of a shelf and let the coldness sink into her skull while she counted to ten.

Betsy untied her apron as she returned to the kitchen. Penna still waited for her, but now with a peculiar expression.

Betsy stopped and tossed her apron on the table. "You know something."

Penna looked over her shoulder at the garden door, then nodded. "Miss Bell said a young woman in the village has been courting Mr. Bell for years. I believe she is the woman who came by the shop, asking for him."

"*She's* been courting *him*?" Wooing usually worked the other way around. But then, few men were as devastatingly handsome as Isaac.

Penna nodded. "She's an heiress."

"But I am an heiress," Betsy cried. "If that's what he wants, why not me?"

"This young lady is the only daughter of Mr. Guest, His Majesty's Lord-Lieutenant for the County of Cumberfordshire."

"Oh." Betsy certainly couldn't compete with that prestigious position. She was merely the granddaughter of a wealthy nabob. "If she's an heiress and her father is His Majesty's Lord-Lieutenant for the County, whatever does she want with a poor tailor like Isaac?"

"He's Mr. Bell to you, Miss," Penna said sharply.

Betsy rolled her eyes. "She could have any gentleman in Cumberfordshire, by the sounds of it."

Penna cast another look about, then lowered her voice and said, "Surely you noticed what a fine-looking gentleman Mr. Bell is?"

Betsy's cheeks heated. "A bit," she muttered.

"And…." Penna glanced about again.

"And what?"

Voice lower still, Penna said, "There's a rumor that his father is a high-ranking member of the peerage."

"Do you think that's true?"

Penna shrugged. "I have no idea, but many in the village seem to believe the rumor. You must admit, being so upright and charming of features, Mr. Bell looks like a nobleman."

Betsy nodded, but she'd met members of the peerage—seen them, rather, as they stumbled in and out of her parents' parties. None of them had appeared particularly upright, handsome, or noble. Not like Isaac.

Then again, who but a member of the peerage would presume to treat a woman with such cavalier disregard as Isaac's father had treated his mother?

Betsy sighed. "Not that his lineage matters. What matters is that, if he doesn't return, he'll have a good reason, and most likely a feminine reason, and I shall not go begging him to choose me." At least, she hoped she wouldn't, for the longer he remained away, the more tempting the idea became.

"Well then," Penna said brightly. "Hopefully Miss Bell is correct, and Mr. Bell will arrive soon. For now, come see the rehearsal of the play. We've likely missed half the first act."

Betsy scooped up her apron and hung it on a hook as she followed Penna outside. They continued on the path through the garden toward the hill, where her grandmother and Miss Bell's Lady Ellen had caused a stage to be constructed with impressive speed. In truth, Grandmother had also seen a great many improvements done in the past few weeks. Once she and Mr. Relógio had agreed Betsy was reformed and Rodchamb in good hands, Grandmother had unleashed her connections, fortune, and managerial skills on the estate. Grandmother had stunned Betsy with what could be accomplished in such a short period of time.

Grandmother had seen the roads fully repaired. The tenant houses as well. She'd hired in farmhands and staff. Purchased quality livestock and set up a supply of fodder and foodstuffs for until Rodchamb's farms were producing well again. Almost as much as she wished for Isaac's return, Betsy now longed to be like her grandmother. She could readily see why Grandpa Adams had left everything to his wife rather than his dissolute son.

They reached the hill where the newly constructed stage stood against the backdrop of the orchard. They'd selected that location so that all of Grandmother's and Lady Ellen's guests could picnic on the slope of the hillside while watching the play. A natural amphitheater, Lady Ellen had called the hillside when she'd toured the property. Betsy didn't know Lady Ellen well yet, but she seemed to sooth Miss Bell and she'd been very polite when she'd arrived in her fancy carriage several days ago, introduced herself, and then disappeared into the office with Mr. Relógio and Betsy's grandmother.

Her ladyship reclined on the hillside now, seated on a blanket in the grass, alongside Isaac's mother, while they watched her daughters and their friends act out *A Midsummer's Night Dream* on the stage. Lady Ellen's reddish-brown curls gleamed in the sun beneath a blue ribbon-bedecked bonnet. Her hair showed not a hint of gray, although Betsy guessed her to be at least halfway through her third decade. She had two daughters but had made no mention of a husband or son. She pointed to the stage and laughed. Miss Bell joined her.

Despite her seeming friendliness, Betsy felt uncertain about Lady Ellen. Neither Betsy nor her grandmother were previously acquainted with her. Lady Ellen's reason for being at Rodchamb and encouraging her daughters to put on such a lavish production, complete with an array of fantastical fairy costumes fashioned by Isaac's mother, remained a mystery to Betsy. She suspected Grandmama knew more, but she wouldn't share anything about the conversation in the office with Lady Ellen, so Betsy lacked even a surname. Her ladyship had simply asked to be addressed as "Lady Ellen."

"There you are," Miss Bell said when Betsy and Penna reached them. Miss Bell regarded Betsy with more warmth than her mother ever had. "Come, sit with us. They're doing beautifully."

"The children seem to have memorized nearly all their lines," Lady Ellen agreed. She turned to Miss Bell. "Did you not say something about a picnic?"

Miss Bell clapped her hands together. "Oh yes. I nearly forgot. How delightful."

"Perhaps you should speak to the cook about our picnic before the hour grows too late?" Lady Ellen suggested.

Miss Bell popped to her feet. "A splendid notion. I adore

cooks." She twirled and started up the hill. Singsong words about cooking and cakes trailed behind her.

Betsy stood alongside Penna and watched as Miss Bell danced her way up the incline.

"I hate to send you off again so soon, Penna," Lady Ellen said. "But perhaps you should go with Miss Bell? She's a dear creature and a talented modiste, but I do not believe we can count on her for our lunch."

Penna dipped a curtsy. "Yes, my lady."

"Thank you ever so," Lady Ellen said, and Penna hurried after Miss Bell. Lady Ellen patted the blanket beside her. "Please, sit, Miss Adams."

Betsy had the strangest feeling that Lady Ellen had deliberately sent the other two women away. She lowered herself onto the blanket. On the stage, the cast continued to rehearse. Some of them, all youths between eleven and fifteen, showed real flare in their performances. Others stumbled. They all appeared invested in the occupation, regardless of ability.

"Your daughters have a great love for theater, Lady Ellen?" Betsy asked.

"No. This undertaking is more of a whim."

Betsy raised her eyebrows and pointed toward the stage and elaborate costumes, complete with shimmering wings. "All this for a child's whim?"

Lady Ellen shook her head. "Oh no. For mine." She continued to regard the stage.

Betsy digested that new information. "If I may be so bold to ask, why here at Rodchamb?"

"Miss Bell's fairy costumes elevate the play's performance to a level of magnificence. She had so much trouble coming to me earlier this year, I thought instead I would come nearer to her."

"How kind of you," Betsy murmured, though she didn't trust that reply for a moment.

To move twenty young house guests, have a stage constructed, get Grandmama to go along with the idea, and purchase all those fantastical fairy outfits for a children's play seemed ridiculous. Were all members of the peerage simply a bit mad?

"I hear that you had the honor of meeting Miss Bell's son?" Lady Ellen said.

"Yes," Betsy startled. "That is, yes, I have."

"He resided here for a time, I believe, to assist you with the estate?"

"He did." Not that what Isaac did was any of Lady Ellen's concern.

"His mother speaks of him as quite competent."

"He is." Betsy studied the other woman with discreet side glances. "Will his lordship be joining us for the performance this weekend?"

"My husband? That would be a dreadful sight. He passed away several years ago."

"I'm sorry for your loss," Betsy said, then was struck with a horrifying thought. Was her ladyship searching for a handsome replacement like Isaac?

"I, for one, am not sorry," Lady Ellen replied. "My father forced me into marriage with a cantankerous old fool."

"Yours was an unhappy union, then?" Betsy said, then sensed another route to discover the woman's intentions. "Surely, there is someone out there who would better suit you?"

"Not every woman is cut out for matrimony."

That bold declaration told Betsy only that Lady Ellen didn't mean to marry Isaac. She could still want a man as kind and handsome as him for…other purposes. Heaven knew she had gleaned enough from her odd upbringing to know that noble men and women sought amusements outside of matrimony. She placed a hand on her belly and took a quick breath.

"So, you would say that Mr. Bell is an honest, upright young man?" Lady Ellen went on as if not noticing her discomfiture.

"Honest, upright, and *moral*," Betsy supplied.

"I also heard he's quite handsome."

A fresh wave of worry washed over her. "I—I couldn't say, my lady."

"Truly? How odd."

Betsy flushed.

"My brother is quite likely to attend this weekend's festivities," Lady Ellen said after a moment.

"You got him to agree, then?" Grandmama said.

Betsy twisted to find her grandmother and Mr. Relógio approached arm in arm. Now that Mr. Relógio spoke to her and no longer evaluated her every action, Betsy liked him much better, and her heart lifted to see him walking with her grandmother.

Lady Ellen, too, looked over her shoulder at them. "Yes. He'll likely arrive this afternoon."

Grandmama nodded. "Excellent."

"Would you care to sit with us, Grandmother—you too, Mr. Relógio, and watch a rehearsal of the play?" Betsy asked. "The next act will begin soon."

"Thank you, but no" her grandmother answered. "I will save the spectacle for the day of the performance when they will hopefully be at their best."

Mr. Relógio raised a brow. "We shall save the pleasure of watching for the day of the performance, when they shall *undoubtedly* be at their best," he said, his subtly rounded vowels adding a delightful lilt to the words.

"That is what I said," her grandmother muttered.

"Nearly." He smiled broadly and waved an elegant hand toward the rose garden. "Shall we?"

Grandmama returned his smile, then nodded. With a tip of his hat to Betsy and Lady Ellen, Mr. Relógio escorted her away.

"Hopefully, Mr. Bell will likewise arrive to watch the performance," Lady Ellen said.

Lady Ellen specifically wanted Isaac to attend the party? Had an invitation been sent to him? Betsy's heart fell. How would he be able to resist a sophisticated woman like Lady Ellen?

CHAPTER 17

Isaac walked down the forest road. Tall trees fashioned a brilliant green arch above, through which soft sunlight filtered. Many times, he checked and rechecked his way, astonished by the wide, even roadway he trod. Had only a few weeks passed since he'd last walked this road? Had Betsy defied her grandmother and taken a loan for repairs? He had seen some minor improvement in the roadways while he resided at Rodchamb, but only a great deal of money could have affected such a remarkable renovation.

Far from soothed by the good repair in which he found the roadways of Rodchamb, concern prompted him to quicken his pace. With the roads in such a fine state, the Lord-Lieutenant's carriage could have him at Rodchamb manor in under four hours. Worse, whatever conveyance Doctor Fox might bring in with which to cart off Isaac's mother and Betsy's grandmother would have no trouble reaching Rodchamb now.

Isaac reached the wall around the manor house late that afternoon. Adding to his dismay, the tall iron gates stood wide and the drive was tended and clear of debris. Anyone could drive a carriage right up to the front door now. Isaac suppressed the urge to run.

He rounded the curve of the drive to find a large, elegant carriage before the house, rigged six in hand. Isaac's heart thudded even as his mind scrambled for logical thought. The carriage could not possibly belong to the Lord-Lieutenant or Doctor Fox. Fox likely hadn't even been summoned yet, and the Lord-Lieutenant would have needed to pass Isaac on the road to beat him there. Besides which, Isaac didn't recognize the conveyance from about town, and the driver wore the wrong livery.

Still, the brightly lacquered carriage and team of six signaled the presence of someone important. Isaac paused to order his garments and redon his hat. He hadn't thought to wear his gloves, but in the country that omission could be overlooked. As Isaac adjusted his coat's sleeves, the carriage rolled into motion and pulled away from the grand front entrance of Rodchamb's mansion. Isaac started forward once more.

The carriage rounded the drive to reveal several people on the wide steps. His gaze caught on Betsy. She'd gained more weight, so that her sky-blue gown fit properly now, and her fuller cheeks added even more loveliness to her face. Instead of a braid, her rich locks had been coiled into perfect spirals, pinned up to reveal a long, delicate neck.

She stood between an older woman he assumed was her grandmother and Mr. Relógio. To his right stood Isaac's mother, Penna Chaff, and a woman Isaac didn't know. She descended the steps, hands outstretched to greet a tall, impeccably clad gentleman, who must have arrived in the elegant carriage.

Isaac hurried his steps. He was immensely relieved to see his mother and he'd missed Betsy. The sound of her voice. Her face. The way her blue eyes glowed with inner light when they beheld him.

They all seemed to notice him at once.

"Isaac," Betsy cried.

Isaac's steps faltered. The dowager's gaze flicked from the gentleman to him and back. Isaac's mother appeared so white, he thought she might faint. Penna took her arm, apparently fearing the same. The unknown woman simply stared at Isaac, arms still outstretched. Mr. Relógio, smiled.

"Isaac!" Betsy darted down the steps.

Isaac rushed to meet her.

Betsy skidded to a stop on the gravel of the drive as she reached him. Breath rapid and cheeks pink, she dipped into a curtsy. "Mr. Bell, it's marvelous to see you."

Her happiness sparked equal joy in Isaac as he bowed. "The feeling is entirely mutual, Miss Adams."

"It is?" Her eyes shimmered.

"So, this is Mr. Isaac Bell," a cultured male voice said.

Isaac looked past Betsy at the well-garbed gentleman, and into a face startlingly similar to his own. A face not unlike, if memory served....

Isaac addressed his mother, who now clung to Penna. "Is this...." He choked on the words.

The gentleman strode to Isaac and stopped in front of him. "Mr. Bell, permit me to introduce myself. I am your uncle, Martin Winston, Duke of Midleharton."

Isaac gaped.

Betsy faced the duke. "You are Mr. Bell's uncle, Your Grace?"

The duke nodded. "Indeed, and though we'd only now commenced introductions, I presume you to be Miss Elizabeth Adams."

Betsy flushed and lifted her chin. "I am, Your Grace, but I don't understand. You are a duke...and Isaac's uncle?"

"I do believe it is possible to be both," His Grace said in a mild tone. He looked over his shoulder. "Ellen, do come here and explain."

"As if you cannot," said the woman. She started down the steps.

Isaac watched her approach and wondered anew how she could fit into the gowns his mother had made for her. Not that she appeared oversized, but that the gowns appeared rather undersized. Too small, even, for Betsy at her thinnest.

"Lady Ellen is my sister," the duke continued as Lady Ellen approached. "Your father was our older brother."

"Was?" The single syllable cracked in his dry throat.

"Was," Lady Ellen confirmed as she reached them. "Sadly, your father died many years ago."

Isaac's mother sagged against Penna. Mr. Relógio put an arm around her waist and he and Penna took her inside the manor. Isaac knew he should go to his mother, but his legs had turned to stone.

Betsy threaded her arm through Isaac's. "I am sorry about your father," she whispered.

Isaac shook, unable to speak. He'd assumed his father was dead. In a way, believing his father had passed had been the easier alternative. No one wished to think their father had simply grown weary of them. Yet, knowing for certain that he was gone…. Isaac swallowed.

Lady Ellen and her brother exchanged a look. "We've been searching for you," she said. "Charles never told anyone who you were or where we could find you. We only knew in what direction he headed when he went to visit."

Isaac's breath grew ragged. "He was that…ashamed?"

"Ashamed? Charles?" His Grace's brows shot up. "Certainly not."

"Father forbade the relationship and would have ensured Charles never saw you or your mother again, if he could have found you," Lady Ellen clarified.

"What do you mean, made sure he never saw them again?" Betsy gasped. "What would he have done?"

Isaac could well guess. Men like that, dukes and His Majesty's lieutenants, did as they pleased to people like him and his mother. "What befell my father?"

Lady Ellen glanced at the duke, who nodded, and she said, "Your grandfather put spies on Charles, so Charles adopted dangerous measures to avoid them. Climbing from towers. Jumping his horse over gullies. Anything to evade Father's men." Sorrow pulled at her features. "He took one risk too many and ended up at the bottom of a cliff, paintbrushes scattered around him." She frowned again. "We never knew why he had paintbrushes. For years, we searched for an artist, when in your mother is a modiste."

Isaac stifled a sob.

Betsy squeezed his arm tighter. "Isaac paints. He's brilliant."

"Oh." Moisture appeared in Lady Ellen's eyes. "Well, I should like to see your work, someday."

"Yes, my lady," Isaac managed.

"Yes, "Aunt Ellen"," she corrected.

Isaac swallowed again against the hard lump in his throat, unable to do more than nod.

"But how did you finally find him?" Betsy asked. "You…you don't mean to take him away, do you?"

"Take him away?" Lady Ellen chuckled. "He's a man grown. He can very well go where he pleases."

"Ellen located Miss and Mr. Bell through some rumors she heard in London, I believe." His Grace's tone held a touch of censure, though for London or for rumors themselves, Isaac couldn't guess.

Lady Ellen nodded. "The Adamses came to London this winter full of wild stories of rustic living. One of Mr. Adams' favorites was a ribald anecdote about a country modiste and a duke's son. Very inappropriate for dinner parties, I must say. I apologize dear," she added to Betsy, "but I refused to associate with your father again after he told that story. Still, the tale stuck in my mind and when I investigated, I discovered some fact behind his tale. So, I encouraged my daughters to put on a play, thinking special costumes would be just the thing to suss out the truth without doing any harm."

Costumes, Isaac registered dully. Too small for adults. Costumes...for girls. His...cousins.

Lady Ellen leveled a satisfied smirk at her brother. "I found our nephew, after all our years of searching."

"Yes, you did." The duke cleared his throat. "That's all very well, but I came because of your inheritance, Mr. Bell. We left the funds right where your father invested them. Been nearly fifteen years, you know. We were about to give up. I'd decided fifteen years was long enough to search."

"I hadn't," Lady Ellen stated.

"We found him, so we need not have that argument again."

"*I* found him," she corrected.

His Grace waved a hand toward his sister. "Nevertheless, he is found." He fished inside his coat pocket. "Here is the information about the account. I'll have my man help you take possession when next you're in London, or we can move the funds to any bank you like." He handed Isaac the paper.

Isaac's hands shook as he unfolded the page.

Betsy gasped. "Why, that's more than my dowry."

His Grace beamed. "Yes, well invested, that sum was. Charles had a good sense for such things."

Isaac refolded the page and held it out to the duke. "I cannot possibly accept this money."

"I cannot imagine why not, young man," Grandma Adams said.

They all turned at her approach.

"In fact, I demand you accept that money," she continued.

"But I, that is, I don't know them. They owe me nothing."

"You are our nephew," Lady Ellen said at the same moment

as His Grace protested, "Charles desperately wished to provide for you."

"I daresay you won't be leaving them insolvent, boy," Grandma Adams added.

"Not to say that account isn't a tidy sum, Bell, but the funds won't be missed," His Grace assured him, though he added a grimace. "Sordid topic, money, but be assured the family fortune is well intact. Overflowing coffers and all that."

"We don't need the money," Lady Ellen added.

"Oh, and you do, Isaac. For your shop," Betsy said.

Grandma Adams snorted. "If the amount is more than your dowry, he'll hardly require work as a tailor any longer."

"Oh," Betsy mumbled.

Isaac became acutely aware of Betsy's arm twined with his. The scent of lemon that wafted off her hair. Her smooth cheeks. Her full, curved lips. Those amazing blue eyes, framed in dark lashes.

"As I was saying," Grandma Adams reiterated loudly, "I *require* you to accept your inheritance."

"Why?" Isaac asked.

"Do you believe I will permit a penniless tailor to wed my granddaughter and sole heir? Or even a brilliant, but as of yet unknown, painter?" She snorted. "I think not."

"W-wed your granddaughter?" Isaac stammered.

"You'd best mean to do so, the way you've been looking at her, boy."

Isaac stared at the wrinkled, tanned face. Though not very tall, Grandma Adams could be rather intimidating. But he didn't need anyone to intimidate him just then. He faced Betsy and dropped to one knee.

Betsy let out a squeal of joy. "Yes. I will marry you."

"Let the lad ask, my dear," the duke said.

"Oh." Betsy said. "Yes, Your Grace."

Isaac caught her hands in his. "Miss Elizabeth Adams, you

are the most beguiling, most wonderfully stubborn, and kindest person I have ever met. It would be my privilege to be your husband, should you be willing to have me. Will you do me the great honor of becoming my wife?"

Tears filled her eyes. "I will, Isaac. You know I will."

Lady Ellen let out a happy cry and caught Isaac in a hug as he rose. She released him into a similar embrace by Grandma Adams, who actually smiled. His uncle, clapped Isaac on the shoulder.

"This calls for a celebration," Grandma Adams declared.

"Then I have your permission, Mrs. Adams?" Isaac belatedly thought to ask.

"If that is the question, then the answer is no."

Isaac's heart paused mid beat. He gawked at Grandma Adams, once again unable to speak.

"What?" Betsy demanded. "But, Grandmother, you said that if he accepted his inheritance, he could marry me." She balled her hands into fists at her hips. "You are not making me earn another rose. I'll run off with Isaac before I do. You see if I won't."

"Hush, child. You are too quick tempered." Grandma Adams addressed Isaac. "You will have to watch that, my boy."

"I like Miss Adams just as she is," Isaac said firmly. "But what do you mean, the answer is no?"

"Have you decided the lad isn't suitable enough after all?" His Grace asked. "I'll have you know our lineage dates back seven centuries. Legitimate or not, the boy comes from fine stock."

"Hot headed, the lot of you," Grandma Adams proclaimed. "I merely meant the question was incorrect."

Mr. Relógio emerged from the manor house door and descended the steps. "We've taken Miss Bell to the parlor, for she refused her room. Miss Chaff is with her." He nodded to the duke. "I believe the shock proved a bit much."

"Understandable," Lady Ellen murmured.

"Harold, you are exactly on time, as usual." Grandma Adams grasped Mr. Relógio's hand. "Now, as I tried to inform you when we arrived, my quick-tempered Elizabeth—"

"You mean, as I attempted to tell you earlier, 'my dearest granddaughter,'" Mr. Relógio corrected.

Grandma Adams frowned. "That is what I said."

"Nearly," he agreed.

Grandma Adams laughed and addressed Betsy. "As I tried to tell you when we arrived, I am no longer Mrs. Adams. I am Mrs. Relógio. Harold and I married last summer, a year ago this weekend to be exact. One of the reasons we returned is so he might meet you."

Betsy shrieked and threw her arms about her grandmother, then Mr. Relógio. "I am so pleased you are my grandfather."

Isaac extended a hand to the gentleman. "You have my best wishes."

"Once we're married, Mr. Relógio will be your grandfather," Betsy exclaimed.

Isaac blinked rapidly. He'd come up the drive with his mother as his only relation. Now, he had a whole family. "So he will." He grinned so wide his face hurt. "I…I've never had grandparents."

"Well, you have an aunt too," Lady Ellen said. "Two aunts, if you include Her Grace, and your uncle here, and I have two daughters and Their Graces have three sons and a daughter, so you've six cousins."

"My sons and daughter will arrive tomorrow," His Grace added. "I have them a day behind, in case the lot of you proved unsuitable."

"Six cousins?" Isaac wondered if his new cousins would be friendly to him? Hope in his eyes, he looked at Mr. Relógio.

Mr. Relógio seemed to understand and said, "I have three grown, married daughters and twelve grandchildren."

Betsy clapped her hands. "Marvelous. We shall have such a lovely time meeting them all."

Isaac looked about the ring of faces, mind numb of anything but joy.

"About those celebrations?" His Grace said. "Not that you don't have a lovely drive here, Mr. and Mrs. Relógio, but I'd enjoy seeing more of the estate. Particularly a comfortable parlor and a snifter of brandy."

Mr. Relógio smiled. He made a sweeping gesture akin to a bow. "It would be our honor, Your Grace."

The duke offered his arm to his sister as Mr. Relógio offered his arm to his wife, and the four proceeded indoors. Isaac stared after them. He had aunts and an uncle and cousins and grandparents. But most importantly, he had—

"Isaac?" Betsy touched his sleeve.

"I missed you," he blurted.

Betsy gave him a radiant smile. "I missed you too."

"Even though I made you empty chamber pots?"

She winkled her nose. "You didn't make me do that. One of the housemaids did. The one who's sweet on you." She grimaced. "Well, one of the ones who's sweet on you."

"I doubt any of them noticed me," he said.

"Liar."

"But if they did notice me," he continued, "I did not, and will never, encourage them."

"I know."

"Don't be too long, children," Mrs. Relógio called over her shoulder from the top step. "I am about to convey the happy news of your betrothal to the staff. I believe the announcement will be met with universal delight. Especially by Mr. Côte." She waved Isaac's aunt and uncle before her through the manor house door, held open by a young footman.

"Especially by Mr. Côte?" Isaac asked in a low voice as the four disappeared inside.

"He's not entirely convinced, that without you, I won't revert back into the monster I once was," Betsy replied.

Isaac stroked her cheek with the backs of his fingers. "Surely *monster* is a bit strong."

Eyes half-closed, Betsy nuzzled his hand. "I doubt *monster* is strong enough. I was an absolute *beast* to him and the others. To you."

"I shall never credit such talk." He cupped her cheek.

"I'm certain I could still be a bit beastly, if necessary." Her full mouth grazed his palm as she spoke.

Isaac's chest tightened. "Oh?"

She nodded. "As you'll find out soon enough, Isaac Bell, if you don't stop teasing me and let me kiss you."

With a growl, Isaac swept her up against him and covered her mouth with his.

CHAPTER 18

Isaac buried his hands in Betsy's hair and angled her mouth to better receive his kisses.

"Ahem."

Betsy's arms twined about his neck.

"Ahem!"

Isaac pulled her closer. He needed to feel her pressed against him more than he'd ever needed anything else in his life.

"I said, 'ahem'," Penna cried as she hurried down the steps toward them. "Mr. Bell, Miss Adams, stop that this instant or I…I shall get a bucket of water."

Isaac lifted his head to find Betsy's companion glaring at them.

Penna stopped beside them. "I came out to tell you it's time to join everyone in the parlor."

"Isaac?" Betsy tugged his head back down to hers.

"I, ah, believe we best rejoin the others," he said.

"Others?" she murmured.

Isaac caught her hands and unwrapped her arms from about

his neck. He kept one hand clasped in his and reordered her curls with his other.

"Let me." Penna pulled Betsy away from him and smoothed her glossy locks. "See to your cravat, Mr. Bell, and pick up your hat."

Isaac scooped up the hat and recalled his reason for coming there. In the shock at meeting his relations, the joy of his engagement, he'd forgotten all about Filomena Guest, the Lord-Lieutenant, and Doctor Fox.

"Isaac, whatever is the matter?" Betsy batted Penna's hands aside and stepped closer to him.

He frowned. "I'd forgotten why I came here."

Betsy stilled. "It wasn't to ask for my hand?"

Isaac captured her hand and brought her fingers to his lips. "That was not why, but you agreeing to marry me is a most...." He took in her wide eyes. "Rather, *the* most fortuitous, wonderful, marvelous turn of events I could possibly have imagined."

"I should hope so."

"Yes, well." Penna pulled a handkerchief from her skirt pocket and dabbed at her eyes, then tucked it away. "Here." She straightened Isaac's cravat. Her back to Betsy, Penna whispered, "Please be good to her, sir. She is kind at heart."

"I know she is," he whispered back.

Tears welled in her eyes.

Done with his cravat, Penna pulled out her handkerchief again. "I'm so joyous for you both."

"Our union is nothing to cry over, Penna," Betsy said, and Penna cried harder.

"I must speak with your grandmother," Isaac said as Betsy gathered Penna to her. "Come in when you may."

Betsy rolled her eyes skyward. "We won't be long. Penna is being silly."

"I was so afraid no one would ever love you." Penna wailed.

Isaac smiled as he jogged up the steps.

When he reached the top, Mr. Côte opened the door and stepped aside so Isaac might enter. He stepped in and marveled at the chandelier, which positively dripped crystals, no longer a naked spiny armature. Rodchamb had clearly undergone as great a change as had the roads.

"May I take your coat, sir?" Mr. Côte asked.

"Thank you."

"No. *Thank you*, Mr. Bell," Mr. Côte said, more effusive than Isaac had ever seen him, tears in his eyes. In a voice that radiated relief, he continued, "I never thought anyone would love her, either. Leastwise, no one of good character." Mr. Côte took Isaac's outerwear and hat, and said, "You won't change your mind about wedding her, will you, sir? Now that you're wealthy in your own right?"

Isaac raised his eyebrows. "News traveled fast."

Mr. Côte squared his shoulders. "It is not idle gossip, sir. I could hear His Grace from the entrance hall."

"I am certain you could." Isaac grinned. "Especially if you cracked the door open."

Côte had the good grace to avert his gaze.

Isaac clasped the elderly gentleman on the shoulder, aware of how he'd born up under years of mistreatment, all for his love of Rodchamb. "Be assured, Mr. Côte, that I love Miss Adams fully and deeply and that no amount of income will alter my regard for her."

"Thank you, sir."

Isaac regarded the man. "You had the crystals for the chandelier the whole time, didn't you, Mr. Côte?"

Mr. Côte pursed his lips. "I did, sir, along with a great deal more that went *missing*, to keep everything out of harm's way."

Isaac grinned again then remembered his mission. "The Relógios and their guests are gathered in the east parlor?" he asked.

"Yes, sir."

Isaac had guessed they'd be in that particular parlor, for the room offered a view of Mrs. Relógio's splendid rose garden. He headed east. As he walked the long halls, footfalls muted by thick runners, he took in anew the silk-clad walls. Elegant sconces graced the walls at regular intervals. Every so often a small ornamental table stood against the wall, topped with a rose-filled vase. Oils of landscapes, bouquets, or bowls of fruit hung from the walls. He was startled to realize that all of this grandeur would be Betsy's, and now his—if she'd reassembled the rose pendant her grandmother had given her.

Not that he cared. He would love Betsy in any type of home, anywhere. Yes, he'd come to view Rodchamb with a certain fondness. He longed to see the crops come in. To know how well the orchard bore this autumn. Or if more of the tenants had returned as hoped, and how their farms might be made to prosper. He didn't need Rodchamb's riches, however. All he needed from Rodchamb were his paints and Betsy, and the paints could be replaced.

A weight lifted from him. He also did not need the shop. Or Miss Guest's patronage. If he intended to remain in Cumberfordshire, he did require the favor of her father. Still, the Lord-Lieutenant seemed a reasonable man. It could be his greatest sin was spoiling his daughter after her mother died.

Isaac reached the parlor and halted within the doorway to find a celebratory atmosphere. His Grace and Mr. Relógio spoke in low tones near the fireplace, each with a tumbler of dark liquid in hand. Mrs. Relógio and Lady Ellen sat at a low table, set with tea and sweets, his mother with them. She appeared pale but composed and oddly subdued.

"There you are," Mrs. Relógio said. "I've a grievance with you, Mr. Bell."

Isaac couldn't tell from her tone if she spoke in jest. "Yes, Madam?"

"You forgave the tenants two quarters rent. Two quarters!"

"I did."

"Well, what have you to say for yourself?"

"That I believe forgiving the rent was the right decision."

Mrs. Relógio frowned, but Mr. Relógio chuckled. "I like this lad," he said.

"Only because you agree with what he did," Mrs. Relógio snapped. "Which is why I have the better head for business."

"You have the more ruthless head for business," Mr. Relógio countered. "Sometimes, the quickest path to income is not the path that leads to the greatest success."

Mrs. Relógio shook her head, but Isaac read both fondness and amusement under her dour façade.

Her gaze shifted back to Isaac. "Barring that one rather large exception, I approve of how you managed Rodchamb, Mr. Bell."

"Of how Miss Adams and I managed Rodchamb," he corrected.

"You raised the boy to be confident," Mrs. Relógio said to his mother.

Mother, still dazed, simply stared at him. Footfalls approached behind Isaac. Betsy and Penna had arrived. Despite the news he must give them, fresh joy shot through Isaac when he stepped into the room and turned as Betsy halted beside him. Isaac captured Betsy's hand in his and Penna continued to the couch where she sat beside Isaac's mother.

Mrs. Relógio reached for a bell. "Now that we are all here, we must celebrate your engagement."

"Oh yes," Lady Ellen agreed. "We can have a toast here and then Mr. Bell can come out to the garden and meet his cousins."

Before Mrs. Relógio could ring for a servant, Isaac said, "Please wait…if I may?"

Everyone in the room looked at him.

"I have news of some import." He scanned the faces before him. "Miss Filomena Guest and her father, His Majesty's Lord-

Lieutenant for the County of Cumberfordshire, met with Mr. and Mrs. Adams early today. They...." He hesitated. "Miss Guest and the Adamses are of a mind that my mother and Mrs. Relógio must both be declared insane and taken to an asylum in Bristol, and that Miss Adams

should be sent, as they put it, somewhere far away, such as Australia."

"What?" Betsy gasped.

Isaac squeezed her hand. "Your parents met with the Lord-Lieutenant to persuade him to agree to have your grandmother and my mother declared mad and to summon Doctor Fox to remove them." To the room, he added, "The Adamses offered to maintain the roads better and to supply Doctor Fox's asylum with a generous donation, once they are restored as masters of Rodchamb and all of Mrs. Relógio's holdings are handed over to them."

Silence stretched out for a long moment. Then Mr. Relógio chuckled, again. "You mean, they are having documents drawn up to declare Mrs. Adams mad and to turn over her holdings to her son?"

Isaac nodded. "I believe so."

Mr. Relógio raised his brandy glass in mock salute. "Let them do as they may. I believe the only *Mrs.* Adams currently associated with Rodchamb is Miss Adams' own mother. As she has only whatever allowance her husband gives her, he's welcome to it."

"Oh, but they are so awful," Betsy cried. "How can they mean to say anyone is mad or send anyone to Australia? Why must they be so horrible?"

Isaac squeezed his betrothed's hand again.

Mrs. Relógio sighed. "I'm afraid your father's horribleness is my doing, child. I left to see the world when he was five, and I rarely returned."

"Nonsense," His Grace said. "Half the peerage is raised by tutors and nannies."

Isaac privately deemed half the peerage also guilty of horribleness but had no notion whether being raised by tutors and nannies was the cause.

"Well, if anyone is mad, they are," Betsy declared, chin at a defiant angle. "They drink so much and use so very much laudanum and have those parties. I say that if anyone should go with Doctor Fox, they should."

"Here, here." His Grace raised his glass.

Mrs. Relógio appeared thoughtful. "Mr. Fox's treatment may do them some good. Could you accomplish that turn of events, Your Grace?"

The duke cocked a wary eyebrow at his sister.

"They are reprobates of the worst sort, Martin," Lady Ellen said. "Immoral, opium-soaked blights on society, and I am willing to swear to that fact."

Everyone gaped at her.

Her ladyship shrugged. "Well, they are. You all know as much."

His Grace cleared his throat. "Ah, yes, well, if they attempt to take legal action against the no-longer-in-existence Mrs. Adams, I will exercise my powers to see they do a stint with Doctor Fox to reform them."

Mrs. Relógio nodded with satisfaction. "Thank you, Your Grace."

"But he will still take me," Isaac's mother said softly.

"Oh, no, certainly not," Penna assured her.

"They cannot, can they?" Betsy clenched Isaac's hand.

"You know they can." His mother put a trembling hand to her heart. "Everyone says I am mad. Doctor Fox will have an entire village of witnesses ready to swear as much."

Isaac was startled at the lucidity in her speech—and in her eyes. He hadn't known she understood her disconnection with reality or how others saw her. He'd been glad for the moments when she seemed suddenly aware of the world around her but the anguish in her eyes made him wish this wasn't one of those moments.

Isaac released Betsy and went to kneel before his mother. "No, Mother, Dr. Fox will not have the villagers as witness against you."

"He will." Tears shimmered in her eyes.

"You are not mad," Isaac insisted. "You are free and happy and full of life, but not mad." Not fully mad at any rate, and certainly not mad enough to be committed to Dr. Fox's asylum.

"You thought my gowns were the work of a madwoman," she sniffled. "I know you did."

Isaac forced a neutral expression. He had no idea his mother had so easily read his thoughts. Was it not a positive sign that she was that aware? Mad people didn't know they were mad, did they? If Dr. Fox did try to commit her, her awareness would prove she wasn't mad.

He took her hands. "I did not think you mad. Though I did resent the gowns, I admit. But only because you never told me they were costumes."

"And I may as well go to the asylum, because now you will marry Betsy and leave me, and I shall be all alone." She pulled her hands free from his and covered her face.

Isaac started to say that she was worried over nothing, then realized that to say she could live at Rodchamb was to impose upon Betsy his will, which went against every lesson he'd taught in the weeks he spent with her. But surely, any woman would expect him to care for his mother, and Betsy already cared for her.

"Now no one loves me best in all the world," his mother sobbed.

"Mother, you must have realized that someday I would marry. Give me time—"

"No, no," she keened through her fingers. "Filomena wanted you, and you did not want her, and she wouldn't let any other girl in the village near you. They were all afraid of her. That's why I encouraged her. I can't lose your love too, Izzy."

"You…what?" Isaac stared.

"Miss Bell, how could you?" Betsy cried. "I thought you were a kind person, full of joy and love, but you conspired against your son's happiness?"

Isaac pushed to his feet. "Betsy, she does not understand—"

"She understands perfectly," Betsy cut in. "She carried on an affair all but certain to result in a child born out of wedlock, despite knowing the hardships that child would suffer. She then thrust upon you the responsibility of running that shop at age *nine*. She flits about doing precisely what she wants, while you shoulder every responsibility. Every burden. She is not mad, Isaac." Betsy swung her gaze onto his mother. "She's cunning and selfish—and quite brilliant at getting her way."

"Betsy," Isaac gasped.

"I told you I would discover your flaws, Mr. Bell, and you have two," Betsy continued. "One is that you become so obsessed when you paint that I daresay lightning could strike and still you would not notice. That flaw, I can bear. What I cannot countenance is the way you allow your mother to control you."

Isaac stiffened. "Given the way you were raised, Miss Adams, you would resent anyone who acceded to the wishes of their parent. Why do you not know how to ride? Or speak French? Or sew?" His mind shouted for him to halt, but he finished, "Because you were determined to thwart your parents."

"Mr. Bell, Elizabeth," Mrs. Relógio cut in.

"At least I learned how to stand up for myself," Betsy cried. "You would give up everything for your mother, when she has never given up one thing for you."

"I don't want anything," Miss Bell cried. "Only to come live here with you, where I can have Isaac's love and I won't be alone."

Isaac inwardly grimaced. The petulance in her voice was only proving Betsy's point. "Mother, you cannot simply invite yourself to live in Miss Adams' home, even if I am her husband and an offer might be expected. You must wait for it to be made, at least."

"But you must permit me, Izzy. What will become of me, if I am alone?" Her voice dwindled into a sob again. "You know I am not well enough to live on my own. What if something unfortunate were to happen to me?"

Isaac stared at her. He'd sometimes felt she might be deliberately swaying him, but nothing like this. How—

"I will make this choice very simple for you, Mr. Bell," Betsy declared. "Your mother may not reside at Rodchamb. With your inheritance, you can afford for her to live anywhere she likes. I can afford for her to live anywhere she likes. Anywhere, but here." Betsy spun and marched from the room.

His mother clung to his arm with both hands. "Oh, Izzy, I am sorry."

Isaac flushed poker hot. Would his new relations still want him after that display? Would the duke send word to turn back the carriage that carried Isaac's cousins?

"It is best this way, dearest," his mother continued in a soothing voice that conjured memories of him as that nine-year-old boy being told *"It is best that you keep our ledger, dearest. You know how terrible I am with numbers."*

"We're wealthy now," she continued. "We do not need Miss Adams. We can live by the sea. Wouldn't that be lovely, Izzy? A cottage by the sea with gulls and waves and the ocean and the moon?"

The anger and hurt in Betsy's face filled his mental vision

and he realized she had seen what he had been blind to for twenty-two years. His chest tightened.

He looked down at his mother. "Yes, Mother, you will be happy in your cottage by the ocean. Rest assured, I will find the perfect one for you. But I will only be happy with Betsy." He pulled his arm free and bowed to the room at large. "If you will excuse me?"

For the first time in his life, Isaac ignored his mother's sobs.

CHAPTER 19

Betsy stood before the fountain and watched water tumble, the early evening air thick with the full, rich scent of roses. Footfalls approached from behind, but she didn't turn. She dashed at her wet eyes and cheeks. Why had she still not learned to sew? Not learning no longer defied her parents, and she required new handkerchiefs.

She hadn't meant to yell at Isaac or to give him an ultimatum, but Miss Bell had made her so very angry. Usually, she enjoyed Isaac's mother. If the other woman had asked, Betsy would have offered her a space at Rodchamb without a thought.

But she hadn't asked. She'd cried and cajoled and threatened and sought to take advantage of Isaac's kind nature, and Betsy simply wouldn't tolerate her manipulations.

She knew without looking it was Isaac who stopped behind her and when he proffered his handkerchief, she took the square of cloth as she tried to hold back a sob. She would not be like Isaac's mother and use tears to control him.

Still, her voice cracked when she said, "I must learn to sew." She dabbed at her eyes with the handkerchief.

For a moment, only stillness met her words. Fear twisted her stomach.

I must learn to sew? Not, *I am so sorry, Isaac, please don't decide not to marry me.* Or *I promise to work harder to control my temper.*

Isaac slid his arms about her waist and pulled her against him. He rested his chin on the top of her head, his long form solid and strong against her back. "You'll never need to know how to sew. You have me."

Betsy slumped against him. "Wouldn't it be a waste of your skill to hem handkerchiefs?"

"Nothing done out of love is a waste."

Betsy couldn't quite stifle a shaky giggle. Isaac always had an answer.

He squeezed her tighter. "You don't agree?"

"I do," she said, but her voice shook with something between laughter and tears. "Only, who taught you so many ridiculous things to say?"

He didn't reply, and she regretted the question for the saccharin, impractical saying could only have come from one place.

"She will not come live with us," Isaac stated.

Fresh relief filled Betsy and dizzied her. Not because Miss Bell wouldn't live with them, but because Isaac had said, "us." Her fear he'd changed his mind about marrying her had loomed large, despite his promise to sew her handkerchiefs.

"She can for a time, and she may certainly visit. I am not certain she can be on her own."

"She's a grown woman, and we'll hire her a staff." His jaw glided over Betsy's hair as he shook his head. "I think, perhaps, by taking care of her, I encouraged her to have her way, but I had to take care of her after my father left us. How could I not?"

"Certainly, you had to help her," she said, and mentally added, *even if you were nine and she was a grown woman.*

He squeezed her to him and pressed a kiss to the top of her head.

Betsy turned in his arms. Her breath shallowed as she studied his face. "Sometimes, you must take care of yourself."

He offered a half smile. "And you?"

"Sometimes, yes, that would be nice, but not too often."

The other corner of his mouth ticked up. "But you will let me sew you some handkerchiefs."

Betsy nodded. "That would be very kind of you."

"You'll let me do this?" He lowered his lips to hers.

Betsy slid her hands up his chest over his shoulders and around the back of his neck to tangle in his hair. She stood on her toes and leaned into his kiss, now far wilder than the one he'd given her in the front drive. Isaac pressed her closer.

With a groan, he released her, backed away and looked over his shoulder.

"Isaac?" Betsy said in a breathless voice. Behind her, she braced her hands on the edge of the fountain, her legs weak. "What is wrong?"

He turned back with another lopsided grin. "The thought flashed through my mind that Penna might come up behind me with a bucket." His expression grew more serious. "And that I shouldn't disrespect you so."

She hadn't felt one bit disrespected. She'd felt worshipped. She licked her lips and forced her next words. "Yes. Well. It's right to…to wait."

Isaac nodded and clasped his hands behind his back.

Betsy wanted to say something more but could think only of Isaac's kisses. She'd enjoyed the first one, but the second proved even better. She had the suspicion they would get better still.

"I forgot to ask," he said abruptly, seeming more rattled than she ever recalled him. "The rose? It seems you must have, but did you complete it?"

"You know about the rose?" She couldn't recall telling him about her precious pendant, and she recalled every moment with Isaac.

"Mr. Côte and Mrs. Calic told me."

"Oh." Betsy liked to watch his lips while he talked. And while he didn't.

"So, did you?" he asked.

"Did I?"

"Finish the rose."

"Yes."

The fountain bubbled and gurgled. The scent of roses saturated the air. The sun painted the sky behind Isaac a brilliant array of pinks.

"The next time I paint you, you should wear the rose," he said.

"The next time?" She tried to focus on her words, rather than dream about his kisses. "You haven't finished the first painting."

"Now that I am here, I will. Then I shall want to paint another." He stepped closer again. "And another."

"Hmm."

"That is, if it does not trouble you that when I paint, it would take a sudden strike of lightning for me to notice the world about me."

Her fantasies of another kiss shattered. "Forgive me. I didn't mean to criticize."

"No, you are right. I become much too absorbed in my work."

"You love painting."

More than he loved her? He'd implied she needn't worry about other women, but did she need to compete for his affections with painting? Now that he'd inherited a fortune, and soon would marry into another, he didn't need to work. He could paint all day. Every day.

He stroked her cheek again, sending a delightful shiver down her spine. "What if we agree that I may focus on my paintings, so long as you may interrupt me whenever you wish?"

Betsy twined her arms about his neck again. Her heart resumed its frantic beat. "I can agree to those conditions."

Isaac dipped his head closer.

"Miss? Betsy? Mr. Bell?" Penna's called from somewhere near the house.

"She's still far away," Isaac whispered, and he kissed her.

When Penna finally found them, they were walking out of the rose garden, side by side, not even holding hands. In fact, Isaac had clasped his behind his back again, as if to ensure he couldn't reach for Betsy. She hoped that in the fading daylight Penna couldn't discern the blush that heated her cheeks.

"There you are." Penna's gaze raked over them. "You've been gone quite some time."

"We had a lot to talk about," Isaac murmured.

Penna sniffed. "Talk, is it?" She leveled a look of suspicion on Betsy.

"Yes. We talked about Miss Bell," Betsy supplied.

"Well, I hope you didn't settle on too much. It's been decided she's to go live in a cottage on His Grace's land."

Isaac halted. "That's been decided? And she agreed?"

"His Grace and Lady Ellen insisted. They said their brother would want them to take care of the woman who should be his widow."

"Oh, how kind of them," Betsy breathed. "What a good man His Grace is, to honor the memory of his brother."

"Aye," Penna agreed. "It's easy to see where Mr. Bell gets his noble streak." She waved in the direction of the house. "Now come in and make ready for dinner. I, for one, wish an early night. We have *A Midsummer Night's Dream* tomorrow, and then the ball. Mr. Bell, we still have the suits you left when last you returned to town, so you should have no trouble readying for dinner. I will take Betsy with me." Penna ushered them both forward.

Isaac chuckled as they walked, and the sound filled Betsy with delight.

"You needn't worry, Miss Chaff, I will not drag Miss Adams off to my room to change for dinner with me," Isaac said in a nonchalant voice.

"No, you most certainly are not," Penna retorted, though Betsy rather liked the idea. Her mind filled with all sorts of images.

Regardless of Betsy's imaginings, they soon separated and changed for dinner, which proved a convivial affair where Isaac enjoyed meeting those of his cousins who had accompanied Lady Ellen. The dinner set the tone for the following day, begun in good cheer which continued on through the play, where Miss Bell's fairy costumes, complete with shimmering wings, proved the star of the production. Many more guests had arrived before the show, including the remainder of Isaac's cousins on his father's side and many of the tenant farmers, and everyone gave the cast a standing ovation. Isaac handed a rose to each of Lady Ellen's daughters, and Betsy could see the girls had already become enamored with their handsome older cousin.

Then, finally, the part of the day for which Betsy had longed arrived. The ball her grandmother had promised. Betsy had never been permitted to attend a ball in Rodchamb's ballroom. Now, she was glad of that previous ban, for she understood her parents' events as debaucheries she shouldn't have ever witnessed. Besides which, waiting meant she might have her very first dance with Isaac. No ball could be complete without Isaac.

She'd been practicing. Ever since her grandmother had sent the invitations out, over two weeks ago, Betsy had practiced dancing with the eager help of Chef Dramm, the kitchen maids, and Penna, who'd also danced with Rodchamb's chef. Their practices had been fun, but Betsy secretly hoped Isaac would be lighter on his feet than Chef Dramm.

Betsy descended the curved staircase in her best gown, her grandmother's rose necklace at her throat, and Penna a few steps behind. Isaac paced the foyer, hands clasped behind his back, but halted the moment he saw her. He stood motionless, incomprehensibly handsome in his dark tailcoat and trousers, sapphire waistcoat, and white cravat.

The utter intensity in his gaze reminded her of how he looked while painting. He watched her as if nothing else existed in the world. Heat bloomed in her cheeks. How had she lived before Isaac came into her life?

When she reached the bottom, he executed a low bow, then straightened and offered his arm. Betsy's hand trembled as she placed her gloved fingers lightly on his sleeve.

"You look exceptional," he murmured as he started them in the direction of the ballroom.

Betsy beamed. "So do you."

"I cheat. I make my own suits, so I may tailor them perfectly."

"While it is a very flattering suit, I do not believe a few layers of fabric can take credit for how handsome you are," she said.

He looked down at her. "If you are not careful, I shall think you seek to flatter me."

"I do."

"But you already have my heart."

Her heart tripped over its next beat, but Betsy pressed on, delighted with their banter. She'd never before been able to banter.

"Yes, but perhaps there is more I want from you," she murmured.

He halted them several paces from the ballroom door, his

expression a charming mix of amusement and challenge. "What, exactly, might that be?"

Heat traveled from Betsy's toes right up to her scalp.

Isaac raised both eyebrows. "As an unwed miss, it's quite scandalous for you to be thinking such things."

"How do you know what I'm thinking?" she blurted.

Penna sighed. "I daresay we all know what you're thinking, and I agree with Mr. Bell, you ought not be having such thoughts. *Yet.*"

Betsy hadn't thought her cheeks could get any hotter, but she'd forgotten Penna. "I think I need some air."

"I'll escort you to the terrace," Isaac said.

"I will escort Miss Adams to the terrace," Penna corrected. She took Betsy by the arm and pulled her in the direction of a small side parlor that also opened onto the terrace. As they left Isaac behind, Penna muttered, "We'd best get those banns read right quick."

They stepped out into the cool night air and Penna released Betsy's arm.

Betsy pressed her hands to her warm cheeks. "I forget myself when I'm with him."

Penna laughed. "No need to apologize. I am pleased you're so taken with him."

"Then why are you so strict?"

Penna glanced about, but the only people in sight mingled together far down the terrace. "Associating with your peers will be difficult enough," she whispered, "even with so upright a gentleman as Mr. Bell as your husband and even though he is the acknowledged nephew of a duke. So, to avoid the repercussions of your mother's reputation…"

Betsy hadn't fully considered her precarious social standing. "Are my parents' reputations really so terrible?"

Penna groaned. "Worse—and you know it is your mother

who bears the weight of any scandal, as men can be as scandalous as they please and still be considered gentlemen."

Betsy sighed. "Well, then, I shall do nothing to encourage such sentiments and everything to refute them."

"I think that would be best."

Betsy shrugged. She didn't care much what people thought. After all, she would never be a London socialite. The only reason she had wanted her time among the *ton* had been to find a gentleman so she might escape her parents. Now, she was free of them and didn't need a husband...but she wanted one. A very specific one.

"May we go back in now? I vow to behave, but I should very much like to dance with Isa—" She caught Penna's censorious expression. "With Mr. Bell. To whom I am affianced, I may remind you."

"Yes, we may go in," Penna allowed.

Instead of returning as they'd come, they walked to the far end of the terrace, where guests spilled out into the night from the crowded ballroom. As Betsy entered, she smiled and nodded at the guests, many she didn't know. She realized that she'd missed her formal entrance with Isaac. Near the front of the room, Mr. Côte continued to bellow names as guests entered. Betsy scanned the room but didn't see Isaac. Was he awaiting her outside? She turned to Penna to suggest they go back outside to find him.

"His Majesty's Lord-Lieutenant for the County of Cumberfordshire," Côte boomed. "Miss Filomena Guest. Mr. Dougal Guest."

Betsy whirled to face the door. A broad-shouldered gentleman of middling years strode in, a young woman about Betsy's age on his arm. Another young man stood to the woman's left. More willowy than Betsy had ever been, even when she hadn't been able to scrounge enough food, Miss Guest stood tall and whip straight beside her father. All three were dressed not for a ball but in regular evening clothes so fine the difference hardly mattered. The Lord-Lieutenant glanced around in mild confusion, but Miss Guest glared as if she might commit murder. Dougal Guest glanced around the room, then slipped away into the crowd.

Betsy's grandparents emerged from the crowd. They moved at a stately pace, as if to greet expected guests, not intruders. Isaac and his uncle came into view, angled to intercept the Guests as well. Betsy caught Penna's arm and set out across the room.

Before Betsy and Penna could reach them, her grandparents, Isaac and his uncle reached the Lord-Lieutenant and his daughter, and the six disappeared out the door from which they had entered. Betsy pushed through the crowd in an effort to overtake them but reached the hallway to find them gone.

"They went to your grandmother's study, Miss Adams," Mr. Côte said in a low voice.

"Thank you, Mr. Côte," Betsy said. "Truly." She started to walk past him, but he lightly touched her arm, expression grave.

He cast his eyes about the immediate area, then gestured them a few paces down the hall. In an even lower voice, he said, "Miss, please do not permit any harm to befall your grandmother or, heaven help us, allow the return of your father as master of this house."

Betsy gasped. "My father?" she whispered.

Mr. Côte grimaced. "He is here, as well. He didn't enter the ballroom but lurked in the hall."

Betsy pressed her lips into a hard line. "Do not fear, Mr. Côte. Things will not return to how they were. You have my word."

"But you are not yet of age, Miss. You are still under the dominion of your father."

Betsy clamped her teeth, then recalled Lady Ellen's words of the evening before. "I am not. He is unfit to govern himself, let alone me. Lady Ellen said she would vouch for that fact. Please, find her and send her to the study, Mr. Côte."

An eager gleam lit his eyes. "Right away, Miss."

"Thank you," Betsy said, again. "Come, Penna."

Betsy turned and walked toward her grandmother's study.

CHAPTER 20

The study door stood closed and a footman blocked the way.

"I was told not to permit anyone to enter or to listen at the door, Miss," he told Betsy.

Penna drew in a breath, but Betsy held up a staying hand. "You were told, I assume, not to permit any of the guests near? I am not a guest. In fact, in a few months, I shall be mistress of this house. You are aware of my position in this household, I assume?"

The footman lowered his gaze.

Betsy gentled her tone. "My place is in there, alongside my grandmother to help defend Rodchamb from the ravages of my patriarch. Surely you can see reason?"

"Y-Yes, Miss," he stammered.

"Now, tell me, did they lock the door?"

"No, Miss. I do not believe so."

Betsy raised her chin. "Good. Lady Ellen will be here soon. When she arrives, send her in immediately. Do you understand?"

He nodded. "Yes, Miss."

"Thank you."

Betsy stepped around him and eased the door open enough to see inside the large room. Her father stood before the desk on the other side of the room, behind which sat her grandmother, Mr. Relógio at her side. The Lord-Lieutenant and his daughter sat on one of the deep leather sofas, His Grace and Isaac on the other.

"I won't ask again, Mother. Vacate that chair. This is my house and that is my desk, and I shall conduct this meeting. You are here to be tried by the Lord-Lieutenant for lunacy so a doctor can remove you."

"Ridiculous," Betsy's grandmother declared. "If anyone here is mad, it is you, much to my sorrow. I did this to you, by not raising you right and by letting you marry that hedonistic creature you selected."

"Charlotte has nothing to do with this," Betsy's father snapped.

"Clearly not, as she isn't even present." Grandmother sighed. "Was she too intoxicated to bring out in public, or too sunk in a laudanum-induced stupor?"

"You will not speak of the mistress of Rodchamb in that fashion, Mother."

She stood, braced her hands on the wide desk, and leaned forward. "I am mistress of Rodchamb, boy. You'd do well to remember that."

"You are a mad old hag," he spat.

Grandmother laughed. "I daresay I have more wits about me than you can lay claim to in a decade."

"I have wits enough to take my rightful place from an old woman." Her father started around the desk.

Mr. Relógio stepped in his way.

"Tell your lacky to step aside, Mother."

Penna gripped Betsy's arm.

"I ask you not to speak that way about your stepfather." Her tone remained mild, though her eyes sparked.

Betsy's father rocked back on his heels. He whipped toward the Lord-Lieutenant. "You see how mad she is? She's married one of her servants."

"Harold owns the farms alongside mine," Grandmother retorted. "But it would not matter if he were a servant. He is a wonderful man, and I love him even more than I once loved your father."

Betsy's father threw up his hands and giggled. "You see? Mad!"

"Father," Miss Guest urged. "Do something. Think of all Mr. Adams has promised."

The Lord-Lieutenant came to his feet with a little cough. "Yes, well, perhaps I should take that seat, Madam, while I conduct the inquiry into your, uh, sanity."

Betsy's grandmother settled back into her chair. "What could possibly lead you to think, a woman as successful and wealthy as I am, is mad?"

The Lord-Lieutenant cleared his throat again. "Yes, well, there is the, ah, reported fact that you freed every plantation worker under your care and then hired those who wished to come back and work as free men."

"And women," Betsy's Grandmother corrected. "Free men and women. Women have the right to earn and hold income, as well."

Miss Guest gasped. "You see how deranged she is, Father?"

Isaac glared at Miss Guest.

"That is a radical idea, Madam," the Lord-Lieutenant said.

Betsy's Grandmother snorted. "But hardly mad. It is an idea my own late husband held and acted on when he left everything to me, deeming our progeny too lacking in good sense to be handed so much responsibility."

Betsy's father sputtered.

Grandmother continued over his protest. "I plan to continue this course of action when I leave my late husband's holdings to my granddaughter, Elizabeth."

"Ha!" Betsy's father cried. He pointed at Mr. Relógio. "As if *he* will permit Betsy to inherit. By marrying this interloper, you have handed everything that should be mine to him." He turned to the Lord-Lieutenant. "Is a wedding conducted in the Caribbean legal?"

"It cannot be, Father, surely?" Miss Guest cried.

"It, ah…." The Lord-Lieutenant faltered.

Miss Guest surged to her feet. "A Caribbean wedding is not legal. You will see that it is not, won't you, Father?"

"Oh, do hush, you insidious child," Grandmother said. "Harold has no rights over my holdings, nor I over his, which, I might add, are the more prosperous of the two estates. We decided that when we die his wealth will be divided between his daughters, and mine will go to Elizabeth." She waved a toward Betsy where she still peered around the door.

Everyone looked, but only Mr. Relógio evidenced no surprise to see her. Betsy opened the door wide and she and Penna stepped into the room. Isaac jumped to his feet and hurried to her. Miss Guest stepped between them. He stopped short.

"So that is why you want this deranged little tramp." Miss Guest cast a murderous glance Betsy's way. "Her wealth."

Isaac frowned. "Her wealth is meaningless to me, and I would ask you not to insult her."

"You expect me to believe her wealth means nothing to you? I know you went to the bank. I know your shop will not last the winter."

"I daresay he is closing his shop," Lady Ellen said as she entered the room. She angled he head in acknowledgement to Betsy and Penna, then turned her attention onto her brother, who still lounged on the couch. "Why do I have the impression proper introductions have not been made?"

"Who is this?" Miss Guest shrieked loud enough to make Betsy's ears ring. "I thought you put a footman outside the door, Mr. Adams."

Betsy shook her head and realized she'd never needed to worry that Isaac could care for the woman.

"While I find your manners lacking, I shall still honor you with a reply." Lady Ellen spoke with a hauteur Betsy had never heard from her before. "I am Lady Ellen Cardale." She pinned Miss Guest with a hard look. "You have my permission to curtsy."

The Lord-Lieutenant made a hasty bow. "It is an honor, Lady Ellen."

She angled a beatific smile at him and murmured, "Indeed. The gentleman seated there with that smug smile is my brother Martin Winston, Duke of Midleharton."

The Lord-Lieutenant bowed to His Grace as he muttered from the side of his mouth, "Filomena, you must curtsy."

"In addition to being prominent members of the peerage," Lady Ellen continued, "we are Mr. Bell's aunt and uncle. He is the son of our eldest brother and, as the only child of the woman Charles intended to marry, recipient of our late brother's inheritance." She returned her cold eyes to Miss Guest. "He, therefore, is in no need of a tailor's shop."

Miss Guest blinked, then grabbed one of Isaac's hands. "Oh, but Isaac, how wonderful. Did I not always tell you that you must be the son of a duke? And now you are wealthy too. We can be so happy."

"I am starting to have a better idea who among this lot is mad," His Grace murmured.

"As am I," Betsy's grandmother agreed.

"Miss Guest." Isaac used a far kinder tone than Betsy would have as he tried to pry his hand away from her. "You and I will never be happy together. I do not love you. You do not love me. I daresay we don't even like one another. Even if you do not believe marriages and love have any real connection, you cannot imagine a good one can spring from active disdain."

"Dis-disdain?" she stammered. "You *disdain* me?"

Isaac pulled free of her hold and stepped back "You tried to ruin my business. You yet plot to have my mother locked away, and the woman I love carted off to Australia. Yes. I disdain you."

Never had such harsh words been spoken in so soft, so pitying, a tone. Betsy would have shouted them.

But Isaac must have known Miss Guest well, for rather than return to rage, she seemed to deflate. Her lower lip trembled as she looked up at Isaac. "You will never marry me, will you?"

"No, Miss Guest, I will not."

"Even if she were in Australia?"

"Even then. I am sorry."

She sniffed and lowered her head. When she raised her face again to looked about the room, she grimaced. "Yes. Well." She dropped a curtsy. "My lady, Your Grace, it is my honor to make your acquaintance." The words barely out, Miss Guest rushed past Betsy and fled the room.

The Lord-Lieutenant cleared his throat. "This appears to be quite the misunderstanding."

"Indeed," His Grace murmured.

"No," Betsy's father cried. "I see no misunderstanding. My mother is mad. My daughter is depraved. You already wrote Doctor Fox. He will take them away and I will be master here."

Lady Ellen locked eyes with Betsy's grandmother. Grandmother nodded and Lady Ellen addressed the Lord-Lieutenant. "We do believe Doctor Fox's services to be quite necessary. He shall still receive a generous donation to his asylum for his time."

"You see?" her father cried, eyes wild. "You see? Her lady-ship agrees with me."

Betsy's grandmother sighed. "We have much to discuss, but first, Miss Chaff, would you escort my granddaughter and Mr. Bell back to the ballroom? I believe they promised one another a dance."

"If you are all certain?" Isaac said.

"I may, at some point, need Miss Adams' private testimony," the Lord-Lieutenant said. "But that need is not urgent." He managed a half smile. "Enjoy the festivities, Mr. Bell."

Betsy wondered if perhaps they should stay, but her grandmother looked at her and gave a slight nod. Betsy wanted to run to her grandmother and throw her arms around the older woman's neck but knew this was not the time for such a personal show of affection. She would save that for later. She broke free of Penna's now-loose grip and hurried to Isaac, then pulled him in the direction of the door.

"Come," she urged. "Grandmother is correct. You promised me a dance."

Isaac's hand tightened about hers and he lengthened his stride as they hurried from the room. He smiled at Betsy. She smiled back.

"Oh, you ought not be holding hands," Penna scolded behind them.

Betsy laughed through tears, but didn't let go of Isaac's warm, strong hand. They neared the ballroom and Dougal Guest stepped away from the wall and into their path.

"Bell, a word?" he said.

Betsy cast Isaac a quick look, but he showed no disquiet as he released her and extended his hand to the other man. "Dougal. Good to see you."

They shook hands.

"And you, Bell." Dougal Guest grimaced. "I tried to stop them."

"I know." Isaac nodded to Betsy. "Mr. Guest, this is my betrothed, Miss Adams. Miss Adams, Mr. Guest."

Betsy dipped a curtsy, something else she'd been practicing. "Mr. Guest."

"And this is Miss Chaff, Miss Adams' companion." Isaac gestured toward Penna as she reached them, a bit red in the face.

"How do you do, sir?" Penna managed.

"Quite well, so long as Bell here managed to stave off my sister's schemes."

"We were on our way to the ballroom, Mr. Guest," Betsy said. "Won't you join us?"

"I should be honored and, if I may request a set? After you dance with Bell, that is."

Betsy nodded. He seemed kind, this friend of Isaac's. "Certainly."

Isaac now offered Betsy his arm, which she accepted.

"What of you, Miss Chaff?" Mr. Guest said. "Would you honor me with a dance?"

Penna's stammered acceptance as Betsy floated down the hall on Isaac's arm. She glanced back to see that Dougal Guest had now offered Penna his arm as her gallant escort.

"I believe I shall introduce Dougal to my new cousins," Isaac murmured.

"What of Miss Guest?" Betsy teased. "Will you introduce her to His Grace's sons?"

"I doubt I'll have to do so myself. By now, she's likely already danced with at least one. She can spot an unwed member of the peerage from half a mile away."

Betsy laughed, and Isaac joined her as they hurried into the grand ballroom for their very first dance.

EPILOGUE

Betsy stood on the prow as their ship cut through the white-capped swells, headed into a morning sunrise streaked with pinks, blues, and oranges. Strands of her hair had broken free from the single, utilitarian braid she'd adopted for the voyage, and she had given up trying to tuck them back behind her ears.

Isaac wrapped his arms about her from behind and pulled her against his chest. He placed a kiss atop her head and murmured, "I can make out buildings along the coast."

Betsy nodded. "We're nearly there."

Isaac gave her another light kiss at the nape of her neck. "Shall I wake the children? They will never forgive us if we do not let them watch us dock."

Betsy hugged her arms about Isaac's. "In a moment. First, let us enjoy the sunrise in peace."

This journey marked their third trip to her grandparents' island home, though it had been over two years since the last. At first, Betsy had been nervous about sea voyage, but she'd wanted to see where her grandparents called home, and to meet her new aunts and their husbands and all of her cousins.

They'd met Isaac's side of the family as well, though that effort didn't entail such long journeys, and they'd twice now visited his mother in her lovely cottage by the sea on the edge of the duke's holdings.

They'd seen Dougal Guest, too, as he'd fallen quite in love with His Grace's daughter, a match that only moderately pleased the duke, but which enthralled both young people and to which Lady Ellen had clarified, His Grace must acquiesce.

"After all," she'd said, *"You do not want your daughter sneaking off to meet her love, as our brother used to do."*

Dougal seemed infinitely happier than his sister who, a year ago, had pointedly declined to invite them to her wedding. She'd finally married the village's new tailor, the patient, middle-aged gentleman to whom Isaac had sold the shop.

A white gull screeched high above them, then swooped down into the water. The gull popped to the surface of the water, blazed white in the bright Caribbean sun, and tipped its head back to swallow a still-wriggling fish. Betsy laughed as she let the past scatter behind them and returned her gaze to the docks. As always seemed to be the case, the great seagoing vessel took longer to dock than expected. As the sun lifted higher and the day grew sultry with the humid Caribbean air, Betsy knew their sons would soon clamber to play in the clear blue-green water with their cousins.

An hour later, Betsy stood with Isaac out of the way while their boys ran about the deck and tried in their young way to help unload the ship. As the deckhands gathered their luggage, a myriad of Relógios disembarked from carriages at the end of the dock. Their boys jostled down the gangplank to be the first to greet their extended family.

"That must be the new baby." Betsy pointed to one of their cousins, who climbed from the carriage holding a squirming bundle. "Can you believe Grandpa Relógio is a great-grandfather already?"

"He is nearing his seventh decade," Isaac replied.

Her grandparents stood side by side at the end of the dock and watched the greetings unfold. Even from the prow of the great sailing ship, Betsy could see their smiles.

"Do you think when we are both in our seventh decade we'll have great grandchildren to come visit us and fill our days with laughter and joy?" she asked.

Isaac slipped an arm about her shoulders. "I believe bringing the boys with us when we travel ensures that we will."

Betsy snuggled nearer to him. "I do wish Penna could come too."

Isaac laughed. "She's terrified of the ocean, and she and Chef Dramm have their own family to care for now." He paused, then said, "Perhaps when we return to England, the boys can finally meet your father."

Betsy frowned.

Isaac squeezed her shoulder. "Or not."

"We shall see how he fares…when we return."

Since leaving Doctor Fox's care, her father did seem much improved. He lived in a small townhome in London and socialized little. She and Isaac paid for his townhome and gave him a yearly stipend of fifty pounds. They'd offered more, but Father had refused. He read a lot, wrote Betsy weekly and, every other month, returned to Bristol to visit her mother, who Doctor Fox did not believe would ever recover from the ravages of her addiction. She'd gone through considerable struggles without her laudanum to sustain her and come out the other side with a constant tremble and an inability to string together enough words to form a full sentence. It seemed too great a burden to ask Betsy's father and the staff to tend to her, and she seemed happiest seated in the window of her little room at Dr. Fox's asylum.

On the dock below, their sons hugged their cousins. The sound of her boys' giggles on the sea breeze warmed Betsy's heart. She stepped free of Isaac's arm and grasped his hand. "We should disembark. I daresay the crew is ready to be rid of the Bells for a time."

"I shouldn't have brought your father up in this moment," Isaac said softly. "I apologize. Seeing so much of our family together and happy made me feel sorrow for him."

"Though unneeded, your apology is accepted, and it is a good thought. We will visit him in London and, if he does not relapse, we can invite him to Rodchamb for a weekend. He has intimated he would like to meet his grandsons."

Isaac squeezed her hand as they started across the deck at their waiting family, and onward, into their future.

EXTENDED EXCERPT FROM BALLAD OF DISCORD

SONGS OF REBELLION BOOK ONE

TARAH SCOTT AND SUMMER HANFORD

BALLAD OF DISCORD BLURB

If the man you love won't trust you with the truth, how can you ever again trust him?

The pieces of Elizbeth McKinley's world scatter when her father, in an act of pure madness, joins forces with a mysterious Frenchman in an attempt to claim the Scottish crown. Now, pawns in a game far vaster than they can imagine, Elizbeth and her sister must flee or be shipped off to France to wed strangers. To make matters worse, the one man who should most wish to help her, the man Elizbeth loves, refuses to believe she's in danger. His betrayal will cut deeper than any sword.

CHAPTER 1

Giggles and rapid footfalls sounded in the corridor outside the sunny parlor. Elizbeth smoothed a stitch in her needlework while she waited for the bittersweet prick of tears to subside. It had been two years since their mother died. Laughter and joy were long overdue in their household.

"You know we ought to chide her for running," Aunt Davina said.

Elizbeth glanced at Davina, who sat across the parlor.

"She's nineteen," Davina went on. "A child no longer. When the two of you come out this autumn, we can hardly have her running about in company."

Elizbeth nodded as her strawberry-haired little sister charged into the room. Elizbeth wouldn't reprimand Margarette, and she doubted their aunt would, either. Only four years Elizbeth's senior, Aunt Davina was more an older sister than a matronly aunt and was as apt to join in their schemes as curtail them.

"The mail came," Margarette cried. She slid to a halt in the center of the Kidderminster carpet and waved a handful of letters.

Aunt Davina smiled down at her book, her bowlike lips pressed closed, her only censure to ignore the display.

"Oh?" Elizbeth looked up with feigned disinterest even as she tried to discern familiar handwriting on the flapping envelopes.

Her dear friend, Mister Robert McFarlan, was away on business for their father. Their three-week separation was the longest they'd been apart since...she fought down a blush... since he'd kissed her a month past. Although writing her was inappropriate—they weren't officially engaged—she considered a letter far less scandalous than his single, decidedly unchaste, embrace. So, she'd wheedled from him a promise to write. Though he was due to return that evening and she'd searched the mail for such a letter every day, he had been remiss thus far.

Smile wide, Margarette twirled on her toes, letters held aloft. Somehow, she'd noticed Elizbeth's recent interest in the mail and was determined to tease.

"Margarette, dear, shouldn't you be at your lessons?" Aunt Davina asked sweetly.

With a final spin, Margarette twirled over to the settee and plunked down beside their aunt. "After I see who's written." She began shuffling the envelopes. "Father," she said, and tossed two in a pile. "Father again." Another followed. "And again."

Elizbeth returned to her stitching. Attempts to contain her sister would only fuel her teasing. Perhaps Aunt Davina was correct and they should try to instill more decorum in Margarette. What man wanted a wife who ran giggling up and down the corridors of his home?

An intelligent one, she decided, who wanted a home full of joy. Not the same sort of man who would marry their aunt, but similar. She suppressed a grin. Little did Aunt Davina know, but as Elizbeth had already settled on a suitor, she planned to use her delayed season to find a man for Davina. It wasn't right that one disastrous romance, undertaken nearly a decade ago when Davina was just seventeen, should prejudice her against all gentlemen.

Margarette's sudden silence caused Elizbeth to look up. Her sister's blue eyes sparkled, her grin full of mischief. She'd finished her sorting and held two letters back from the pile for their father. Seeing she had captured Elizbeth's attention, Margarette pried one open and unfolded the pages within.

"Now, this one is interesting," Margarette drawled. "Great Aunt Saundra writes that she's returned from Italy for another visit."

"Has she?" Aunt Davina raised one delicate brow. "What is she now, eighty? I am surprised she made the journey."

"She says she wishes to see us, when we can." Some of the joy left Margarette. "She's of the opinion this will be her final visit to Scotland." Margarette blinked rapidly. "She means then to return, to die in Italy and be laid to rest there."

Aunt Davina plucked the letter from Margarette and scanned the page. "I know she's pious, but I will never understand how a good Scottish noblewoman grew so enamored of Italy."

"She is not even our real great aunt," Margarette said with a sniff. "It's not as if we will lose a real family member." Margarette's unspoken words echoed through the room: *as we did when mother died.*

"True enough, but our families were close, and she has never forgotten that." Aunt Davina folded the letter. "She's been Great Aunt Saundra since before I was born, and we shall visit her as she asks."

"Yes, of course, we shall," Elizbeth said. "What is the final letter, Margarette?"

As hoped, her sister's frown disappeared and mischief lit her eyes. "This?" Margarette held up the envelope, careful not to reveal the handwriting. "This letter must be an error. I shall have it returned. After all, only an engaged miss would receive a letter such as this one."

Elizbeth smiled before she could stop herself. Robert had written? Her soon-to-be betrothed cared more for her than for propriety, and more than he feared her father's wrath. Not that Father had ever indicated displeasure in their courtship... assuming he'd noticed.

Margarette popped to her feet. The pile of letters for their father toppled in her wake and spilled across the settee toward Davina. "In fact, such a letter as this is so scandalous, could do such harm to a lady's reputation, that I say we must burn it." Margarette whirled toward the tall fireplace at the far end of the room.

"Margarette," Elizbeth cried before she could help herself.

Her sister turned back with a victorious grin. She thrust the letter behind her back and took two steps backward toward the hearth. Elizbeth didn't know if she should laugh or shriek. She felt caught between the girl she was at twelve, tormented by her little sister, and the woman she'd become at twenty-two.

"For Heaven's sake." Aunt Davina laughed, her chocolate-colored curls a jumble as she shook her head. "Give me that letter and take yourself off to your lessons, Miss. I believe 'tis Italian today."

"French," Margarette said, then clamped her lips closed with a grimace. She crossed to their aunt and proffered the envelope, which Davina accepted with a smile.

Although she still didn't have her letter, Elizbeth couldn't contain a smirk. Margarette hated French.

"Well, off you go to the library." Aunt Davina made a shooing gesture. "I will quiz you later."

"Yes, Aunt Davina." Margarette made a great show of becoming somber before she smiled and skipped from the room.

Aunt Davina gathered the scattered letters, placed Elizbeth's on top, and held out the stack. "Will you take these to your father? He likely wishes to have his mail."

Elizbeth set aside her needlepoint and stood. Eyes on the top envelope, she took the pile and hurried from the parlor. She reached her father's office to find the door closed. The thick wood panel shutting him away meant he didn't wish to be disturbed, so Elizbeth deposited his mail on the small table outside his office door. She couldn't help but recall a time when their golden-haired mother had been alive and his door was always open. Elizbeth sighed. Mother was not alive, and their father's office door was nearly always closed.

She turned from the door to find Mary hurrying toward her. The maid took in the closed office and proffered a card. "There is a Frenchman here to see your father, Miss. Claims he's a lord of some sort, or I wouldn't have let him in."

Elizbeth took the card. Etched on the surface was simply *Seigneur Faucon.*

Lord Hawk, she thought, her French considerably better than Margarette's.

She looked at the maid. "Do you think he truly is a French lord?" A lord would be worth disturbing her father.

"Well, Miss, he seems quite fancy, to be sure, and very French." This last, Mary delivered with a wrinkle of her nose.

"Show him to my office," came her father's clipped voice behind the closed door.

Elizbeth winced. She'd forgotten about her father's keen hearing. She offered the card back to Mary. "Bring him to Father."

"Yes, Miss." Mary took the card and scuttled away.

Elizbeth stood for a moment, gaze on the door. Should she ask her father if he needed anything? He had a bell pull, and servants to fetch for him, but since their mother's death, he'd taken to skipping breakfast. Now, they rarely saw him outside the dinner table, if then. She shook her head. He knew she was there. If he wanted to see her, he would ask her in. Besides, she had Robert's letter to read.

Elizbeth turned on her heels. Though guilt assailed her, she went to the little room that had been her mother's office. She withdrew the key from her bodice—a key none knew she possessed—opened the door, and slipped inside.

Stuffy heat warmed her arms. Her mother had kept the window open nearly year-round. Elizbeth preferred the fresh air, as well. Today, however, she dared open the curtains and beveled panes just enough for a sliver of light and a flicker of breeze. She couldn't risk being caught. Her father, who thought he had the only key, would be livid.

Elizbeth understood his feelings. He wished this room, where Mother was once so often found, to remain undisturbed, in some fruitless hope to preserve a glimmer of her spirit. But it didn't. When mother was alive, light poured in through the open window. Her household notes and correspondences lay scattered about the desk and the second table, which over-crowded the little room. Father had pressed her to take one of the parlors for her office, but Mother liked her cramped little space with its lavender walls and flowery upholsteries.

Now, desk and table were bare, their papers long since sorted by Aunt Davina. After Mother's death, Aunt Davina arrived with their wayward, unpredictable Uncle Graham, and she'd taken over running the household. While Elizbeth appreciated Aunt Davina and was daily grateful for her competence, she had no real notion why Uncle Graham was there. All he did was soak up Father's whisky—when he could pry himself away from his harlots long enough to come home.

Shrugging off her now-grim mood, Elizbeth settled into the armchair by the window. She ran a finger along Robert's concise handwriting then, carefully, she opened the envelope.

This was her first letter from Robert and she wished to cherish every word.

Elizbeth:

As promised, I am writing. I comply only because I abhor breaking a promise. However, I must remind you how inappropriate it was for you to ask me to write. Your father would be displeased not only that you asked me, but that I allowed you to extract my promise to write. Be warned, in the future, I will not give in to your pleading.

Elizbeth rolled her eyes. If there was one little flaw in Robert, it was that he was too serious, but that was also what she cherished about him. His seriousness drew her in. To call forth his laughter made her heart sing, and she knew, when Robert spoke, he meant each word. Still, he could stand to be a touch less severe.

Her eyes went to the final line.

With the very greatest affection, yours always, Robert.

Elizbeth pressed the letter to her chest. Those words made the rest of the letter worthwhile. Her gaze caught on the quill sitting on the desk. The quill had been her mother's favorite. Tears unexpectedly pricked. It was terribly unfair that she had died without seeing Elizbeth fall in love. Elizbeth recalled the delight in her father's eyes whenever her mother walked into the room. Elizbeth wanted a love like that. She'd found a love like that.

"You would have loved him as much as I do, Mother," she whispered.

Elizbeth held the page back in the line of sunlight to reread the short missive.

"This request to speak in the garden is ridiculous," her

father's voice, speaking French, emanated from somewhere outside, near the window.

Elizbeth snapped her head up.

"Not ridiculous, but necessary," a man replied in the same tongue. "The manor has ears."

"I assure you, none of my staff speak your language," her father snapped back. "Half of them barely speak English."

Movements slow, least the chair creak, Elizbeth grasped the window and drew it back toward the sill. Father would not appreciate being made a liar of.

"Humor me, *Seigneur*, for my news is life shaking," the Frenchman said. "Any who hear it will face mortal danger."

The window clicked quietly closed, muting her father's reply into unintelligibility.

Face mortal danger? Elizbeth would have laughed had *Seigneur* Faucon's tone not been deadly serious. What news could possibly be of such importance? Her fingers tightened on the latch. She hesitated a heartbeat, then drew her hand back.

Eavesdropping was unacceptable. Doubly so when the two men were going to great lengths not to be overheard, and especially if the information they shared was truly somehow dangerous. If the Frenchman's words were for Father's ears alone, Father alone should hear them.

A thought struck. The library windows also opened onto the garden. Margarette!

Elizbeth surged to her feet. She folded and tucked Robert's letter into her skirt pocket as she crossed the room. She poked her head into the corridor—empty, as hoped. She slipped from the room and hurried down the hall.

Halfway to the library, she came up short. Lord, she'd forgotten to lock the door. Elizbeth hurried back and secured her mother's office, then again headed toward the library. She pushed the door open, stepped in, and nearly collided with Margarette. Elizbeth stumbled back.

Her sister recoiled. "Elizbeth," she cried. "You cannot believe what I heard."

Elizbeth contained a sigh. She leveled a frown on her sister. "You listened in on Father's private conversation."

Margarette gaped. "How do you know?"

"I heard them talking and came to stop you." Elizbeth grasped her sister's arm and pulled her into the center of the large room, away from windows or door, then realized the Frenchman's words had truly rattled her. "It is wrong to eavesdrop."

Margarette yanked free. "I do not care. 'Tis a good thing I heard. I don't want to go." Margarette's voice broke off in anguished tears.

Elizbeth stared. "Go where?"

"To France," Margarette cried.

"Why would you be going to France?" Elizbeth asked, unable to follow Margarette's tearful declarations.

"The Frenchman said we must." Margarette rubbed at her eyes. "He said we are to marry Frenchmen so Father can have an army."

"What under Heaven are you talking about?" Elizbeth demanded. "What do you mean, 'we'?"

"You, me and Aunt Davina," Margarette said. "Father is going to send us to France so they will send back an army to help him become king of Scotland."

"Margarette," Elizbeth hissed. "Do not say such things. That is treason. Stop making up stories."

Margarette lifted her chin. "It is not a story. The Frenchman said Father is the secret descendent of the Jacobite kings, and so we are princesses—which would be great fun—except that France sent him with a ship to take us away."

Elizbeth planted her hands on her hips. "Did you fall asleep over your lessons?"

Margarette grimaced. "Aye, because French is so boring, but that is *not* the point."

"It is exactly the point," Elizbeth corrected. "That is what you get for eavesdropping—and for not studying properly. Your French is terrible, which is why you so badly misunderstood their conversation."

Despite her admonition, a thread of unease wound through Elizbeth. Margarette might not speak French well, but Elizbeth did, and she hadn't misunderstood the Frenchman's warning about mortal danger.

Margarette's gaze sharpened. "You heard something, too."

Elizbeth groaned inwardly. Margarette eschewed books, but she was too intelligent for her own good.

"If I am wrong, why were they talking in the garden rather than Father's office?" Margarette demanded.

"There could be many reasons," Elizbeth said, but doubt persisted. While Margarette's story was obviously a mad mixture of dream and miscomprehension, the meeting was odd. Why was a French lord speaking with their father to begin with?

"My French may be atrocious, but I comprehend much more than I speak," Margarette said. "I know what I heard. We cannot let Father send us away to France. Especially you. What about Robert?"

"Mister McFarlan," Elizbeth corrected absently as she sought to make sense of Margarette's story.

"We must warn Aunt Davina," her sister urged. "The Frenchman said they want her, too." Elizbeth shook her head and started to tell Margarette to return to her French lesson, but Margarette grasped her hand. "Please, we must tell Aunt Davina."

The fear in Margarette's eyes stopped the refusal that leapt to Elizbeth's lips. Margarette feared nothing.

Elizbeth gave her hand a gentle squeeze. "You must try to see that you dreamed up this silly story."

Margarette stubbornly shook her head. "Aunt Davina can decide."

Elizbeth bit her lip. Their aunt was forgiving, but eavesdropping on Father's private conversation was a graver transgression than running down a hallway.

Margarette's hand clutched harder. "Elizbeth, I am afraid."

"We may have to tell Aunt Davina," Elizbeth allowed. "Or we may be able to keep your misbehavior between us. Tell me everything you think you heard, as near the original as you can, in French, and I will decide."

Margarette hesitated, then nodded and launched into her tale.

CHAPTER 2

D avina closed Debrett's *The New Peerage*. She weighed the etiquette book in her hands. Debrett's, and all of Britain, agreed that a proper chaperone must be wedded or widowed.

Due to Bhradain's betrayal, Davina was neither.

Mister Haywood, she corrected. He never should have been Bhradain to her. After nine years, some other woman must have the honor of addressing Mister Haywood by his Christian name.

She rubbed eyes tired of reading Debrett's dry, restrictive words. Across the room, the mantle clock ticked off slow minutes. The dinner hour approached, and Elizbeth hadn't returned. Margarette wouldn't. She would hide from a French exam for as long as possible. If the girl devoted as much effort to learning the language as she did to avoiding her lessons, she would be fluent.

Elizbeth, though, should have returned to her sewing. The envelope from Mister McFarlan had been thin. How many words could the page contain, and how many times could Elizbeth possibly read them? Davina considered fetching her niece.

A smile flittered across her lips. Elizbeth, as conscientious a young woman as Davina had ever met, thought no one knew where she hid when she wished to be alone. Sweet Elizbeth had no idea Davina—who had never been very well behaved—routinely followed, snooped, and spied on her nieces. In their best interests, of course.

She drummed her fingers on the book in her lap. Nae, Debrett would never condone her as a chaperone. But she was all her nieces had, and she was determined to safeguard their wellbeing.

Which brought her to Mister McFarlan. A kind man. Intelligent. An attorney. Not a true gentleman, though from a genteel family. Born the same year as Davina, so not too old for Elizbeth, nor so young as to be foolish. In truth, she felt him a good match for her niece. There would be no trouble there, except that Davina had no idea how her eldest brother felt about the notion of his daughter wedding one of his attorneys.

One might assume, as James permitted the courtship to continue, he was pleased. That would be, if one didn't know James. Or rather, the man he'd become since Maryanne's death. With his wife's passing, James had lost all attachment to the world. Like as not, he hadn't noticed the glaringly obvious affection between his daughter and the attorney.

Hurried footfalls, growing in volume, sounded in the hall without. Davina stilled her fingers. The footsteps were too heavy to be Elizbeth or Margarette. Her brother James burst into the parlor. His gaze darted about the small room, minnow-like. A strange pallor had leached all color from his face and his normally neat brown hair was wind tossed, as if he'd been outdoors. Of late, James never went outdoors.

"Whatever is the matter?" She set the book aside and rose. "James?"

"Where are my daughters?" he barked.

"Not here, as you can see. Is something amiss?" In view of his distress, she tried to keep a check on her temper, a thing more easily accomplished were it not the case that James was continually brusque these days. "James?" she repeated.

"What? Nae. Nothing is amiss." He raked long fingers through his dark hair.

At forty, James was still a handsome man. Only a hint of gray touched his temples and his broad shoulders and arms were well muscled. Unlike many other men his age, he had no paunch. She saw the way women looked at him, even young women. He could find happiness again. If only he would try.

He looked about the room again. "Where did you say they are?"

"Margarette is most likely in the library." She would not betray Elizbeth's secret. He would be furious should he learn his daughter possessed a key to her mother's office. "I have no notion where Elizbeth is."

James's mouth thinned. "Is not your one purpose in this household to know where my daughters are?"

She tamped down harder on her anger. "Indeed. Shall I launch a search, or would you rather wait an hour and see if they join us for dinner?"

His frown deepened into a scowl. "A husband would have curbed your tongue years ago. But I suppose it's better this way." He turned on his heel and stomped from the room.

Davina stared at the empty doorway. "That was rude even for James," she murmured.

Should she go after him? Was something truly amiss, aside from his self-absorbed sorrow over Maryanne? Before she could decide, new footsteps filled the corridor. Recognizing both sets, Davina retook her place on the settee. Perhaps the answers were on their way to her.

"Aunt Davina." Much as her father had, Margarette hurtled into the room.

Behind her, Elizbeth entered, her lovely face marred by worry and her steps considerably more graceful. Instead of sitting, they stopped before Davina. She looked up at them, expectant.

"Aunt Davina, Margarette has overheard something that concerns us," Elizbeth's voice was grave.

"Overheard?" Davina cocked a brow. "How did you manage that, dear?" Davina understood all too well how one *overheard* things.

Margarette had the grace to blush. "I did not do it on purpose. I was in the library, studying French. I truly was."

Davina nodded.

"The window was open, and Father and that Frenchman started talking in the garden."

"Frenchman?" Davina asked.

"Yes," Elizbeth said. "He arrived shortly after we left you, and asked to speak with Father. He gave the name Seigneur Faucon."

"Lord Hawk?" Davina didn't like the sound of that. The name was obviously false. She turned back to Margarette. "What did this Lord Hawk have to say to your father, and how does it concern you both?"

"It concerns you as well." Margarette popped up on her toes as she spoke, hands clasped before her. She shot Elizbeth a look.

"Tell her," Elizbeth ordered. "Only, do try to make sense."

"He said it all in French." Margarette scrunched her nose. "Elizbeth says I must repeat it as nearly as I heard, so you may interpret the words for yourself, since my French is abominable." This last, she accompanied with a supplicative glance upward.

Davina didn't know if she should be amused or alarmed. James's harried visage came to the forefront of her thoughts. "Let's have it, then."

Margarette embarked on a monologue. She used two voices, one apparently her idea of her father and the other the Frenchman. Some of the syllables that left her mouth resembled no language.

As Davina took in the half-intelligible babble, her pulse quickened with each word. Lord Hawk had told James he was the descendent of Henry Benedict Stuart, Cardinal-Duke of York, and the last of the Jacobite kings? Davina clenched her hands in her lap, for the tale grew even stranger. Seigneur Faucon had asked, and James agreed, to be given custody of her, Elizbeth and Margarette. He planned to take them and their considerable dowries to France and marry them to men of power. Their new husbands would raise an army, and return with it to Scotland, to fight for James, the Jacobite king. Davina stared up at her nieces. Tall, lovely young women whose hands would be a prize for any man but…princesses?

"And then they went deeper into the garden," Margarette concluded.

Davina looked at Elizbeth. "You heard none of this?"

She shook her head. "Nae, but I did hear the Frenchman say they must discuss something very secret and dangerous."

Margarette stared, her blue eyes filled with uncharacteristic worry. "Aunt Davina, what are we going to do?"

Davina shook her head, dazed. She had no idea. "You are sure that is what they said? You weren't dreaming? I know how French puts you to sleep."

Margarette blew out a frustrated breath. "I repeated the words to you—badly, I might add. How could I have dreamt all that? I don't even know some of those words. Please, I do not want to go off to marry some horrible French lord."

Davina scrubbed at her forehead. It couldn't be true. They were not royalty, not even gentry, though possessed of considerable wealth. Even if Margarette had heard correctly, it simply couldn't be true. The most shocking part was that James might believe any of the tale. His frantic eyes, his pallor, rose in her memory.

"Let me think on this. Please," she murmured.

"Yes, of course," Elizbeth said.

"But, what if Father tries to send us away?" Margarette demanded.

"He will hardly have us abducted," Davina soothed. "Go ready for dinner. We will see how your father is then. Like as not, he'll tell us the tale of this strange Frenchman and his bizarre ideas, and we will all laugh together. Tomorrow, Seigneur Faucon will be but a memory."

Elizbeth smiled. "You are quite correct, of course." Margarette looked mutinous, but Elizbeth caught her arm and tugged her toward the door. "We'll see you at dinner, Aunt Davina."

"Yes," Davina murmured absently as they stepped from the room into the hall.

She hadn't wanted to further alarm her nieces by speaking of their father's odd behavior, but there was someone to whom she could report the entire series of events. Her brother, Graham. Davina rose and went in search of him.

Davina found her brother sprawled face down and shirtless atop his bed. Beside him, curled to one side and, blessedly, fully clothed, though grass clippings decorated slippers and hem, lay a blonde woman Davina had never before seen. Nor, if she knew Graham, would she ever see the woman again.

Nose wrinkled at the stale sweat that permeated the chamber, Davinia crossed the room to the window. She yanked back the curtains and unlatched the windows. As fading daylight and fresh air spilled in, a groan sounded behind her.

"Davinia, what the devil are you doing?"

She turned to find Graham seated on the edge of his bed.

The blonde, snoring softly, didn't stir. Graham blinked rapidly, eyes bloodshot in a face still striking, despite his lack of sleep and what had undoubtedly been an abundance of whisky. Bare chested as he was, Davinia was reminded why her brother remained a favorite of the ladies. She would have thrown a shirt at him, but the one discarded on the floor looked too sweat-infused to touch.

"What am I doing?" she repeated. "I am here to tell you to ready for dinner. You have avoided consciousness long enough for today."

He pushed a hand through tangled brown locks, then cast a look over his shoulder. When he turned back, he wore a perplexed frown, as if he didn't quite know what to make of the unconscious blonde.

"Consider me told, sister dearest."

"That is not all," she said in clipped tones. "I must also, though Heaven knows why I bother, ask your opinion on a matter that may be significant."

Graham groaned and fell backward onto the bed. He fumbled for a pillow, found one, and pulled it over his face.

Davinia hurried back to the bed and kicked him in the shin. "Graham, this is important."

He lifted one half of the pillow. "I'm listening." He dropped the down-stuffed fabric back into place.

"I cannot very well discuss this in front of her." Davinia waved at the woman on the bed.

Graham lifted the pillow and craned his neck. Again, that perplexed look crossed his face.

"You *do* know her?" Davinia's voice dripped sarcasm.

"I suppose I must." He stretched out an arm and poked the slumbering woman in the shoulder.

Thick lashes fluttered open. Blue eyes focused on Davinia. "Hello."

With one word, the woman revealed her English

origins. Davinia grimaced. Leave it to Graham to bring home an Englishwoman. Offering Davinia a shrug, he tucked the pillow under his head. The Englishwoman sat up and looked about, appearing just as perplexed as Graham.

"Hello, Miss…" Davinia let her voice trail off in question.

"Ingram." She offered a bright smile. "Anastacia Ingram. And you are?"

Davinia bit back a sharp retort. "Miss McKinley. If you could excuse my brother and me, Miss Ingram, I should like to speak with Graham alone."

Miss Ingram's head snapped toward Graham. "*You* are Graham McKinley?" She frowned. "I was told to stay away from you. You're a terrible rake."

"Posh." Graham smiled his most charming smile and tucked his clasped hands behind his head. "If I am such a rake, why are we clothed?"

Miss Ingram looked about again. "If you aren't a rake, why am I in this bed?"

"I haven't the foggiest." Graham shrugged. "But if you would care to remain, I can think of several ways to test my fortitude. We must put this rake business to rest."

"Graham," Davinia snapped. Between James's half-madness since losing Maryanne and Graham's devotion to sin, Davinia sometimes felt as if she were responsible for the entirety of their family's wellbeing—and sanity.

Graham pointed toward the door across from the bed, leading to an antechamber. "Go in there, sweetheart, and ring for a servant to ready you a bath. I will come to you shortly."

Miss Ingram stood. She tugged her skirt straight and squared her shoulders. She was tall for a woman, her build slender. "I will give you your privacy, but you will not find me waiting for you in the bath." Her blue eyes snapped. "Just because we ended up in this bed, does not mean I am here for your frivolous pleasure, sir." She cocked her chin in the air and marched from the room.

Graham watched. A slow smile stretched across his face.

"You have no idea who she is or how you both ended up here?" Davinia asked once the door clicked shut behind the woman.

"You heard her. She's Miss Anastacia Ingram."

Davina had a few choice things to say about that, on the heels of which, she launched into the details of both their nieces' story and her encounter with James. Halfway through, Graham's brow furrowed. By the time she finished, he sat upright on the edge of the bed, his features hard with thought.

"I suppose it is possible," he murmured.

"That we are decedents of the Stuart family and James is a Jacobite king?" Davinia snorted. "Hardly. My only fear is James might believe the mad tale and turn our nieces over to some strange Frenchman. Likely, this is some sort of ransom plot to get at his wealth."

Graham regarded her with worried eyes. "And you."

"Me what?"

"If he really believes the Frenchman's tale, he could turn you over as well."

"I am six and twenty. I am no more subject to James's will than I am to that of a random passerby." *Unlike Elizbeth and Margarette.*

Graham shook his head. He levered himself to his feet, towering over her. "I cannot imagine James being taken in by some Frenchman's tale. Besides, Margarette likely dreamt the whole thing."

Davinia nodded. For all his debauchery, Graham was dependable when it came to family, and he, if anyone, knew their older brother well. "Of course, you are correct. I am going to prepare for dinner." She glanced toward the door through which Miss Ingram had departed. "Do not let your English harlot keep you."

"She is not a harlot. She is Miss Anastacia Ingram."

Davinia raised her brows. "Graham, I found her asleep in your bed. She is a harlot." Without another word, she left the room.

CHAPTER 3

E lizbeth entered the dining room arm in arm with Margarette. As with every informal meal, Aunt Davina sat at her place to the right of their father's seat, which, as usual, stood empty. A small measure of relief loosened the knot in Elizbeth's stomach at sight of her Uncle Graham. He occupied his place at the opposite end of the table. He met her gaze and gave a reassuring smile.

Elizbeth's pulse skipped a beat.

He knows.

Aunt Davina must have told him what Margarette heard. That meant Aunt Davina was worried. Was Uncle Graham there to ensure their father didn't send them to France? Elizbeth took her seat to the left of her father's chair. Was it really possible he might agree to marry them to strangers? What of Robert? Surely, her father wouldn't tear her from the man she loved. Robert would never permit it. Her stomach cinched tighter. Could he stop Father?

Margarette sat beside her. "Father isn't here," she said, tone relieved.

Elizbeth fought to keep her thoughts clear. His absence had

to be a good sign, didn't it? She exchanged a glance with Davina. Her aunt smiled encouragingly.

Margarette leaned close to Elizbeth. "Do you think he has already ordered our trunks packed?" she whispered.

"Hush," Elizbeth hissed.

Three maids entered, each carrying platters of food, but Elizbeth scarcely paid attention as they filled her plate.

"You appear refreshed, Graham," Davina said.

He laughed. "I always appear refreshed."

Davina gave him a look Elizbeth couldn't interpret. Were they mentally communicating about Father?

"Aren't you hungry, Elizbeth?" Margarette asked.

"Are you ill?" Uncle Graham regarded Elizbeth.

He waited, expression gentle. He was a good uncle. He looked out for them, particularly since her mother's death and their father's retreat from the world. He would never allow Father to send them to a foreign country to marry strangers.

She shook her head. "Nae. I am just not particularly hungry tonight."

His eyes twinkled. "I smelled blueberry buns baking earlier. Surely, you want one? No one makes a better bun than our Missus Henderson."

She smiled. Uncle Graham always made her feel better. "I do love blueberry buns."

He winked. "I know. At least taste a bit of the pheasant. It is quite good."

"I will."

She was being silly. She'd allowed Margarette's dream to influence her reality. She forked a piece of pheasant and lifted it to her mouth, then halted when Father strode into the room.

"Well, this is a pleasant surprise." Uncle Graham lifted his glass of wine and downed a mouthful.

Ignoring his brother, James looked about the room. His gaze fell on the waiting servants. "Leave us, and ensure neither you nor any other stand outside these doors, on pain of death," he said, voice grim enough to send a shiver down Elizbeth's spine. "I will ring when you may return."

Eyes wide, the staff hurried out. Elizbeth watched them depart with mounting fear, a fear reflected in Margarette's eyes. Aunt Davina stared at their father through narrowed eyes. Uncle Graham leaned back in his chair, expression sober.

Her father went to the hall door, then to the servants' door, peering out each before closing them firmly. Finally, he took his seat. "I am glad everyone is here. That will save me the trouble of having to repeat this announcement."

Aunt Davina exchanged a look with Graham.

Elizbeth's uncle turned and met her father's gaze. "You look far too serious, James. Have some wine." Graham lifted his glass again and emptied its contents.

To many, the action would appear cavalier. Elizbeth knew better. Her uncle's keen mind seldom dulled, even with great quantities of liquor.

Her father reached for a nearby platter of potatoes and spooned some onto his plate. "You could use with a dose of responsibility, Graham," he said. "But that will come soon enough." He reached for the decanter of wine.

"Responsibility?" Graham repeated. "It's rather too late for that, don't you think?"

Her father slowed in filling his glass and flicked a glance at his brother. "You had best hope not." He set the decanter down, stabbed a slice of pheasant, and transferred it to his plate. He began cutting the meat. "What I am about to tell you, remains between us." He flicked a glance at Graham.

"Surely, you are not accusing me of being a gossip monger?" Graham laughed.

"No man can be assured of keeping his own counsel when he drinks too much."

Uncle Graham laughed again. "I heartily agree. Luckily, I

never drink too much." He reached for the decanter and refilled his glass.

Aunt Davina shot him a warning look.

James forked pheasant into his mouth. "I will get straight to the heart of the matter. Our great Aunt Saundra is not truly our aunt."

"If that is your big announcement, then it is you who have been drinking too much," Uncle Graham said.

Her father didn't so much as glance at him. "In fact, Saundra is our" –he pointed his knife at Davina, Graham and himself— "grandmother, and you girls' great-grandmother." The knife darted menacingly toward Elizbeth and Margarette.

Aunt Davina gasped in unison with Margarette's cry of surprise. Elizbeth could only stare. What they'd overheard indicated nothing like *this*.

"What could possibly give you that idea?" Graham asked.

"I have seen the ledgers, records of marriages, of real names and births," her father replied.

Graham regarded him. "Why are we only learning of this now?"

Her father ate more pheasant. "Because her husband, Henry Benedict Stuart, Cardinal Duke of York, was still living."

Even Elizbeth couldn't refrain from a loud gasp this time.

"*James*," Davina breathed, "Henry Stuart never married. He was a priest, sworn to celibacy."

"Davina is correct," Graham said.

"She might be naïve enough to believe that would stop a man, but not you, Graham," Elizbeth's father said, his attention on his food. "He would not be the first priest to marry in secret."

Elizbeth's mind raced. Henry Benedict Stuart was the last legitimate descendant of James VIII, and younger brother to Charles. What year had Charles Stuart last tried to take the throne? Her thoughts muddled. 1759. Yes. To the Jacobites, he had been the Young Chevalier. Dear God, Margarette hadn't dreamed the conversation between their father and the Frenchman. It was true. Nae, it wasn't true. It was ridiculous to think they were descendants of kings. But their father believed the Frenchman's story.

"Birth certificates can be forged, James," Graham said. "Where did you get this information?"

"That is not important at this time."

Graham snorted. "I beg to differ. Never has it been more important than now."

Her father took a drink of wine. "You may take my word. It is all true."

Elizbeth held her breath in anticipation of Graham's demand of proof.

Graham picked up his wine glass, leaned back in his chair, and studied her father. "What has Father to say of this?"

"He knows nothing of it," James replied.

Graham's brows rose. "I should think a man would like to know that the woman he called mother *isn't* his mother."

"He will be told when the time is right."

"When will that be?" Graham asked.

Under the table, Margarette's hand found and clasped Elizbeth's.

Their father laid down his utensils and looked at them. "Once I have laid claim to the Crown.

AFTER DINNER, IN THE PARLOR, DAVINA TRIED TO marshal her thoughts, to plan out what she must say to reach through the madness engulfing James, but she couldn't think with Elizbeth pacing the parlor carpet. "Elizbeth, please sit down," she said, tone terse.

Elizbeth whirled to face where she sat on the divan. "Aunt Davina, this means everything Margarette heard is true."

Davina heard the tears in her niece's voice and jumped to her feet as Elizbeth sobbed. Margarette, too, sprang from her chair. Davina reached Elizbeth first and pulled her into a hug. Margarette threw her arms around Elizbeth's back and hugged them both.

"Shh," Davina soothed. "Graham will not let your father do anything foolish." Neither would she. "You know he hasn't been the same since your mother's death. He simply isn't himself, that is all." Perhaps Davina didn't need the perfect words. Maybe, while the gentlemen took their port, Graham was already reasserting reason.

"But Papa thinks he is the King of Scotland," Elizbeth said through another sob. "It is madness, pure madness."

She was right and that frightened Davina more than anything else about the absurd tale. How could James believe such insanity? Worse, how could he possibly think he would succeed? England would crush him—and them along with him. In the meantime, however, he very well might try to ship the girls off to France.

Davina coaxed her nieces to the divan and sat between them. They each clasped one of her hands and laid their heads on her shoulders as they used to do as children.

"I will not go to France or marry some Frenchman," Margarette finally said.

"Of course you shall not go." Davina gave her hand a squeeze.

"If Papa tries to make me I'll... I'll jump off the ship," Margarette declared.

"You most certainly will not," Davina replied. "Besides which, there will be no ship from which to fling yourself. Your father is not sending anyone to France."

Elizbeth lifted her head from Davina's shoulder and swiped

at her eyes with a finger. "But Father seemed so determined. I cannot leave Robert." Her voice cracked.

"Mister McFarlan," Davina corrected with mock severity.

A sad smile lifted a corner of Elizbeth's mouth.

"Neither of you need worry," Davina said. "Graham will know exactly what to do." She hoped.

Elizbeth shifted to face them, expression brightening. "Robert can help, as well."

Davina frowned. "I do not know--"

"Just consider, he is an attorney, so he knows the law." Elizbeth leaned forward, intent. "Not to mention, he is exceedingly intelligent."

Davina nodded. "Perhaps you are right," she said, more to humor her niece than out of any real belief in Mister McFarlan's abilities. "Between him and Graham, we are assured of a solution."

"Robert returns home this evening," Elizbeth said. "We could speak with him tomorrow."

Davina released a breath. "We will see what Graham learns from your father, then decide."

"Perhaps we should leave tonight," Margarette said.

"Leave tonight?" Elizbeth frowned. "Where would we go?"

"We will not leave tonight," Davina said. "Nothing can happen tonight." As the words left her mouth, Davina prayed she was right.

Elizbeth rose. "I would like to compose my thoughts." She smoothed the front of her gown.

Davina nodded. "Write nothing about your father." Elizbeth frowned, but Davina added, "Nae, Elizbeth. If anyone were to read your journal your father could hang."

The girls looked at each other, wide eyes bright with fear.

Elizbeth sucked in a deep breath and nodded. She turned toward the door.

Margarette jumped to her feet. "May I come, Elizbeth? Oh,

please do not say no. I may not have a gentleman like you do, but I no more want to go off to France to marry a strange Frenchman than do you and I would like to organize my thoughts, as well."

Elizbeth looked at Davina. Davina gave a tiny nod of approval. She read the mutiny in her elder niece's features and realized Elizbeth had planned to sneak off to her mother's study, a place she wouldn't take her little sister. Davina raised her brows, all but daring Elizbeth to admit her secret.

"You may come," Elizbeth said and turned back toward the parlor door.

Margarette skipped across the room, but Davina recognized the worry in her eyes. She watched until the door closed behind her nieces and left her alone with her thoughts. Should she retire for the evening, as well? She glanced at the mantle clock. Eight thirty-five. Far too early to sleep, even if she weren't a bundle of nerves. What had happened to James to push him over the edge of delusion? She knew—everyone knew—a part of him died with Maryanne. But this... She shivered.

When the clock struck ten, Davina could no longer stand the suspense. She went to the dining room, where they'd left the men, but found the room empty and the table cleared. Her heart began to beat fast. Where had they gone? Her brother's study, perhaps? She checked but found the room empty.

Davina hurried up to the fourth floor where their private chambers were located and went to Graham's room. Her quiet knock brought no answer. She slipped inside and closed the door. She turned, then stopped short at sight of her brother's long legs stretched out in front of the chair before the hearth. Anger bubbled up. Had Graham retired to his room to drink himself to sleep? She marched toward the chair.

"He has gone quite mad."

Davina halted, alerted by his tone. "You do not mean..."

Graham gave a heavy sigh. "Aye."

Davina hurried across the room and sat in the chair opposite him. "James truly believes he is the King of Scotland?"

Graham's gaze shifted to her. "He may be right."

Davina gasped. "You cannot be serious. This-this is…"

"Treason?" He nodded. "I know."

"But you said he is mad."

He barked a humorless laugh. "Of course he is mad. Even if we are descendants of Henry, to lay claim to the Crown is the height of insanity. There isn't the slightest chance of success. Only the eventuality of the gallows."

"You are saying we are truly descendants of the Cardinal Duke of York—that great Aunt Saundra is really his wife?"

Graham shrugged. "The documentation certainly seems genuine. I would have to have it examined by an expert." He grunted. "Though where I would find one, I have not the foggiest idea."

"I know someone who might have an idea," Davina said. "Elizbeth suggested we enlist Mister McFarlan's aid."

"Robert McFarlan, James's attorney?" Graham's mouth thinned. "Is Elizbeth still pining after that pup?"

Davina frowned. "He is no pup, Graham. He is only five years your junior."

"Seems more like ten years. The man has no backbone. I would no more ask his help then I would a footman's."

"What do you suggest, then?"

His expression grew even more grim. Trepidation slithered in her belly.

"James truly intends to marry off all three of you."

Davina blinked. "He intends to marry off *me*?" She stiffened with indignation. "I am his sister, *not* his daughter. Not to mention, I am of age. He cannot force me to marry anyone."

His expression softened. "In fact, he can, and quite easily."

"But how?"

"Davina, he need only truss you up and toss you into a

carriage with that fool Frenchman who has promised to launch the war that will win James the crown."

Davina stared. "He would take me by force?"

"What is the difference in taking you by force and sending his daughters against their wishes?"

He was right, of course, and she would no sooner see her nieces wed to strangers in another country than she would herself, but the idea galled her. "I pity the man who tries to force me into marriage, much less his bed," she said more to herself than Graham

A hint of the smile she was accustomed to seeing in Graham's eyes appeared, then vanished. "Such a man would not be kind, Davina."

She hated that he was right. "We must save the girls."

He nodded. "Unfortunately, there is only one way to secure their safety, and yours."

Unfortunately? A dread unlike any she'd ever known took root in her heart.

"Forgive me," he whispered. "But you three must wed."

Scarsdale Publishing